CW00730074

Requiem

Requiem

Iris Collier

PIATKUS

First published in Great Britain in 1997 by
Judy Piatkus (Publishers) Ltd of
5 Windmill Street, London W1

*A catalogue record for this book is available
from the British Library*

ISBN 0-7499-0381-3

Set in 11/12 pt Times by
RefineCatch Limited, Bungay, Suffolk
Printed and bound in Great Britain by
Biddles Ltd, Guildford & King's Lynn

Five and twenty ponies trotting through the dark,
Brandy for the parson, baccy for the clerk,
Laces for a lady, letters for a spy,
Watch the wall, my darling,
While the gentlemen go by!

Rudyard Kipling

Chapter One

London to Auckland. To the Auckland morgue. He'd been travelling for twenty-five hours incarcerated in a Boeing 747, hurtling along at five hundred miles an hour at thirty-five thousand feet, all for this girl, Bridie Ransome, lying there in her metal box like an effigy in a church. He stared down into the yellow, shrunken face framed by wisps of reddish hair, brittle as straw.

Chief Inspector Douglas McBride had seen more than his fair share of corpses in his thirty years in the police force, but this one was different. To start with, he'd known her when she was alive. He'd chatted to her, shared a pot of tea with her, back home in his native Northumberland. He'd always thought her unconventional, no more: maybe smoked the occasional joint; nothing worse. The girl Clare, her daughter, Bridie had said was a joy. Terrible to have to go home and tell her what had happened to her mother.

He turned towards the young New Zealand morgue attendant. 'There's no doubt that she took an overdose?'

'She topped herself, all right. Her body was full of the stuff. Heroin. Perhaps it was an accident, perhaps not – makes no difference. Seen enough?'

'Yes. Cover her up.' *Shut her up in her final resting place*, he said to himself. *Pull the plastic sheet over Bridie Ransome*.

Back in the police car, he turned to Detective Inspector Terry Jamieson. 'Thanks for waiting. Scene of death next, if you don't mind.'

Stocky Jamieson, red-faced and red-haired, almost a replica

of Douglas but younger by twenty years, looked at his senior in surprise.

'You don't mean that, surely? It's a hell of a journey. The Maoris found her up in the rain forest, up the Wanganui. It's hot up there, *bloody* hot, and humid.'

'I admit I hate the heat, but I've got to go. I'll need to talk to the people who found her.'

'That'll be difficult. They don't like policemen. Especially Pommie policemen.'

Douglas started stolidly out of the window. He knew the New Zealand police resented his presence. They'd told him as soon as he landed that they could do without him. But Douglas had his brief. The dead girl, Bridget Ransome – known as Bridie – had been Edith Laker's chief assistant, and Edith Laker was a JP. You couldn't trifle with her. And, more importantly, she was a friend of his Superintendent. They would both want answers. Who was responsible for Bridie's death? And what was she doing in New Zealand in the first place? It would be easy for Douglas to agree with Jamieson and his colleagues that Bridie had killed herself with heroin, pack his bags, get back to the airport and face another hellish twenty-five hours in the Boeing 747. But he wouldn't be able to face Superintendent Blackburn and Edith Laker at the other end. Or little Clare . . .

'Scene of death, Inspector, if you please,' he said decisively. 'And straight away. The sooner we go, the sooner I'll be out of your hair.'

Jamieson knew when he was beaten. He started the engine. 'Right you are, Chief Inspector. I'll lay on a jet boat.'

He'll regret this, thought Jamieson as he put the car into gear. But he'd been told to humour the bastard. Two more days, and they'd be rid of Douglas McBride for good.

The trip wasn't as bad as Douglas had expected. February in New Zealand's North Island meant a temperature of 80° Fahrenheit with a soft, moist breeze caressing his face: a paradise when he thought of his forbidding stone house in Berwick surrounded by swirling fog and an icy east wind. He was too hot in his lightweight tweed suit; he envied the Maori driver in his brief shorts. Jamieson, sitting next to him, had taken his jacket off, but Douglas couldn't bring himself to change the habit of a lifetime and follow his example.

The boat cleaved its way through the tea-dark water of the Wanganui. There hadn't been much rain over the last few weeks and the river was low. A continuous series of shallow rapids made navigation difficult, but the driver, Jimmy Hohepa, knew all the deep channels and hardly slackened speed when white water showed ahead. Douglas clung on to the sides of the boat and looked up at the thickly wooded cliffs on either side of the river. Giant, primeval ferns grew side by side with the mighty Nikan trees, the most obviously tropical of all New Zealand's trees with their slender dark green stems and massive heads of shiny palm leaves. Underneath hung necklaces of long, pink flowers which pierced the gloom of the forest like swarms of tropical birds. A strange country, Douglas thought. Nothing really seemed to have changed since dinosaurs roamed the forest.

Suddenly the boat altered course and made towards the left-hand side of the river, where a landslide of shale had provided a makeshift landing place. Hohepa brought the boat's nose against the mass of fallen rock and jumped out, offering his hand to Douglas. Hohepa pointed upwards to where the path ascended through the dense undergrowth; Jamieson set off and Douglas followed, struggling a little, his feet sinking into the soft, moss-covered soil. As soon as he had disembarked he was attacked by thousands of insects, attracted to his perspiring face. He swiped at them impotently as he stumbled in Jamieson's wake. All around him, strange trees dripped moisture; he was dimly aware, as if in a dream, of contorted, moss-covered tree trunks, the distant sound of water cascading over boulders.

Up, up, they climbed. Douglas finally surrendered his principles and took off his jacket. Immediately the insects pounced in jubilation on his sweat-soaked shirt. He stopped for breath and smelt the moist, dank smell of rotting wood, heard the eerie, piercing cry of the bellbird.

Jamieson turned round and looked at him. 'Not far now. There's an old settlement up here. A government idea to create a back-to-nature village for hopeless cases. Give them a new start. It didn't really come to anything. They couldn't stand the loneliness. Here we go. The last bit. Keep away from those vines. We call them bush lawyers – they've got hooks on them, and once they get hold of you they're the very devil to get rid of.'

Suddenly they came to a clearing in the forest. The dappled light revealed a couple of huts, mere shacks with wooden, moss-covered walls and corrugated tins roofs now half-buried under a thatching of lichen. The doors had long since mouldered away and Douglas, ducking his head, went into the nearest hut. He noted the mud floor, partially covered by a pile of dried palm leaves. He looked at Jamieson who stood framed in the doorway.

'She was here?'

'That's where Larry found her. On that pile of leaves.'

'Larry?'

'Jimmy's son. He was up here hunting for possums. They're vermin in this neck of the woods and the Maoris sell the pelts.'

'How long had she been here?'

'Two to three days. Decomposition wasn't far advanced'

'Any sign of a syringe?'

'Yep. Larry handed it in. And there were track marks all over her arms and legs. They found a stash of stuff over there, in the corner. Enough to keep her going for a couple of weeks if she took it steady.'

Douglas said nothing. He felt a desperate sadness; it was a terrible way to die. A sinful waste of a young life. That girl in the morgue, with her angel's face and young, slender body – somewhere she had a husband. Where the hell had he been when she needed him?

'Any sign of the husband?' he said to Jamieson.

'Nope. We're broadcasting appeals. We know he's in New Zealand – he checked in at the airport several months ago.'

'He's a New Zealander, I gather.'

'That's right. Half Maori. They married out here ten years ago. He was a stockman. We lost track of them, so they must have travelled a bit.'

'And she ended up on my patch. Until she made this final journey.'

'Perhaps she came looking for him. She was out of luck.'

'Maybe she did find him and he didn't want to know,' said Douglas.

Jamieson shrugged his shoulders. 'Even if they met, had a

big row, he didn't have to bring her all the way up here to bump her off. No, she'll have come here of her own accord.'

'I'm still not convinced,' said Douglas stubbornly. 'I want to see this Larry. How far away is he?'

'Just down the river. But Jimmy won't take to the idea. The Maoris like their privacy.'

'I respect that, but I still have to be sure of the truth. Let's get out of this God-forsaken place.

Jamieson looked at Douglas sharply. 'I warned you not to come.'

'I had no choice. Now, let's get on.'

They left the desolate place and went back to the jet boat. Jimmy took some persuading to take them further down the river, but finally capitulated. Douglas was aware of a slight subservience in Jimmy's attitude towards Jamieson; he thought it possible that the Hohepa family could be in the pay of the Auckland police. After all, Jimmy owned a fleet of power boats and was up and down the river all the time, with or without a boatload of tourists. He'd see plenty of what was going on. Douglas wondered what the Auckland police would have felt, knowing someone like Bridie was on their manor. Would they have cared enough to protect her? Or did they decide to let Nature take its course?

They arrived at the Maori settlement half an hour later. There wasn't much sign of any activity. An old woman going about her domestic chores paid them no attention as they got out of the boat and made their way to the collection of wooden huts. Jimmy spoke to her and she – obviously reluctantly – dumped the pile of washing she was carrying. She filled the kettle, slammed it down onto the wood-burning stove and got out three mugs. Douglas sat at one of the long wooden tables, grateful for the rest after his exertions, and Jamieson sat next to him. When the kettle boiled, Jimmy brought them their tea. Outside, it began to rain.

A young boy emerged from one of the huts and hurried towards them. About sixteen, he was dressed smartly in jeans and a blue shirt, with an orange baseball cap set at a rakish angle on his dark hair.

'He's turned up,' he said to Jamieson, whom he appeared to know well. 'It's just come on the radio.'

'Ransome?'

'Who else? They're not holding him for questioning because he says he knows nothing about the girl's death. And he's got an alibi. He was away down on South Island, sheep-shearing. Been there for several months. Wants to know about his daughter. He's waiting for you, sir,' he said, glancing at Douglas, 'hoping you can tell him how she is. No need to hurry,' he added as Douglas stood up ready to depart. 'He's not going anywhere, not until he sees you.'

'So that's it,' said Jamieson with a note of quiet satisfaction. 'Seems we were right all along. She did do herself in.'

'Serves her right,' said the boy morosely, 'she shouldn't have . . .'

'Shouldn't have what, lad?' said Douglas, his policeman's instinct alert.

'Nothing.' Douglas waited. 'Well, all I meant was that she shouldn't have come here. We don't like strangers on our patch.'

So that *was* it! Douglas felt a surge of triumph. *Maoris don't like strangers*, Jamieson had admitted . . .

'Did she try to sell you anything? Grass? Coke? Smack? You know what I mean, laddie. Come on, out with it. Did you kill her because she was undercutting your pushers? Or was it that you just didn't want someone like her around? That's it, isn't it?'

The boy's face clammed up. Douglas realised his mistake; he'd gone too far, too quickly.

'We never did it! What right has he got?' the boy said angrily to Jamieson. 'He can't come here accusing us of bumping off tourist druggies, can he, Terry?'

Douglas tried to save the situation. 'Don't get het up. It was just an idea.'

'Well, it's a bloody daft idea. Why should we kill her? She was up to her eyeballs with the stuff. It was only a question of waiting.'

There was no more to be gained. Douglas would never be able to find any evidence that someone from the Maori settlement had deliberately set about killing Bridie. He'd arrived too late. The Maoris had closed ranks and probably the police had agreed to turn a blind eye. After all, there were bigger, more dangerous fish in the sea than Bridie Ransome round these parts and the Maoris were the ones who'd catch them. It wouldn't do for the Auckland police to antagonise the Hohepa family. Douglas couldn't say he altogether blamed them.

Douglas turned to Terry Jamieson. 'Come on – let's get back. I'd like to meet this chap Ransome.'

Back in Auckland, Douglas met the quiet, soft-spoken New Zealander with more than a dash of Maori blood in him. He was handsome and vital, with his long wavy hair, lean tanned body, and the expressive eyes of his Polynesian ancestors. No, he said, he hadn't seen his wife for over a year. They'd separated because of her refusal to seek counselling for her drug habit. He hadn't got in touch because he didn't know where she was; as far as he was concerned, she'd signed her own death warrant years ago. But he wanted to see his daughter again. He wanted her to have a different sort of life from her mother's. He listened with interest as Douglas told her where Clare was now living, and promised to go and see her as soon as he could. They parted, Billy Ransome saying he would be over to England as soon as the shearing season finished.

'Did Bridie sell stuff to other people?' said Douglas as he walked with Ransome to the entrance hall of the police station.

Ransome looked at him keenly, his dark eyes giving nothing away. 'I never saw her. But how else would she have got the money to come out here?'

'She was in full-time employment.'

'She was never the type to save. I expect she sold a bit on the side. She wasn't clever enough to be part of an organised gang, but she could be enterprising when she got desperate. Like most druggies.'

The end of the trail, thought Douglas, as he made his way back to his hotel. No evidence that the Maoris had bumped off Bridie Ransome; they'd made certain of that. The case was well and truly closed. Death through an overdose of heroin – probably accidental, suicide at the worst. Now there was nothing for it. It was back to England and he had twenty-five hours to think about what he was going to say to Edith Laker and Superintendent Blackburn.

*

7

Clinker turned up the collar of his donkey jacket and glanced up at the steely sky. The wind, straight from Eastern Europe, tore at his hair with icy fingers and his eyes watered as he thrust his hands further down into his pockets. What a climate, he thought gloomily; what a hellish time of the year. Even Mac, his comfortable mongrel, seemed dispirited. February: a dead month. Frozen sky, frozen sea, frozen marshes.

It was all Hilda's fault, of course. She'd prised him out of his snug cottage on Holy Island and brought him to this place. And all because she'd taken one look at *Sirius*, a neat, gaff-rigged wooden sailing boat which she'd spotted for sale in Higgins' Boat Yard, and gone and bought it. Then she'd installed him in a cottage down on the quay and told him to get the boat ready for the spring. By April, she'd said, they'd be off cruising south. This year, round the British Isles; next year, the Med. *Silly old fool*, he muttered to Mac, who, used to Clinker's confidences, twitched an ear sympathetically. A pity her husband died when he did, he thought for the umpteenth time. He might have been Ambassador in Brussels, might have picked up a gong or two at Buckingham Palace, but that hadn't stopped him from having a heart attack as soon as he retired.

And now he had Hilda on his hands. Hilda, Lady Nevill: as fit as a flea, and determined to go sailing. At least she paid him well. That 'annuity', as she called it, set him up handsomely. Not that he didn't deserve it. She was always on at him, demanding progress reports on *Sirius*. Even in this weather, when his fingers ached with cold and the inside of the cabin dripped with condensation. She was a demanding old soul, all right.

There was no joy in walking today. He'd go on just a bit further, up to the old barge lying on the shore, its woodwork rotting into the mud, its ribs showing like the skeletal remains of some primeval animal. Like the pictures he'd seen on television of animals in Africa killed by drought and picked over by vultures.

Suddenly, Mac growled. That wasn't like him, Mac knew the ropes: no racing ahead; no stopping to sniff at interesting holes in the bank; and definitely *no* growling or barking.

Clinker stopped. Mac began to whine; obeying some savage instinct, he began to slither forward on his belly. Clinker called to him, but Mac appeared not to hear.

Perplexed, Clinker stared at the dog. All around them the mud creaked and bubbled like a live thing; the tide was out. He saw the shells of millions of crustaceans heaped along the edge of the channel, thought of the billions of organisms eating, procreating, dying. Mac's growl turned into a whine.

'Stop that, you old bugger,' said Clinker angrily. 'You'll frighten the birds.'

Mac took no notice. The whine turned into a terrible howling as Mac raced urgently along the path towards the rotting hulk. Clinker ran after him. He stumbled over a clump of coarse grass, cursed, and looked out across the mud. Mac was down at the edge of the creek. And there, on a shelf of mud which would soon be covered by the tide, he saw a man, lying face down. Mac, his face turned towards the sky, began a terrible ululation which seemed to epitomise all the sufferings of his species. Clinker rushed up to him.

The man was lying spread-eagled some six feet out in the channel. He had been tied at both hands and feet to stakes driven into the mud. A rope, stretched tight across his back and fastened to two more stakes, held him down. With horror, Clinker realised he'd been left there as the tide gradually crept towards him, licked round his head, caressed his neck, back and legs, until it covered him like a blanket. Then the water had filled his nostrils, his mouth and lungs and slowly, inexorably, choked him to death.

Dear Christ, thought Clinker. *The smugglers' hanging*. He'd read about it somewhere. It was what smugglers used to do to anyone who grassed to the Excise men. It was a terrible warning to other would-be informants.

But this man belonged very much to the present. He was a big man, six feet at least, Clinker reckoned. He wore baggy trousers, now water-logged and clinging to his long legs, and a black T-shirt. There were tattoos on his outstretched arms. On his feet were trainers, filthy, pressed down into the mud. Only the limp pony-tail which hung over one shoulder like a piece of seaweed could have belonged to an earlier time. *Poor devil*, thought Clinker. Whatever he'd done he didn't deserve to die like that, alone, listening to the mud creaking as the tide approached, knowing there was no escape.

Clinker called to Mac, who was trembling and cowed. The tide was no more than ten feet away, ready for a repeat performance.

'Don't fret, old chap,' said Clinker, bending down to pat the dog reassuringly. 'There's nothing we can do for him now. We'll soon get him out of there and on his way to a decent burial.'

Depressed and sickened by the find, Clinker ran back to where he'd left his bike hidden in a clump of grass. He hauled it upright, got on it, whistled to Mac and peddled back to Hernmouth and the police station.

Chapter Two

'Hope this isn't too early for you, ma'am,' said Douglas apologetically, feeling his confidence drain away, as it always did when he was with Edith Lake. 'I thought I ought to come straight away.'

'Thank you, Chief Inspector. I appreciate it. When did you get back?'

'Last night. I'm still a bit fazed.'

'Poor man. I expect you are. I know how exhausting those long flights can be. Let me get you some coffee.'

She walked across to the open door, called some instructions to an invisible person, and rejoined Douglas, who was standing awkwardly in the middle of the room.

'Do take a seat. I'm sorry, I should have asked you before. Una won't be long with the coffee.'

Douglas perched uneasily on the edge of the settee. He was not only jet-lagged, but nervous. The gentry didn't usually have this effect on him; his good friend Willy Graham, who lived near Coldstream, always made him feel at home when he went to dinner at his place, or took part in his shoots. But there was something about Edith Laker that made him edgy. She made him conscious of his blunt, Edinburgh-manse upbringing, where folk always spoke their minds. She also made him feel clumsy; he'd have to take care not to send his cup of coffee flying like he had the last time he was here. Looking out at her beautiful garden, part of the Northumbrian landscape which had been tamed and manicured to suit the genteel elegance of St Oswald's Hall, once again he felt out of place. Edith was, as always, intimidating; even though it was only half past eight in the morning, she was perfectly groomed. Oh, she had style, he had to admit. Her iron-grey hair was immaculate and she had carefully applied lipstick and eye-shadow. He reckoned that he and Edith must be about the same age. Both had said goodbye to their forties; but looking at her now, he thought ruefully how much better she was wearing than he was.

He shifted uneasily on the settee, but was saved from the need to make small talk by the arrival of Una, Edith's housekeeper. Now Una was the sort of woman he *could* get on with. With her good-natured plump face, and frizzy permed hair that was a mixture of reddish colours. She wasn't in the least bit intimidating. She smiled at Douglas as she put the tray of coffee down in front of Edith. He liked Una better than her husband, Derek Rose – everyone called him Delrose – who was Edith's chauffeur and handyman. The pair lived comfortably in the lodge down by the front gate. Delrose always seemed a bit off-putting, somehow, though he was pleasant enough when Douglas bumped into him in the pub.

'Clare's ready,' said Una to Edith. 'Shall I send her in?'

'Of course. The Chief Inspector here won't mind.'

'Have you told her yet?' he said hesitatingly. 'That her mother—'

'Not yet. I've decided to leave that until after I've heard what you have to say. Has Derek brought the car round?' she asked Una.

'Aye. He's waiting.'

'Then tell her to come quickly. She mustn't be late.'

Douglas knew that Clare went to a posh school in Alnwick, St Hilda's Convent, but he hadn't realised that she was driven there each day in a chauffeur-driven car. The bairn had really landed on her feet.

Suddenly a small girl, about six years old, erupted into the room, and hurled herself at Edith. The child was dressed in a uniform of grey skirt and royal blue blazer trimmed with gold braid, which set off her bright face and red-gold hair to perfection.

'Bye, Aunt Edith. See you soon!'

'Have you got your lunch-box?'

'Yes. Blackcurrant yoghurt!'

Edith smiled at Una, and Douglas caught a brief glimpse of the stunning woman she had once been.

'You know what's good for her, Una. Thank you for your trouble.'

'No trouble, ma'am. Clare's a mighty yoghurt eater.'

'Be good,' said Edith to the child, giving her another hug. 'And be nice to Sister Anna. Don't tease her because of her Irish accent. There's nothing wrong with being Irish. Now, off you go. Don't keep Derek waiting.'

Una took hold of Clare's hand and led her away as Edith handed Douglas his coffee. He felt uneasy. People had said that Edith spoiled the child. He knew she paid for her education; but he hadn't realised the extent of her involvement.

'Such a bright wee bairn,' he said. 'Terrible to have to tell her such a dreadful thing.'

'I shall be here for her. She knows that I'll never let her down, not like her mother did. She'll get over it. Tell me the details, Inspector, please.'

Douglas was shocked. A small bairn had to be told that her mother was dead and all Edith Laker could say was that the child would 'get over it'! *Aye, maybe she will*, he thought grimly. *In time. But there'll be much grieving first*.

Edith came over to ply Douglas with more coffee. 'You saw her?'

'Aye, I did that. In the Auckland morgue.'

Edith's gaze never wavered. 'Are you certain she took her own life?'

Douglas shifted uneasily. Edith was just a bit too cold-blooded for his liking.

'It seems pretty certain. The New Zealand police took me to the place where the Maori found her. They found a sizeable stash of heroin in the hut. And her body was full of it.'

Still no reaction from Edith, though he noticed she hadn't touched her coffee.

'And what do *you* think, Chief Inspector?' she said.

'I have to believe what the New Zealand police say. They conducted a thorough investigation.' Douglas hoped this would impress Edith, who was a stickler for correct procedure.

'I'm sure the New Zealand police did everything they should have done. But you seem – unconvinced.'

God woman, thought Douglas irritably, *if only you'd stop staring at me I'd feel a lot more convinced!*

'Not really,' he shrugged. 'It's just a feeling . . .' He paused. How to tell her without being ordered back to Auckland again?

'Well, out with it, man.' Her voice was sharp; Douglas winced.

'Well, the Maoris were a bit defensive, like. She could have been poaching on their patch.'

'How do you mean – poaching?'

'Selling drugs, ma'am. To their people. They like to take care of their own, you see. It's only natural.'

'Bridie, a drug pusher? Is that what you're saying, Chief Inspector?'

'Just a theory, ma'am. She was a persistent user, after all. She wouldn't be the first.'

'I thought I'd put a stop to all that. But they say that once you've got a taste for hard drugs you never give them up. I rescued Bridie, you know, Chief Inspector. She was a poor thing when I took her on, and that husband of hers was less than useless. He soon left her when the going got rough.'

'He knew she was an addict, of course.'

'How can you be sure of that?'

'We interviewed him – the New Zealand police put out a call for him. He had nothing to do with Bridie's death – he was down on South Island at the time. That's been confirmed. He didn't seem too upset about his wife, but he does want to see Clare. I reckon he'll be over soon. We're in touch and I'll let you know any developments on that front. There's nothing to worry about,' he said, noting the look of alarm on Edith's face. 'He'll not want to take the bairn away. He'll be only too pleased to see her so well cared for.'

'Clare's his daughter.'

For a moment Douglas felt sorry for Edith. Her face had crumpled; suddenly, she looked a lot older than her years. Obviously the bairn meant the world to her.

'Aye, but as you pointed out he deserted her and her mother. Probably doesn't want the responsibility. It was sad to see that place where Bridie died. All on her own, in a strange country, amongst the dripping trees. No one should have to die like that. I think she might have gone to New Zealand to find her husband: God knows why. She must have run out of money and decided to earn herself a bit on the side. And that upset the Maoris. We'll never know all the facts. Do you want the New Zealanders to send her body back here?'

'We should have her home. I'll be responsible for the funeral. She must be laid to rest in her own country.'

'That's very good of you, ma'am. Now, I must be on my way. I hope the bairn won't be too distressed.'

'I'll break it to her gently. She was certainly upset when her mother went off like she did. But as she's been let down once already, perhaps she won't fret too much the second time.'

'She's lucky to have you, ma'am.'

'Thank you, Chief Inspector. As you know, I'm very fond of children.' She paused. 'I never had any of my own to love and be proud of. Not that I minded too much – I was always so busy. George was very involved with his job, and there was plenty for me to do as a diplomatic wife. It was only after he died that I came to feel the lack of children. I suppose Clare has become my grandchild – like all the other children I've rescued in Brazil. They've been important to me.'

'We all admire your charitable work,' said Douglas gently, sensing that Edith Laker, despite her formidable self-control, was desperately lonely.

'I've no use for admiration,' said Edith briskly. 'Financial support is what we need. You'll come to my wine and cheese party next Friday, Chief Inspector, won't you? Superintendent Blackburn has accepted the invitation. Seven thirty.'

Douglas felt his good will evaporate. He hated these occasions. Not that he didn't sympathise with Edith Laker's good works; everyone was impressed with her efforts on behalf of the street children of Rio, where she had founded a school for them, enabling them to make a fresh start in life. But holding a glass of warm white wine and chatting politely to the county set was, frankly, not his scene. Still, he couldn't refuse under the circumstances.

Edith watched him waver. 'You will come? De Profundis needs your support.'

'I was taught that charity begins at home. There's plenty of disadvantaged children wandering the streets of Newcastle.'

'Nonsense, Chief Inspector! There's nothing in this country to compare with what goes on in Brazil. Your constables might not help children on British streets, but at least they don't round them up and shoot them. You know why we call our charity "De Profundis"?'

'I can't say that I do, ma'am.'

'I thought as much,' Edith continued. 'It means, "Out of the Depths". "Out of the depths I call unto Thee" – part of a prayer. In this case, the depths refer to the sewers where these children live. I've seen them, Chief Inspector. I was taken down under the streets of Rio and there, in one of the city's main sewers, I found children huddled, just above the waterline, piled in a heap like rats. They tried to scuttle away, just like rats do, but when we spoke to them and told them that our white van was outside with the cross of Jesus painted on the side, they stopped and ran to us, knowing we would take them out of the depths and into the daylight. We are able to rescue just a handful of the Rio street children. They are the lucky ones. It really is your duty as a Christian to support us.'

'I'll always do my Christian duty, ma'am. Never fear about that.'

Douglas, despite his ambivalent attitude towards Edith Laker, could not fail to be moved by her account of the street children. Edith's plea had been extremely convincing, and he would have liked to hear more, but it was time to go. Reports to write: then meet up with Venerables at half past twelve. Another bad business: a man pinned out on the mud and allowed to drown. Was there no end to evil?

He looked out of the large picture window at the bleak landscape. A few skeletal trees were etched against the lowering sky; shabby clouds hung down in festoons. He sighed quietly and made for the door.

'Thanks for the coffee, ma'am.'

'Thank you for coming. You'll let me know when Billy Ransome arrives?'

'Aye, I'll do that.'

'I'll see you on Friday, then. I'll make sure there's a glass of claret for you.'

Douglas's spirits immediately rose dramatically. He walked

briskly out to his car, got in, turned on the heater and drove down the long gravel drive, past the lodge where Derek and Una Rose lived, and out into the main street of the village of Wynwick.

The seemingly endless – and pointless – reports completed, Douglas drove down to the port at Hernmouth and parked his car in front of the harbour wall. The place was deserted; the tide was out and three brightly-painted pleasure boats, tightly wrapped up in bright blue tarpaulins, sat comfortably on the mud, waiting for summer to come. Outside the harbour, along the estuary wall, he saw the masts of fishing boats. *They'll not go out today*, he thought. *Wind's too strong by far*.

He zipped up the front of his anorak and walked over to The Boomers, a pub which was popular with the locals and where he had arranged to meet Sergeant Venerables. It was a squat, Victorian building, built in the local sandstone now pockmarked and streaked with grime. On that freezing February morning, it looked bleak and inhospitable. The sign, showing three swarthy eighteenth-century characters smoking unfeasibly long clay pipes, creaked dismally in the wind. They were said to be three notorious smugglers, known locally as 'boomers' because they came from the village of Boulmer further down the coast. Douglas hated that sign. Smugglers were ruthless, bloodthirsty people: not a bit picturesque or romantic. If today's drug gangs were anything to go by, smugglers were a vicious lot, driven by greed, capable of any villainy.

Inside the pub, the atmosphere was different. A coal fire glowed reassuringly in the Victorian fireplace at one end of the room. Charlie Wheeler, the barman and owner, was busy polishing glasses. A big, powerfully-built man, he was popular because he seemed to mind his own business – but Douglas didn't trust him. He felt he was the kind of man who ran with the hare and hunted with the hounds. However, he had his uses, and occasionally passed on useful hints to the police when it suited him. In return, he asked for nothing except that The Boomers should be left in peace.

Venerables was already there, sitting by the fire. Douglas, who hadn't seen his colleague for ten days, was shocked by his appearance; usually a dapper, energetic man, he now looked the picture of gloom. He almost seemed to have shrunk, judging by the way in which his anorak, tightly buttoned as if he weren't sitting by a good fire, hung loosely round his lean frame. His hair was lank and looked as if it needed washing; his mournful expression reminded Douglas of a slightly seedy bloodhound.

'God, man, you look rough,' he said as he walked over to him. 'What's up?' Noticing his empty glass, he added, 'What are you drinking?'

Venerables raised his head; Douglas tried to avoid his bloodshot eyes. 'Why aye, man, you look in fine fettle. Half of broon, if you please.'

Douglas winced at Venerables' caricature of a Geordie accent; clearly his colleague was in a defiant mood.

'Make that a pint,' Douglas said, turning to Charlie Wheeler. 'The sergeant looks in need of cheering up. Come on, man, liven yourself up,' he said, dumping the glass in front of Venerables. 'What's gone wrong? It's Jenny, I suppose – she's given you the boot. Venerables didn't answer and Douglas went on. 'You're better off without her, man. I warned you that the lass was too ambitious. You want someone who'll stay at home and cook your tea. A proper policeman's wife.'

'Jenny couldn't cook,' said Venerables, stirring himself sufficiently to lift the glass to his lips. 'Not even tetties and bagies.'

'Speak English, man,' said Douglas impatiently. 'I can't follow you.'

'It's all right for you,' said Venerables, with a flash of his old spirit, 'you've been jetting around in the sun, and I've been wading around in freezing cold mud looking at dead bodies.'

'That's your job, man. And there's no need to envy me. Being shut up in a tin box for twenty-five hours is not my idea of fun. Anyway, tell me more. Charlie, don't you have some phone calls to make? Sergeant Venerables and I want a few minutes to ourselves.'

Charlie knew the ropes. He put down the glass he was polishing and left the bar. He knew exactly what they wanted to talk about. He knew who the dead man was: knew who killed him, too. But it was more than his life was worth that he should let on.

'Clinker found him, you say?'

'Aye. It's always Clinker who finds the bodies.'

'Do you know who he was?'

'Newcastle man. Name of Josh Tyler.'

'Who told you that?'

'Chance. He'll be along any minute.'

'John Chance? He's actually done something useful for a change?'

'Seems like it. There's been no sailing for him in this weather, so he's got on with his police work. The dead man was one of his informants.'

'I see. Tyler's friends didn't hold with that, I suppose?'

'Apparently not. But here's Chance now. He's got Lizzie with him – she's a Newcastle lass. Why aye, lassie, what'll you have?' Venerables said, suddenly coming to life.

Douglas sighed. So that was it, he thought: off with the old, on with the new. And Venerables had learnt nothing from past experience. Typically, he'd picked another high-flyer: Lizzie Teal, twenty-seven, as pretty as a peach with her corkscrew curls and baby face, but as tough as nails. Rode a yellow Yamaha motorbike, and was like a Jack Russell terrier when it came to ferreting out drug pushers. Special Branch certainly knew what it was doing when they lent her to the Drugs Squad. He watched her take off her leather jacket and buy her own glass of orange juice from Charlie, who'd miraculously materialised once more. Then she climbed onto one of the bar stools and curled her jean-clad legs round the pedestal. John Chance, a pleasant-looking chap from Durham CID, seemed to be eyeing her with rather too much enthusiasm, Douglas noticed. That wouldn't do anything for Venerables's temper.

'Hi, Douglas,' Lizzie called across. 'Tired of the high life already?'

'Don't you start, lass,' grumbled Douglas, beginning to tire of the leg-pulling. 'As a matter of fact, it's good to be back.'

'Get anywhere?'

'I got there too late. The usual scene. Death through overdose, the Kiwis said, and they're sticking to it. Her employer wasn't particularly cut up.'

'Takes a lot to upset Edith Laker,' said Lizzie. 'She's a tough nut. Dotes on that child, though. Any sign of the husband?'

'He'll be over soon. Wants to take a look at his daughter.'

'About time too.'

'Edith'll not like it. But how are you, lass? This isn't your neck of the woods – bit on the rough side, Hernmouth. Your father won't want to see you here. I'm sure a man of the cloth doesn't like the thought of his daughter nipping round on a motorbike and washing people's hair for a living.'

'He puts up with it. He's got no choice. He gave up on me long ago, when I decided to join the police. Besides, I'm the last person he worries about.' She grinned engagingly at Douglas, whose heart melted. 'His parishioners are forever dying, or having babies, or getting married. Or robbing his church.'

Douglas knew all about Lizzie; her father was vicar of Seaton, a big parish near Durham. No doubt he tried to be proud of his daughter, who'd done well at Durham University – reading Classics, of all things. And now the Drugs Squad had set her up in Hernmouth, working undercover as a hairdresser. She was taking a bit of a risk being in The Boomers with them; but he knew Charlie'd be discreet. He had too much to lose. Besides, he probably thought she was Chance's girlfriend.

There were too many clever lassies around, thought Douglas, as he watched Lizzie run rings round Venerables and Chance. The police force was changing; once, not so long ago, women had been employed just to comfort and console the bereaved. Now they did everything, went everywhere, and made the men restless. Just look at Venerables – he was positively drooling. If you had to have lassies in the force, he thought mournfully, then they ought to wear veils. Aye, and cover their bodies, he added to himself; he couldn't help but notice Lizzie's firm breasts under her tight pullover. Still, she got results. There were no flies on Lizzie, he admitted, albeit reluctantly.

'I hear Clinker's man was one of yours,' Douglas said, turning to John Chance.

'That's right. Bloody nuisance he's gone. We stopped a few deliveries through information we received from him. We found a load of heroin on one of the trawlers the night before the gang got him. Given time, I reckon he would have told us who the top man was. He'd have sold his own grandmother for a tenner. He was a Gateshead man, new to these parts, and he didn't stay long.'

'Know who did it?'

John shrugged. 'Could have been anyone. It's a huge network. Orders went out; someone obeyed. We'll only get on top of the bastards if we find the big man.'

'Where's it all go?' said Douglas. Most people round here can't afford to buy it. Newcastle, I suppose.'

'It goes everywhere. Newcastle, London, Edinburgh, Glasgow. Come the summer, the tourists. This coast has several ports of entry and it's very convenient for Holland, and Eastern Europe. Someone's got something going round here. And now we've lost one of our chief informants, we're back to square one.'

'Plenty more fish in the sea,' said Venerables laconically. 'You've only got to know where to look. Come on, Lizzie, let me buy you egg and chips. You can't survive on orange juice.'

Lizzie laughed and finished her drink. 'It's all I want, but thanks all the same. Anyway, I'm back to work now. Two old-lady perms this afternoon. Fancy a haircut, Frank? You look as if you could do with one. We're unisex, you know,.'

Venerables jumped visibly, then blushed a deep crimson. Douglas looked at him pityingly. *Hell's teeth*, he thought; he's fallen in love again, in just under twenty minutes. Douglas would have to have a word with Lizzie. She was bad for morale.

'Why aye, hinny,' said Venerables, his accent more pronounced than ever for Lizzie's benefit, 'it's time I smartened myself up a bit. When can you do me?'

'Right now, man.'

'Really? Thanks, pet. Just what I need.'

'Now watch it, you two,' growled Douglas. 'Lizzie, leave my Sergeant alone. There's no time for haircuts. I've got an appointment with the Harbour Master at two, and I'd like you to come along with me, Venerables.'

'I'll see he gets there in time, Douglas,' said Lizzie, sliding off her stool. 'It won't take me long to sort him out.'

'I suppose not. He hasn't got that much hair.'

The two left the bar, and Douglas turned back to John Chance, who was staring wistfully after them.

'Don't fret, man. Venerables has the devil's own luck with the ladies. Gets through them like a dose of salts. Anyway, Lizzie's only having him on. She'll make mincemeat of him – you're much more her type. Now, lad, what's the plan? Give it a day or two and the stuff will start coming in again. Superintendent's getting a bit edgy – thinks we're sitting around on our backsides doing nothing.'

'I'll get down to the marina. There's quite a few people around, doing up their boats for the season. Mine's laid up too, next to Clinker's.'

'That's convenient. Do you know him well?'

'Clinker? He's one of the best. Doesn't say much, but he sees things. He'd have been a bloody good policeman. And you, sir? Any developments?'

'Me, lad? I'm going to a wine and cheese party at Edith Laker's house. With the Superintendent, no less.'

'You do lead the *dolce vita*, sir.'

'That's enough of that. In any case, I prefer a good malt myself.'

'Well, keep on hobnobbing with the gentry and you might get offered some.'

'That'll be the day, lad. That'll be the day.'

Chapter Three

It was Friday night and Lizzie stood at her bedroom window looking down into Butcher's Lane. A bit of a do, Annie had said; Lizzie had tried to make her excuses, but Annie, the junior stylist, plump, sexy and full of life, had insisted. So Lizzie, conscious that she had to keep on good terms with the staff of Crokers Unisex Hair Salon, had agreed. It was now nine o'clock – a foul night, and her cottage, which the police had rented for her, was warm and cosy. 'There's nothing for it, Lizzie, old girl,' she said to herself as she turned away from the window and began rummaging through the wardrobe for something appropriate to wear, 'you've got to go. Don't be so bloody middle-aged! It's a sad state of affairs when you'd rather stay in on a Friday night with a good book than go to one of Annie's notorious bashes.' But Annie's friends were not her friends. Mostly local boys who worked at the prawn factory down on the quay, they liked drinking vast quantities of beer and screwing girls. In particular, they liked screwing Annie.

Not that Lizzie was a prude – far from it. She'd had her wild times, but life had suddenly got serious when, six years ago, her lover Mike had died from taking adulterated heroin. It was his death which had decided her career. From the moment she saw the suffering on his white, lifeless face, she knew that what she wanted to do was spend her life hunting down the gangs of pushers who traded on the weak and vulnerable. And Mike had been vulnerable. A shy medical student with gloriously romantic looks and a gentle, loving nature, fear of failure had led him into the shadowy world of drugs which – he claimed –

gave him the necessary confidence to pass exams. Despite all Lizzie's warnings, he'd succumbed. Lizzie still remembered, as if it were yesterday, the shock of finding his body sprawled on his bed in the hall of residence. Since then, she'd been suspicious of most men. She enjoyed watching Annie making the local lads grovel. Only the truly safe, like Sergeant Venerables, attracted her; and then only to flirt with.

And John Chance, she mused, as she pulled out a black jersey shift dress, what of him? He was nice enough, but too dull and plodding, she decided. Give him a few years and he'd turn into a second Douglas McBride. What a prospect.

She dressed quickly: black shift, black tights, and clumpy shoes. She considered taking her radio phone, but her outfit was far too skimpy to conceal it. Besides, she thought dismissively, she wasn't on duty. The prawn packers weren't really criminally inclined – she'd learned to turn a blind eye to the stuff they smoked. That wasn't what she was after.

She pulled on her waterproof jacket, dragged oilskin leggings over her short skirt, and finally donned helmet and gauntlets. Outside in the road stood her yellow Yamaha; as usual, the sight of it thrilled her. She serviced it herself, having been to evening classes to learn the mechanics, and she had full confidence in the powerful 1100 cc engine. It could be relied on to get her out of trouble quickly. Tonight, as always, it started like a dream; she roared off down the street to the council estate where Annie's party was being held.

It was the usual scene: a party getting into top gear and enough booze to stock a pub. Annie, four vodkas down, was flushed and well away with a chap whose chest and arms were covered in tattoos. The music was deafening.

Lizzie knew the ropes. No point in trying to talk to anyone. There wasn't much in the way of eats: a few crisps, some peanuts. Nowhere to sit down. Her safest bet was to choose an older man, or one of the shy ones, and stick to him. She chose the latter, who seemed surprised and delighted with her advances, and was even more enthusiastic when she indicated that she didn't want to dance but would like to go into the kitchen and find something to eat.

In the kitchen they raided the fridge. The boy, who was no more than eighteen, found some sausages and offered to cook them. Lizzie, who loved food and could eat enormous quantities despite her slim figure, buttered some sliced bread of doubtful vintage. Sausage sandwiches would be just what the doctor ordered.

Soon the kitchen was filled with other food-seekers; Lizzie found herself enjoying the good-natured banter. Her youthful partner had disappeared with someone younger and therefore more accessible than herself. Then the tattooed man, who hadn't been able to entice Annie upstairs with him and clearly resented his abrupt dismissal, came across to Lizzie.

'Come on, lass. Get your knickers off,' he said, shoving himself against her.

'I'm not wearing any,' she said.

'Show us!'

'Later, maybe. I'm eating at the moment.'

'Come upstairs with me and I'll show you something you can really get your teeth into.'

'Piss off, will you?'

'Don't tell me to piss off,' he said, affronted. 'You birds are all the same. You lead us on and then you tell us to sod off. What you need is something to relax you. Fancy a smoke?'

'Thanks,' said Lizzie, determined to keep her cool, 'I don't need anything to get *me* going.'

'Well, let me tell you lass,' he said, thrusting his face close to hers, 'upstairs we've got something you might like. A TV – but we're not watching "Neighbours". We've got videos. Good ones. They'll get you going, all right.'

'You mean, you've got blue movies upstairs?'

'Blue, pink – whatever colour you like.'

Lizzie felt the familiar prickle of excitement as her investigative instincts crackled into life. She turned towards the tattooed man, whose name she now remembered: Big Jim, he was called. A porter at the prawn factory. He saw the change in her and reached out to grab her breast. Lizzie came closer; his tattooed chest smelt of sweat and Marlboros. He pulled her to him; she felt his hand run down her back and slide down the back of her tights.

'Come on, let's get upstairs. Cop a feel of this.' And he drew her hand down the bulge in the front of his trousers. She laughed, and began to play with the zip on his flies.

'Eh, lass,' he said, his breathing rapid, 'you know what's what, don't you? You don't need any of them videos. But you'll like the next lot. There's some real hot stuff coming in tonight.'

'Really?' she said. 'I'd like to see them.'

'Would you, now? Well, *Cormorant*'s in port and they'll be along later. Upstairs first – I can't wait.'

'Stay right there. I've just got to go to the loo.'

'Don't be long, pet.'

'I won't. Don't wander off – I need you.'

'Don't worry – I'm not going anywhere.'

She went out of the kitchen, shutting the door quietly. Most people had already made the journey upstairs; she could hear them laughing, cat-calling. She picked up her oilskins and helmet, and left the house. She pushed her bike a little way down the road before starting it, then drove down to the harbour. *Cormorant*: she knew the boat. A ketch, big enough to cope with a force seven gale.

Down on the quay she propped her bike against a wall and went to *Cormorant*'s mooring. A light was on in the wheel-house. Lizzie paused; she knew it was dangerous to board a boat without telling her colleagues. But she'd left her mobile at home. Could she risk it? Lizzie, conscious of her police instructor's words of warning, resisted impulse. Instead, she walked quickly along the quay to the telephone box and dialled the local police station. The person who answered wasn't very helpful: where was she? What did she want to do? No, there were no police cars available. Better wait – someone would come along later and sort things out.

'Later' just wasn't good enough. She might miss a trick – and then where would she be, when her superiors heard that she'd been too cautious?

So she decided to be bold. She walked back to *Cormorant* and hopped over the rail. She tiptoed cautiously along the deck; a man was sitting at a table in the wheel-house, watching television and drinking whisky. All very peaceful.

Suddenly strong arms gripped her from behind, and a hand clamped her mouth. With a swift movement, learnt in her self-defence class, she kicked back, hard. She heard the man grunt; turned, and looked into a dark face and hostile eyes. His small, wiry body, wriggling around inside a fluorescently patterned jacket, made it difficult for Lizzie to grip him tightly. But she was in control. Finally, she got hold of him in a classic judo grip and tipped him over the side of the boat. He slid into the water quite smoothly, making hardly any sound.

Then she noticed the holdall. It was standing by the rail; she had obviously interrupted the man as he was about to leave the boat. She picked up the bag and leapt down onto the quay. Checking to see that her victim wasn't actually drowning – he seemed to be clinging firmly to a dinghy tied to the stern of *Cormorant* – she ran to the motorbike, clipped the holdall onto the back, and drove off to her cottage. Stupid of her not to have brought her mobile! But she'd got the holdall. And she hadn't had to use excessive violence. She'd recognize him again; she'd been trained to remember faces. And she could still feel that bony body wriggling around inside the gaudy jacket, like a crab in an ill-fitting shell.

Douglas looked round the room and shuddered. Bits of cheese stuck on sticks, a choice of white or red wine, polite conversation. Like a scene in a play. The posters were real enough, though; faces of children with great, dark, expressive eyes watched him from every wall. The name of the charity, De Profundis, was painted in stark black letters on a white banner and hung above the fireplace like the Parthenon frieze. He couldn't fault Edith Laker's commitment to her cause, Douglas thought, as he weaved his way through the well-heeled crowd towards Superintendent Blackburn. Edith was certainly queening it this evening. Dressed in a blue silk dress with a necklace of pearls that almost concealed her ageing neck, she stood out as a pillar of elegance in that crowd of comfortable locals who, on the whole, by no stretch of the imagination could be regarded as smart. Her blue-grey hair was newly set and lacquered into place; her face, with its heavily made-up eyes, was an inscrutable, smiling mask.

Blackburn, his well-upholstered figure squeezed into a grey suit of indeterminate age, his thinning hair spread carefully over his ever-increasing bald patch, nodded to Douglas. The Superintendent was trying to be intelligent about architecture.

'This house now, ma'am,' he was saying, 'parts of it must be very old. The tower, for instance.'

'Yes, indeed. The Normans built it to keep out the Scots. It's a pele tower – there are lots of them round here. People sheltered in them when the invaders came over the border. They took their livestock with them and lived in them until the Scots grew bored and went back home.'

'Thank God those days are over,' said Blackburn piously.

'Aye, different sort of invaders today,' said Douglas with a false heartiness. 'The new villains come in by sea and try to poison us with their contraband.'

Una Rose, who'd clearly made some effort to look presentable that evening in a black velvet skirt and red blouse with a ruffled front, came up with a tray of drinks. Douglas helped himself to a glass of red wine: the lesser of two evils as far as he was concerned. Edith turned her head to look at him; Douglas flinched under the gaze of her sharp eyes hooded by metallic blue eyelids. She reminded him of a reptile about to strike.

'Smugglers, Douglas? In *this* part of the country? Surely not. It's the most peaceful spot you could think of.'

Douglas ignored Blackburn's warning look and forced himself to look into those mocking eyes. 'Yes, ma'am. We're not immune to the modern disease. People want their thrills and there's always somebody ready to supply them. And fight over it. Even kill for it.'

'I see what you're getting at, Chief Inspector – that bad business down in Hernmouth. Any more news yet?'

'No, ma'am. And it'll not be easy. People won't talk – they all cover for each other when it suits them.'

'But I'm sure you and the Superintendent here won't have much of a problem! I've heard about your amazing powers of deduction. I shall follow your activities with bated breath. But, please, do try and keep these villains away from St Oswald's Hall.'

Douglas got the distinct impression that she was laughing at him. But Blackburn took her comments at face value.

'Don't worry ma'am. Nothing is going to disturb your peace. Now, if you'll excuse me, I want to have a private word with the Chief Inspector. Is there a room we can use?'

'Of course, Superintendent. The library is free. It's good of you to spare the time to come along this evening, when you're in the middle of a murder investigation.'

'A pleasure, ma'am. I'll leave my donation on the table in the hall, shall I?'

'Why, thank you, Superintendent. Alternatively, you can give it to Derek Rose. He's our treasurer.'

And she left them.

Douglas and Blackburn made their way to the snug, book-lined room on the other side of the hall. The room was softly lit with side lights which complemented the mellow patinas of the antique furniture. Blackburn made himself comfortable in one of the spacious leather armchairs; Douglas, on guard, remained standing.

'This is a disaster,' said Blackburn. 'We can't have an unsolved murder on this part of the coast. Come the summer, the place will be full of tourists – violent death is bad for business. There's nothing for it – I'm moving Venerables down to Hernmouth. Berwick's too bloody far away and we need a few brains around here.'

'What about Chance? He's in charge.'

'*Chance*? Durham CID? Not a chance,' said Blackburn, smirking at his own wit. 'He's only interested in that boat of his. Doesn't notice anything unless it's dumped in his lap.'

'What about Lizzie Teal?'

'She's undercover at the moment. Can't think what those Drugs Squad layabouts were thinking of when they set her up in that hairdresser's. Drug dealing is a man's world, Douglas.'

Douglas, who had finished his red wine and was desperately in need of something stronger, felt compelled to defend Lizzie. He agreed with the Superintendent's sentiments – but he had nothing but respect for Lizzie's ability.

'She's tough, sir. She can cope. So where does this leave me?'

'*You*? Why, you'll stay with me, up in Berwick. We need you to manage the whole circus. You'll have to get off to Hernmouth most days to liaise with Venerables – and galvanise Chance into getting off that fat backside of his.'

Douglas, not enthralled by the prospect of commuting daily along the A1, began to protest – but changed his mind.

After all, it was only thirty-six miles from Berwick to Hernmouth . . .

'Chance isn't doing that badly, sir. In my opinion. He's interviewed and eliminated dozens of suspects in connection with Tyler's murder. I've got a list of them. The usual story: no-one saw or heard anything, and if they did they're not telling. It's just like the smuggling gangs of the past; the locals were terrified of them too.'

Blackburn wasn't impressed. 'This isn't the past, Douglas! It's our job to protect the public and it's *your* job to reassure them. Find an informant. There's always someone who'll squeal on a fellow criminal. One more thing – we've just had a fax from New Zealand, about Bridie Ransome. Something's come up. The Kiwi police still think she willingly took the drugs which killed her, but they've got a new lead which might be of interest to you. Billy Ransome has admitted that shortly before Bridie disappeared, she phoned him.'

'*Now* he tells us! Why the hell didn't he mention it before?'

'Seems he just didn't want to get involved. Anyway, she managed to trace him by contacting sheep farms in North and South Island. She told him that she was frightened. Something had happened in Britain which had caused her to leave the country. He said she sounded confused. He asked her if she was still using heroin, she wouldn't give him a straight answer, and they had a row. He repeated what he'd always said to her: as long as she took smack he didn't want anything to do with her. Then he asked her if she had Clare with her; when Bridie said she'd left her behind in England, with Edith Laker, he refused to help her. He put the phone down and that was the last time he spoke to her.'

'Doesn't sound much of a husband.'

'He'd had a basinful of her, I think. Couldn't stand the thought of her. But that's by the way. It doesn't mean he had anything to do with her death – he was tucked away in South Island, and that's been confirmed. But something serious must have happened here to send her to the other side of the world on a wild goose chase.'

'Have you asked Edith Laker?'

Blackburn stared at Douglas in horror. 'God, man, are you out of your mind? I can't come out with a question like that in the middle of a social function! We're off duty. It's our job to mingle with the public, not ask questions. And don't you forget to give a donation to help those poor bairns. That's what we're here for; and besides, it helps our image.'

Douglas didn't relish the idea. 'Do I have to go back into that room? I don't like drinking wine before dinner. It upsets my stomach.'

'Then don't drink it! It's good for you to go without. In any case, you've got to drive home soon.'

'The sooner the better, sir.'

The sitting room had filled up whilst Douglas and Blackburn had been otherwise engaged in the library. Hilda, Lady Nevill, had arrived and was deep in conversation with Edith Laker; Douglas had a deep admiration for Hilda, whom he'd met in connection with a previous case. She was the sort of person Douglas approved of: straightforward gentry, no side to her. There she was, ready to open her purse. He felt a tiny surge of resentment. It wasn't that he disapproved of Edith's enthusiasm – he'd read in the newspapers about the destitute children of Rio, how they were rounded up by the Brazilian police at night and shot like dogs – but, as he'd told Edith, he'd been brought up to believe that charity began at home. After all, there were hundreds of people sleeping in the streets in towns and cities across Britain, and no one was lifting a finger to help them! Not such a glamorous cause, he supposed. Still, he didn't begrudge helping kids, wherever they were from, and he made a resolution to give generously. He spotted Delrose, Edith's chauffeur and general handyman, and went over to speak to him. He'd never taken to the man, although he couldn't find a good reason why. Delrose, middle-aged with a slight stoop, thinning hair and a disapproving expression, reminded Douglas of an unsuccessful schoolmaster forced, for unsavoury reasons, into early retirement. He wore battered corduroy trousers and a Viyella shirt, just like Douglas's own schoolmasters had worn, back in the fifties. He even had leather patches on the elbows of his tweed jacket – the hallmark of the would-be academic.

'Douglas. Nice to see you. Any news on that poor devil they

found down in the Hern estuary?' His voice was soft; his accent placed him vaguely south of Watford.

'Not yet. But we'll get him. The Devil's not got the better of us yet.'

'He won't get far with you on his tail. You're a veritable St Michael.'

'I do my best. And how's the wee Clare these days?'

'She's well. But you can see for yourself – here she comes.'

Clare, dressed in a fleecy blue nightie and clutching a battered teddy bear, came running into the room. She went up to Edith, who hugged her warmly. Douglas could not help but compare her bright, hopeful face with the tragic, defeated features of the lost children of Rio, staring reproachfully down from the walls.

'Good night, Aunt Edith,' he heard the child say.

'Good night, pet. You remember Lady Nevill, don't you?'

'Of course. Hello, Lady Nevill.'

'I think it's time we dropped the Lady Nevill, don't you? Why don't you call me Aunt Hilda?'

'Then I shall have two aunties. Aren't I lucky?' And the girl laughed, the unconscious, carefree laughter of childhood. Douglas, watching the scene, felt his heart melt; Edith had done her work well. The child scarcely seemed affected by the loss of her mother. How sad it was, he thought, that the poor, bedraggled woman he'd seen in the Auckland morgue had been so little missed by her own family! By all accounts her husband had been relieved at her death, and her child obviously had not suffered a great deal. For a moment he thought wistfully of the children he had never had: never would have, now. Oh, he'd experienced many of life's pleasures: a good meal, a fine malt whisky, a brisk walk over the moors, the excitement of the shoot. But romance? Marriage? Family? No. Not for him. God hadn't planned it that way.

His introspection was interrupted by Blackburn, who was impatient to leave. Douglas, nothing loth, said his goodbyes and left with the Superintendent, though they'd come in separate cars. For a moment they stood together in the drive looking back at the house; through the drawn curtains, they could see the silhouettes of people talking and laughing together. A full moon appeared from behind the scudding clouds, lighting up the garden.

'A fine house, Douglas.'

'Aye, sir. She's done wonders with it. I can remember when St Oswald's Hall was a bleak ruin with a tumbledown tower at one end. Forbidding sort of place. Now look at it – like something out of *Homes and Gardens*.'

'That's what money can do, Douglas. And Edith Laker's got money, all right.'

'Husband must have left her a packet.'

'So they say. He was a diplomat – last post, Rio. That's where she got involved with the street children.'

'Was the husband an Ambassador?'

'I think so. Why?'

'How come he never got a gong, like Lady Nevill's husband?'

'God, man, I don't know! I'm not an authority on the Honours system.'

Douglas shrugged. 'Anyway, whatever he was, it gives her something in common with Lady Nevill. I don't envy her this house, though. Upkeep must cost a fortune. And there's Delrose and his wife to pay. And the fancy car.'

'Aye. I envy her that car, now. A white Mercedes – just what I've always wanted.'

'Not on a policeman's salary, sir.'

It was after ten when Douglas arrived back at his stone house overlooking Berwick's Elizabethan ramparts. As always, he said a silent prayer of thanks to his uncle who'd left him the house ten years ago. It suited him well and had been the main reason why he'd moved from Edinburgh to Berwick. His housekeeper, Mrs Fairweather, had left him a plate of sandwiches in the kitchen; he settled down to eat them in front of the television to watch the tail-end of 'News at Ten'. The phone rang; he was surprised to hear Lizzie Teal's voice. He listened with mounting concern.

'*Videos*, you say?'

'Bad ones, Douglas.'

She paused as if she wanted to say more, but found it too painful. Douglas understood.

'Steady on, lass. The yacht, now – *Cormorant*, you say?'

'That's right. It's left harbour, of course. It took off before the local police got down there. They're tracking it now. It won't respond to radio contact, but they'll pick it up when it gets to Holland. That's the course they're on.'

'*Cormorant* belongs to Bruce Hamilton. Friend of Delrose's.'

'So it seems. But he wasn't involved, apparently. He was in Durham, staying at the Prince Bishop. He's on his way here now. He says he didn't give anyone permission to use the yacht, which was in for a refit. He's furious.'

'I'm not surprised. And what about you, lass?'

'I'm fine. Someone tried to clobber me, but I chucked him over the side.'

'Good for you! They taught you something in police school then?'

'Oh, I know how to defend myself. But the chap I tipped off the boat had gone when the local police got there. The thieves presumably picked him up and took him with them. We shall have to wait and see. Anyway, I got his holdall.'

'How many videos, Lizzie?'

'About forty. How can anyone watch that filth, Douglas? Little kids – they couldn't be more than six or seven—'

For a second, Douglas remembered little Clare, in her nightdress, the picture of innocence.

'Try not to think about it, lass. They're sick, they're not normal, the people who watch those videos. We'll get the bastards. I'll come right down. I'll need to talk to Bruce Hamilton tonight. *Cormorant* won't reach Holland much before midday tomorrow, I suppose.'

'I doubt it. Mind you, she's got fast engines. They'll fly the crew straight back.'

'Try not to get upset, lass. We have to maintain objectivity. It's only a job we're doing.'

'You'd be upset after seeing what was in that holdall. But don't worry. Nothing will stop me from doing my job.'

Chapter Four

Venerables wasn't too pleased about being roused by Douglas at so late an hour, to put it mildly.

'Better bring a bag with you,' said Douglas. 'Seems likely that you'll have to kip down there in Hernmouth.'

'What! In that God-forsaken place? Where'll they put me? In with Lizzie Teal?' Suddenly things looked brighter.

'Not a hope, laddie. In the police house, most likely, with Sergeant Holmes. Now get moving. Bruce Hamilton's on his way from Durham.'

'*Cormorant* belongs to him, doesn't it?'

'It does. And at this moment I bet he's wishing he'd never laid eyes on it.'

It was well after midnight when they arrived at the Incident Room, which had been set up in the police house on the outskirts of Hernmouth. The room was full of people, most of whom Douglas knew. Sergeant Holmes, who lived in the house, whose beat took in the villages of Craster, Wynick, and St Waleric's Haven, nodded in Douglas's direction. Fred Waring, from Customs and Excise, was talking to Lizzie Teal. John Chance came in minutes after Douglas and Venerables arrived. Douglas noticed that John looked solicitously in Lizzie's direction; he also noticed Venerables taking note of the situation. *Trouble brewing*, he thought. Always the case when lassies were around. But he was glad Lizzie didn't seem to be suffering any ill effects from the evening's experience on *Cormorant*.

'Hamilton's on his way,' said Holmes, who, as the occupant

of the police house, felt he should take charge of the proceedings.

'Good. Then we'll keep you company whilst you're waiting,' said Douglas, sitting down heavily in the one comfortable chair. He felt his age entitled him to it. 'Get some coffee on. Sergeant Venerables will tape our conversation when Hamilton gets here. He can't object.'

There was the sound of a car drawing up outside; a door slammed, and Bruce Hamilton marched in. Despite the lateness of the hour, he looked remarkably fresh; righteous indignation had lent colour to his face. Douglas had met him on several occasions: Hamilton, well-known in both sailing and country house circles, was a friend of Willy Graham, whose shooting parties Douglas regularly attended. Douglas knew him as a good shot, an excellent dog-handler, and a lively dinner companion who, with his fondness for malt whisky, could drink them all under the table. Now, with his stocky figure, abundant red hair and gingery beard jutting aggressively forward, he looked like a fitter version of Henry VIII.

'Well,' he said without any preamble, 'where's *Cormorant*?'

He stared impatiently round the room; when he recognised Douglas he strode over and glared down at him. Douglas stood up, trying to regain the upper hand.

'We're tracking her, Mr Hamilton. They're making for Holland. Don't worry – it's difficult to lose a yacht.'

'For God's sake, man, get the coastguards after it! Call out the navy! You can stop a ship on the high seas.'

Fred Waring, middle-aged and stolid, came over to join them. This was his province.

'No need to put the tax-payer to that expense, sir. The Dutch'll pick them up on the other side and bring them back here. And at the moment they're not replying to radio contact. Anything wrong with your electronics, sir? Just checking,' he added hastily; Hamilton looked decidedly explosive.

'Everything is in perfect working order. The radio was new last season. Of course they're not bloody well responding to your radio calls! Only an idiot would expect them to. They've stolen my yacht – they're hardly going to want a cosy chat with the police.'

The thrusting beard was perilously near Waring's face. He backed away.

'We've only got your word for it that they took the yacht without permission, sir.'

'*Only my word?* Do you know who I am? I'm just the owner of the yacht, that's all. I don't have the remotest idea who's on *Cormorant* at the moment! No one had my permission to take her out of Hernmouth. God almighty, it's February, freezing cold, gales imminent. It's hardly the season for pleasure-cruising.'

'We understand, sir. But we have to be quite sure before we start charging people. Only last night, Miss Teal here clearly saw two men on *Cormorant*: one in the wheel-house, and another man who she threw into the sea.'

Hamilton stopped dead in his tracks and stared at Lizzie.

'And who the hell is Miss Teal? What was she doing on my yacht, may I ask?'

Douglas took over. 'Never mind who Miss Teal is, sir. Just know that she's one of us, and that she had a tip-off that someone on *Cormorant* was bringing illegal goods ashore. She caught him red-handed. And now, sir, if you have no objection, we'd like to record this conversation. For our records.'

'Go ahead. I've nothing to hide. Back to Miss Teal – what sort of "goods" did she find on *Cormorant*?' said Hamilton, perhaps realising the seriousness of his situation.

Douglas nodded to Venerables, who turned on the tape recorder. 'Hard-core porn videos. Particularly foul ones, involving children. She confiscated about forty of them. I have to ask you – do you know anything about this, sir?'

Hamilton, deflated, looked around for a chair, spotted the one Douglas had been sitting in, and slumped down. His aggression had vanished; he looked grey, weary. Venerables handed him coffee in a plastic cup.

'Seems like you've had a lively evening, Chief Inspector,' said Hamilton. Douglas relaxed; Hamilton wasn't going to punch Waring in the face after all.

'Yes, indeed. As you say, a lively evening. To sum up: we've got the videos. We don't know what happened to the man who attacked Miss Teal, and we can't do anything about *Cormorant* until she gets to Holland, but you appreciate that we must make quite sure you knew nothing about *Cormorant's* activities. Did you know that the yacht was being used as a contraband vessel?'

'Are you quite mad, Chief Inspector? Of course I knew nothing about the bloody videos! How could I? I was in Durham, I've been there for two days and three nights. You can check, if you like. I was staying at the Prince Bishop and I was attending a conference on how to preserve the national parks of Northumbria from the ravages of the army. The Ministry of Defence are all for blasting our moors to bits with their wretched guns—'

'Aye, I know, and a crying shame it is too. But we're straying from the point. Who else was at this conference?'

'Willy Graham – he's involved because his game park at Coldstream is perilously near to the firing range. He's staying at the Prince Bishop too. Melrose – and Falkland, and Whittaker.'

Douglas nodded. He knew them all: pillars of Northumbrian society, rich and influential. Like Hamilton.

'So you've plenty of witnesses to vouch to your whereabouts?

'I should say so! We ate a damn good dinner together.'

'Well, we'll just have to wait until they bring in the crew of *Cormorant*. Could you stay around until then, Mr Hamilton? They'll be flown over from Holland, so it shouldn't be too long. Sergeant Holmes has a spare bed, I'm sure.'

'I've no intention of leaving here until those bastards are brought in. And I've no intention of troubling Sergeant Holmes. I'll take the car round to the back and sleep there until you call me.' And he stomped off out of the door.

Douglas glanced at Venerables.

'Got that, Sergeant?'

'Aye, I have. He'll not scarper, will he?' he asked anxiously.

'Sergeant Holmes will keep an eye on him. Remember to offer him breakfast, Holmes.'

'Bacon and eggs?'

'That'll do. And better make that . . .' He counted heads. 'Six.'

Holmes looked agitated. 'I'm no cook, sir! And stocks are limited.'

'Then save the bacon for Venerables and me. Right, I need to get my head down for a few hours. Any chance of a bed at your place, Fred?' he said to Waring.

'There's a couple of sofas,' Waring said reluctantly. 'Wife's not going to like it much, though.'

'Shouldn't have married a Customs officer. Life gets quite sociable at times, I should imagine?'

'I'll say so. But usually we make use of the police cells when we're offering hospitality to our – guests.'

Douglas guffawed. 'I think Venerables and I'd rather doss down at your place. Eh, Venerables?'

'I suppose so. As long as Mrs Waring doesn't mind,'

Waring snorted. She'll do as she's told.'

'Then you're a lucky man, Fred,' said Douglas.

As he left the room with Venerables and Waring, he overheard John Chance pleading with Lizzie.

'What about me, where do I sleep? Is there a sofa going in *your* cottage?'

Douglas waited for the answer.

'No. It's too small for sofas. Besides, I've had enough for one night. You'd be better off at your own place.'

Douglas smiled. There'd be no easy ride for Chance.

'Then I'll stay here and keep Sergeant Holmes company.'

'There's always the lock-up,' said Holmes with a grin. 'Bed's comfortable, and I'll bring you a cup of tea at six.'

'Thanks – but I think I'll make do with that chair. I've no desire to find out what it's like on the wrong side of the law.'

By one o'clock that afternoon Venerables, Douglas, Hamilton, Waring, Lizzie and John Chance had reassembled in the Incident Room. The Newcastle police brought in two men, both in their mid-thirties and both from Morpeth: Nicholas Spicer and Alfred Watson. There was no sign of the small, wiry man who had attacked Lizzie.

'Do you know these men, sir?' said Douglas, turning to Hamilton.

'I've never set eyes on either of them. You bastards,' he said, hardly able to contain his rage, 'what've you done with *Cormorant*?'

'She's in safe keeping,' said Douglas soothingly. 'You'll be able to go and get her as soon as Dutch Customs have finished with her.'

'*Me* go and get her?' exploded Hamilton. 'Someone'll have to go across and bring her over. It's not my fault she's over the other side!'

'Tax-payers' money, sir,' said Waring, stiffening. 'She's your responsibility as soon as she's cleared.'

'Let's sort all this out later,' said Douglas impatiently. He was beginning to feel the effects of a disturbed night; and Mrs Holmes hadn't been too generous with his breakfast. 'Mr Spicer, Mr Watson – do you know Mr Hamilton here?'

Both men shook their heads. 'Nope,' said Spicer sullenly. 'We needed a boat and *Cormorant* was standing there, ready to go to sea.'

'Why did you need a boat?'

'To get to Holland.'

'What for, might I ask?'

'We needed a holiday.'

Hamilton snorted and Douglas began to lose his temper.

'Don't make a monkey out of me, man! You don't have to steal a yacht to go on holiday.'

'You do when you've got no cash.'

'And passports? You need passports when you go on holiday. Or didn't you know that?'

'Passports in order, sir,' said one of the Newcastle officers.

'Miss Teal says there was another man on board, a man who attacked her. Now what happened to him, I wonder? Didn't you take him on holiday with you?'

Spicer looked impassive. 'There was no one else with us. The lady must have got it wrong.'

'So you don't know where this bag came from?' said Douglas, pointing to the holdall on the table.

The men shook their heads. 'Nope,' said Spicer, who seemed to be the most articulate of the two. 'Never seen it before.'

Douglas sighed: an impasse. But only to be expected. No one knew anything; no one had seen anything. A straightforward theft of a yacht, followed by a straightforward charge and a formal arrest. Then off to Berwick and the possibility of a decent prison sentence if they were lucky.

'Very well. Arrest these men, Sergeant Holmes. Maybe they'll tell us more when we get to Berwick.'

Despite loud protestations of innocence the men were charged and arrested. As they were led off, Hamilton came over to Douglas.

'Well, that's that. Now, can I get over to Holland?'

'You might as well. The yacht'll be cleared soon.'

'I hope they've not taken up the floorboards.'

'I'm sure the Dutch will have done a thorough job, sir. But you've nothing to fear if there's nothing there to find. If you'll excuse me, I've got to get back to Berwick. Seems like you've landed on your feet, Venerables – I'm the one who's landed with the commuting.'

'You're the one with the posh car, sir. Fancy a pie and chips, lass?' Venerables said to Lizzie. 'I'm starving.'

'Good idea. I could eat a horse,' said Lizzie, suddenly realising she'd eaten nothing since the sausage sandwich at last night's party.

'Mind if I join you?' said John Chance.

'Course not. The more the merrier,' said Lizzie cheerfully.

'Pity you can't come with us, sir,' said Venerables; Douglas was looking distinctly disgruntled. 'They'll have finished serving lunches by the time you get back to Berwick.'

'All right, Sergeant, don't rub it in. Go off and enjoy yourself. Someone has to stay behind to do the work round here.'

'And you do it so efficiently,'said Lizzie, smiling sweetly.

'Aye, lass. You can say that again. I'm glad someone appreciates me. Now be a good girl and save me a chip or two.'

'They're lying, of course,' said John.

Lizzie, deep into hot meat pie and chips, nodded agreement. They were sitting in the main bar of The Boomers, well out of earshot of Charlie Wheeler.

'How can you be so sure?' said Venerables, in confrontational mood, resenting John's air of authority.

'Because I've seen Spicer hanging round *Cormorant* on more than one occasion – although I admit I've not actually seen him with Hamilton. Anyway, it stands to reason that they'd all say they don't know each other. Probably all part of their contract: when caught, deny everything. It's a risk you take in their game. But they'll get even with Hamilton if he has dumped them in the shit. I wouldn't like to be in his shoes.'

'They could get sent down for quite a long time, John,' said Lizzie.

'People like that have long memories.'

'And there's nothing much else to think about in jail apart from settling old scores.'

Lizzie was beginning to see John Chance in a new light. What others said about him wasn't true; somehow he'd acquired the reputation of being a bit of a Northumbrian beach bum, interested in nothing but his boat. But he clearly had more than his fair share of good sense – and he seemed pretty clued in to the local criminal scene. She decided he was really quite good-looking in a rugged sort of way, with his hard body and weather-beaten face. She liked his hair: dark, wavy, a bit on the long side for a cop. Yes, she could go for him, given half a chance.

Venerables, feeling neglected, began to fidget. 'Douglas'll sort out Hamilton,' he said.

'Aye, maybe. But not in the way I'd like. Not yet, anyway. Hamilton's a slippery customer. He's the sort of man who gets others to do his dirty work for him – he can afford it, that's for sure – and then lets them down when the going gets rough,' said John, pushing aside his mushy peas. 'However, that's as maybe. I think we've got shot of Watson and Spicer for the time being. Watson's done time for petty larceny, so they'll hang on to him. That leaves us with *Cormorant* and Hamilton.'

'You don't *really* think he's behind all this, John, do you?' said Lizzie, reaching over and helping herself to John's peas.

'I'm not sure. There's nothing I can pin on him at the moment, but I'm working on it. I'm off in a minute to meet a new informant to take Josh Tyler's place. This chap's called Angus McLoughlin – know him? He's one of Willy Graham's ghillies and he knows Hamilton and everyone else around here.'

'Let's hope he doesn't end up the same way as Tyler,' said Venerables lugubriously. 'My, lassie, for such a slim, wee thing you put away a mighty heap of food. Want anything off my plate?'

'I'll finish off your chips if they're going begging.'

'Help yourself,' said Venerables, pushing his plate across, grateful for even this much attention.

'Does this Angus McLoughlin know what he's up against?' said Lizzie, tucking in. 'Frank's right – he could end up like Tyler.'

'It's a risk they all take. Dangerous games these people play. They run with the hare and hunt with the hounds. To put it another way, there's many a gamekeeper out there willing to turn poacher.'

'Will this one cost you much?' asked Venerables.

'Nothing. It's blackmail, if you like. I said I'd turn a blind eye to his trade in pheasants in return for any information which might be of use to us. I think he's worked it all out. One tip-off equals two hundred pheasants.'

'Saves the tax-payer,' said Venerables, impressed.

'Aye. And saves lives, perhaps, when we get a haul. The stuff's coming in in such large quantities these days – the profits are huge. More and more people are willing to take the risk, especially with unemployment in this area being so high. But we're not doing too badly in Hernmouth. We've caught quite a few small fish lately.'

'Let's hope they get the message and move on elsewhere,' said Lizzie, polishing off the last of Venerables's chips.

'Not much chance of that. They might wait a bit until they think the pressure's off, then they'll be back. These little ports in out-of-the-way places are just what they're looking for, particularly in the summer months when the place is full of small boats. Yes, we've caught a few of the minnows; what we're after now is the big fish.'

'What about Clinker?' said Venerables. 'Is he one of your informants?'

'*Clinker?* God no! He'd not accept money or favours from anyone. He's a valuable ally – he watches and notices; but he'll not accept any sort of payment. Hates the drug smugglers. Hates what they do to the people they prey on. He'll hate those videos too, Lizzie. By the way – why the hell didn't you call me from the quay last night? Or Holmes, even? Why wait until you got home? That's why we lost *Cormorant*. By the time you called us, she'd upped anchor and gone.'

Lizzie stared fixedly at her empty plate, feeling the colour flood into her face. 'Sorry, John. You're not going to like this

. . . You see, I left the mobile behind. I wasn't on duty. I was supposed to be enjoying myself. And, to be quite honest, the dress I had on was so tight I didn't know where to put it. When I realised what was going on, I knew I hadn't time to get home – I had to get down to the quay straight away. I tried to get a patrol car, I phoned from the call box on the quay, but all the cars were out. They told me to wait, but I knew I couldn't do that. I'd have missed the action. I certainly wouldn't have got my hands on that holdall.'

'Once a cop, always a cop, Lizzie. Take that blasted thing with you always from now on. You must realise you're at risk – someone's not going to like what you did last night. Someone's going to have it in for you, and next time it might not be so easy to get away.'

'I know, I know. Message received and understood. But sometimes it's difficult to know where to conceal the phone. It's all right for you blokes – you've always got pockets.'

'Handbag?'

'Don't have one – too much of a nuisance.'

'Armpit? That's where Special Branch conceal their guns.'

She gave him a withering look.

'In your knickers,' said Venerables, greatly daring.

'On a motorbike?'

'That's another thing – its time you gave up that yellow peril of yours,' said John. 'Far too conspicuous. Get a nondescript, second-hand car.'

'I love my bike! I like the fresh air, the feeling of speed. There's nothing likc it.'

'It'll be the death of you,' said Venerables. 'It's time you settled down, took life a bit more seriously. We can't always look after you.'

'Since when, Frank, have I ever needed anyone to look after me?'

'Now don't take on, lass,' said Venerables, realising his mistake. 'We only go on at you because we care. You're our star of the Drugs Squad. Just be careful, that's all.'

'Frank's right,' said John. 'And I'd be a lot happier if you'd carry a gun. You're trained in the use of firearms and these people we're after are tough customers. Anyway, I won't nag you any more. I'm off – for my appointment with

McLoughlin. Fancy a bite to eat this evening, lass? At my place? It's not much to shout about, but there's a stove and a table and two chairs. The bare necessities.'

'Not tonight, John. I need to catch up on my beauty sleep.'

'Tomorrow, then. Chinese take-away do you? You obviously enjoy your food.'

'I've got to keep my strength up!'

'I can appreciate that. It takes more than guts to kick blokes into the harbour. There's no sign of a body yet, I suppose? It'll most likely turn up in one of the lobster pots, or come in with the tide.'

'He was all *right*, I *told* you,' said Lizzie indignantly. 'I left him clinging on to the dinghy which was tied to the stern of *Cormorant*.'

'Most probably the others hauled him out of the water and took him over to the other side with them. Then they'd chuck him back in with weights on his feet,' said Venerables. 'They'd not want to risk Lizzie identifying him, dead or alive.'

'Not much chance of that. Fish'll have him.'

'God, you two are a couple of ghouls! But I'd recognise him, I'm sure of that. I caught a good glimpse of his face, and if the fish have scoffed that, I'd recognise his jacket, if he was still wearing it. It was quite distinctive,' said Lizzie. 'Hideous, in fact.'

'If you can identify your attacker, Lizzie, if he does end up a floater, then those two in Berwick will face a murder charge in addition to theft.'

John got up, zipped up his anorak and left the bar. Venerables turned to Lizzie.

'Fancy a coffee, pet?'

'Not now, Frank. Another time. I've got work to do. A report to write.'

'You agreed to see John tomorrow night quickly enough!'

'That's tomorrow. Anything can happen between now and then.'

'Day after tomorrow, then. Supper?'

'Leave it, Frank. Just leave it,' she said, sighing.

Venerables sighed. It was becoming the story of his life: the older he got, the more difficult it was to chat up the lassies. He shouldn't have let Jenny go. But then, he thought ruefully, he hadn't really had any choice, had he?

Chapter Five

A week after the arrest of Spicer and Watson, the month of March came in, not with the roar of a lion but with the stealthy tread of a snow leopard. Hilda Nevill took one look at the leaden sky, heavy with snow clouds, and decided that the time had come to stop believing that spring was on its way. In her new spirit of realism she put on her sheepskin jacket and fur hat – her heavy-duty winter clothes – and set off to visit Edith Laker. The road from St Waleric's Haven, where she had rented a first-floor flat in an elegant Victorian house overlooking the estuary, was glazed with a frosting of ice; although she had confidence in her beautifully maintained MGB GT and its new tyres, she nevertheless drove with extreme caution. When she arrived at St Oswald's Hall the first snowflakes of the day were landing on her windscreen.

Edith Laker was waiting for her in the sitting room; a log fire roared up the wide chimney. Una Rose brought in coffee as soon as Hilda arrived and the two ladies got straight down to business. It was what Hilda liked about Edith. She recognised a kindred spirit, someone who didn't mince matters, made good use of every minute of the day, and hated time-wasters. A meeting was a meeting: not a social occasion or an opportunity for idle gossip.

'I hear you're going to Brazil soon,' said Hilda, settling back in her armchair, revelling in the fire's warmth.

'I hope to go next week, just for a short visit. I'm opening another orphanage – and I have to advise the local field workers on finding employment for the older children when the time comes for them to leave our care. It's amazing how time flies! The children we rescued five years ago are into their teens already and will soon be making their own way in the world.'

'There's no difficulty in getting work – because of their background, I mean?'

'We do our best for them. I've seen to it that they all get a good education and know how to behave. But even when they leave us, we still keep an eye on them. They are so vulnerable. We try to protect them as long as we can.'

'I do admire you!' said Hilda enthusiastically. 'You make my life seem so utterly selfish. Here am I, doing nothing more challenging than planning a pleasure trip round the British Isles, and there you are, giving meaning to hundreds of young lives. I should like to help all I can.'

'I know I can count on your support, Hilda. The Bring and Buy sale which you so kindly offered to hold in your house on Easter Saturday will be very much appreciated.'

'One day, Edith, I'd like to come with you, to see your work at close quarters. Maybe I could make a covenant to your charity, or sponsor one of your rescued children? I'd like that. Charles and I had no children – it was something we became resigned to but never welcomed. I gather, Edith, that your husband was also in the Diplomatic Service. Where were your postings?'

'Cairo, Damascus – and Rio, of course, our last post, where I became involved in De Profundis. George and I were also without children. These street children of Rio are my family. I think they almost give me more satisfaction than if they were my own.'

'Yes, I can appreciate that. Maybe you will let me share your family! It would mean a lot to me. I'm sorry that you lost your husband so suddenly – he must have been quite young?'

'In fact he was a lot older than me. He died while we were making plans for our retirement, as so many men seem to. We were going to buy a place in Hampshire, on the River Hamble – we both loved sailing. That's where I met Delrose. He used to look after the garden and crewed for us when we wanted to take the yacht out. When George died I decided to move the yacht down to Falmouth so that I could tackle the Western Approaches, perhaps even take part in the Fastnet. I knew I wouldn't want to live alone in Hampshire, not after he'd gone.

I had always loved the north-east of England, and I knew that for the price of a modest-sized house in the south, I could buy a whole estate up here. So I came looking, saw St Oswald's Hall and that was that.'

'Do you get down to Falmouth very often?'

'Once or twice a year, in the summer. I keep a crew down there – they get the yacht ready for me when I tell them I'm coming. They let out the yacht for chartering when I don't want it. In that way it pays for itself.'

'How splendid to have an ocean-going yacht! What do you call it?'

Edith smiled, and Hilda was struck by the way her face softened. She must once have been quite a beauty, she thought.

'George called it *Snow Goose* – he was an old romantic. But I changed it to *De Profundis*. I thought I might use it to entertain the charity's sponsors this coming summer.'

'All this must keep you very busy.'

'Yes, indeed. But I have stalwart assistance in the shape of Delrose.'

'You're lucky to have him. Look – the snow's coming down heavily now. I hope it won't start drifting. I expect the schools will close early.'

Edith looked alarmed. She was still a handsome woman, thought Hilda, despite her age, which must be teetering on fifty. Her figure was pencil-slim and she carried herself well. She wondered why Charles had never mentioned her; he'd always had an eye for the ladies, though fortunately he'd never gone further than looking. Of course, they'd never been posted to Rio – though the diplomatic world was a small one.

'I do hope this snow keeps off until Clare gets home,' said Edith, her anxiety evident in her voice. 'I must tell Delrose to set off in good time to meet her. Roads round here can get very bad at this time of the year; the gritting people never seem to come until the worst is over.'

'Clare's a delightful little girl,' said Hilda. 'She must seem like a grandchild to you.'

Edith's face lit up. 'She's the apple of my eye. I am so thankful that her mother's death hasn't affected her too badly. If you want my honest opinion, I think Clare's better off without her. I took Bridie Ransome on as an assistant out of pity, and to give Delrose a hand, and Clare and I took to each other immediately. Bridie, I'm afraid, was a hopeless case – addicted to heroin. I could do nothing for her. Well, she's gone now. I expect you've heard the details. I shall continue to be a mother to Clare. I won't let her past be a millstone round her neck. In fact, I'm thinking of making her my legal heir, just in case anything happens to me. The plane to Rio could crash. . . . The yacht could come to grief. . . . I'm sorry to sound so doom-laden, but I have no one else to leave this place to. I know I'm too fond, but there it is. Clare is everything to me.'

Hilda put her cup and saucer back on the polished rosewood tray. 'I should be the same, were I in your shoes. We have a lot in common, you and I: both diplomatic widows; both childless; both needing a focus to our lives. I only wish my financial position were as sound as yours! Dear Charles never had much of a head for business. I've got my pension, and a little cottage near Raby Castle, and I can afford to give Clinker something to look after my boat. But I've nothing as magnificent as St Oswald's Hall and a yacht at Falmouth!'

'George had investments and did well out of them. I was very lucky,' said Edith.

'Yes, finance was never Charles's forte . . . I do envy you your possessions. Your beautiful coffee service! Georgian, isn't it? That hallmark on the sugar bowl is as clear as if it were engraved only yesterday. Do excuse my enthusiasm – antique silver is one of my passions.'

Hilda reached out and picked up the little bowl.

'Let me see, now,' she said, examining the side of the bowl. 'Three castles in the shape of a triangle: two above one. That's Edinburgh, I believe.'

'Edinburgh, yes. It had been in George's family for years.'

'Wonderful! But I really don't like the look of this weather,' said Hilda, putting the bowl carefully back on the tray. 'I think I'll be getting along. Don't forget, you can depend on me to give a Bring and Buy sale over Easter. And let me know what you think of the sponsoring idea. How I should love to go to Rio and meet my child . . . Oh, and the best of luck for your trip next week. How are you getting to the airport? If the flight's from Newcastle, I could always—'

'Delrose drives me down to London. He stays overnight at Heathrow and drives back here the next day.'

'Who takes Clare to school when he's away?'

'One of his friends, usually. It's all taken care of – don't worry. Una is always here when Clare comes home from school. She'll never be a latchkey child as long as she's with me.'

Hilda walked quickly through the biting cold to where she'd parked her car under one of the ancient cedar trees which bordered the gravel drive. She brushed a thin layer of snow off the windscreen, then drove off. Before she reached the gates, she stopped and looked back. The house was truly impressive: a whole history of English architecture, there in one building. Edith was blessed to have so much. And to have a child on whom to lavish affection; that was fortunate indeed.

She felt a pang of self-pity. It had been uncharacteristically inconsiderate of Charles to die when he did . . . Still, now she had Clinker. And *Sirius*: not an ocean-going yacht, admittedly, but a very sturdy gaff-rigged lugger with a cosy cabin.

She drove on, feeling more contented with her lot. As she turned out of the gates of St Oswald's Hall and into Wynwick's pleasant High Street, she began to make plans. If the weather held off she would take a trip to Durham, to the reference library. There was something she needed to know.

The snow began to peter out as Hilda approached the coast. Too late now, perhaps, to go to Durham; but not too late to go and see Clinker. She turned towards Hernmouth.

Once there, she drove down to the Marina, parked her car and got out, pulling up the collar of her coat as she did so. The impact of the raw, cold air took her breath away. The tide was coming in and the north-east wind blew straight from Scandinavia. Spring time in Northumbria, and coastal cruising seemed a long way away. She was tempted to drive straight back to St Waleric's Haven and enjoy the North Sea from the warm comfort of her sitting room. But it would be foolish not to visit Clinker, now that she'd made the effort to come all the way to Hernmouth.

She needn't have worried about the cold. On board *Sirius* all was harmony and domestic bliss. Clinker was seated at the cabin table drinking tea; Mac was asleep on one of the bunks. A paraffin stove belched out heat and, over the table, a brass lamp filled the small space with a mellow light. Clinker looked up when he saw her coming, beamed, and reached for another cup.

'Just in time! I knew you'd be along today.'

It had happened again: this telepathy which existed between them. Time and again each knew what the other was thinking. It was uncanny, really, Hilda thought, as she climbed down the companion-way to the cabin, which was so small she could barely stand upright.

'My, you've made some progress since I last saw you, Frank!' she said.

'She's coming on,' he said stolidly, pouring out the tea.

'You've already finished the floorboards?' she said, taking in the newly-sanded and stained cabin floor.

'Aye. There was a right lot of rubbish under them, too! All gone now. Bilges as clean as a whistle.'

Hilda crossed to the sleeping Mac, who woke up and thumped his stubby tail appreciatively.

'Almost ready to go,' she said, scratching the dog's ear.

The hull's nearly finished. But she'll need a new suit of sails, and there's work to be done on the engine. I think the best thing might be to splash out on a new one. Reconditioned, at any rate.'

'Up to you, Frank,' said Hilda, thinking that perhaps Edith wasn't so fortunate after all. For what could be more fulfilling than restoring an old working boat to something approaching its former glory.? 'When could we take her out?'

'Not at all in this weather,' he said hurriedly. 'You'll freeze to death.'

'Nonsense! I've just bought myself some thermal underwear specially.'

'It'll not be enough. This east wind cuts through you like a knife. Another month will see some improvement in the weather, then I can start painting the outside.'

'Just as you say. Cottage all right, Frank?'

'Aye. I'm nice and snug there; and I can see what's going on in the harbour. Hallo – what's this?'

The heavy throbbing pulse of a powerful diesel engine filled the cabin. Clinker stood up and made for the companion-way.

'Who's this coming in, I wonder? Sounds like *Cormorant*.'

'*Cormorant*? said Hilda, following him up on deck. The ketch that was stolen?'

'That's the one. They caught the thieves – they're safely parked up in Berwick awaiting trial. The owner went over to Holland to get her. Looks like he's got back safely.'

'She's Bruce Hamilton's boat, isn't she? Who's his crew?' asked Hilda, watching the fifty-foot boat manoeuvre onto a narrow pontoon only a few yards away from where *Sirius* was berthed.

'Angus McLoughlin. Black Angus, we call him. Part-time ghillie, part-time fisherman, part-time crew for Hamilton. A man of many parts. Most of the time he's got his fingers in as many pies as he can find . . . Mind you, I envy him that engine. That's what we need. We could go anywhere with an engine that size. In any weather.'

'Too powerful for *Sirius*.'

'Sell *Sirius*! Buy a ketch like *Cormorant*.'

'Next year, Frank.'

They laughed, and Hilda felt a lifting of her spirits. No, she didn't envy Edith Laker one little bit.

They stood together on the deck of *Sirius* watching as a Customs Officer boarded *Cormorant*, greeting Angus McLoughlin like an old friend. Then they went below. After a few minutes the engine was switched off and peace was restored.

'Is McLoughlin Hamilton's regular crew?'

'Seems like . . . Customs man's taking his time. Must be having a dram. There'll be nothing to declare, I'll be bound; *Cormorant's* a clean ship. More than Hamilton's life's worth to run foul of Customs and Excise, especially after what happened to Lizzie Teal last week.'

'Who's Lizzie Teal?'

He turned to face her, grinning. 'Well now, do I know something you don't? Must be a first! Let's go below and have our tea and I'll tell you all about it.'

Chapter Six

It was half past three and the car hadn't come. The sky was heavy with the threat of more snow. Clare Ransome, carefully wrapped up against the cold in her grey raincoat with her blue and gold striped scarf tightly wound round her neck, jiggled up and down impatiently on the front steps of St Hilda's Convent. Where was Donald Stirling? Delrose had told her and Sister Anna that morning that she'd be met by his friend tonight, as he and Aunt Edith would be down in London, and he'd promised that Mr Stirling wouldn't be late . . .

Sister Anna, anxious because she liked to see all her charges safely tucked up under parental wings, came down the steps to keep Clare company.

'Let's go inside, child,' she said, in her soft Irishy brogue. 'It's cold enough to freeze the blood in you. What's happened to Delrose's friend, I wonder?'

Clare made a face and hopped down the remaining stairs to tease the convent cat who had come stalking round the corner from the kitchen area. A large, black, neutered tom, he stopped dead when he saw Clare, then flattened his ears and bolted off into the shrubbery.

'Leave the Venerable Bede alone, child,' said Sister Anna, a note of impatience creeping into her voice. 'You children torment the living daylights out of him! Thanks be to God, here comes your car, at last, just before the two of us catch our deaths. Stand here next to me, and don't be rushing to get in now.'

The black BMW, Edith's second car, drew up in front of the steps for the second time that day. A man sat in the driver's seat wearing a dark anorak, the hood pulled up over his chauffeur's cap. Clare wished she had a hood. Sister Anna went down to him, and he rolled down the window.

'Sorry I'm late,' he said. 'Roads are bad.'

'Drive carefully, Mr Stirling. We don't want anything happening to our precious Clare. What would Mrs Laker say?'

'Don't worry, I'll be extra careful. See you tomorrow – unless Delrose gets back in time. But in these conditions, he might be delayed.'

Sister Anna bundled Clare into the passenger seat next to Donald Stirling. They drove off and she watched the car turn into the main road and towards Wynwick.

Flecks of snow were being whipped around by a spiteful wind that crept under Sister Anna's habit and made her bones ache. The Venerable Bede reappeared and slithered round her feet. 'So it's tea-time, is it?' she said, and looked at her watch: ten minutes to four. Clare would be late getting home.

Clare and her new chauffeur sat in silence until they'd left Alnwick behind. Then they drove towards the coast. Clare was tired and cold; she was dreaming of the plateful of Marmite toast which Una would make for her as soon as she got home. Today, as it was particularly cold, she might get hot chocolate too! Then a cuddle with Bear before her daily allowance of television, followed by a hot bath, and a bedtime story. Una liked reading to her and would do so for hours if Clare wanted it.

She looked out of the window at the frozen fields and the solitary trees; more snow was falling. She saw unfamiliar houses and turned anxiously to Donald.

'Delrose doesn't come this way,' she said.

'It's quicker.'

'I'm hungry.'

'Not long now. In fact, you could say you've already arrived.'

'What do you mean?'

'You're a big girl now. Work it out for yourself.'

Clare decided she didn't really like Donald Stirling. She didn't like his voice; it was growly, and she couldn't really understand what he was saying. She wished he'd hurry home.

Suddenly the car stopped and Donald got out and came round to her door. She felt herself seized by strong arms; before she could cry out, something painful and tight was slapped across her mouth. She wriggled and twisted, trying to get free, but Donald produced a rope and tied it around her body so that she couldn't move. He dragged her out of the car and hauled her into the back seat where he covered her with a blanket, leaving a little space round her face so that she could breathe.

Donald drove on; faster now, and Clare's body was flung from side to side as he took the corners at high speed. Some of her hair had got caught up in whatever he'd stuck across her mouth, and it pulled her scalp whenever she turned her head. She wanted to shout, to scream, to fight against the cruel rope that bound her, but she could do nothing. She didn't have the strength. As she gave herself up to terror, she thought of the sad, gentle lady who had been her mother, remembered her laughing, long-haired father. And Aunt Edith. Aunt Edith, far away in Brazil. And then another thought came that calmed her just a little: Aunt Edith always knew what to do. She would never let Donald Stirling get away with this. He would be caught, and punished, and locked away in prison. Because that was what happened to bad men, wasn't it?

The car stopped and Clare caught a glimpse of a darkening sky, heard the sound of water lapping against a wooden jetty, the harsh screech of a seagull. Then the blanket was wrapped even tighter around her body and over her face. As she was hauled out of the car, feet first, fear overcame her and she lost consciousness.

She didn't feel the motion of the boat as it chugged down the estuary and out into the North Sea. She didn't feel the bump as it dropped anchor alongside a rock in a tiny harbour. She was unaware of being dragged ashore, carried up a flight of steps and across a field to a ruined building. She didn't hear the trap-door open, knew nothing as she was hauled down-stairs and dumped on a bed.

When she finally opened her eyes she felt as if she'd turned into one of the characters in the stories which Una read to her: stories of princesses who went to sleep and woke up in magic kingdoms. But this place didn't look magical. The bed was hard and smelly; the small heater, in the corner of the dingy room, belched out paraffin fumes which made her throat sore. She saw a bare, wooden table; and a girl sitting at it buttering slices of bread.

'Here she is, Sammy,' said Donald. 'Now it's over to you. Here, take this.'

Clare saw him throw something across to Sammy, something that shone and made a clanging noise when it hit the table. Clare knew the thing on the end was called a padlock.

'What about my stuff?'

'You stick to what you've got. I don't want to risk the child. You've got something to keep you going. And take it easy. Remember, if anything happens to the child you'll get no more smack out of me. Understand?'

'Sure,' said the girl, not sounding very happy.

Then Donald left them; Clare heard his footsteps going back up the stairs. The next minute she was gazing up into the eyes of the girl called Sammy. And she didn't look friendly.

That afternoon Douglas and Venerables drove to Newcastle. Neither of them was in a talkative mood; the only sound was the mournful clack of the windscreen wiper operating on its lowest setting.

'Back on your own patch,' said Douglas, finding the silence oppressive.

'I'm not a South Shields Geordie. I lived north of the Tyne.'

'All the same to me.'

Venerables snorted indignantly. 'South Shields is . . .' He paused whilst he thought of a suitably contemptuous adjective.

'Beyond the pale,' suggested Douglas helpfully.

'You're dead right. Well beyond the pale. Respectable types live north of the Tyne. Tynemouth's where I come from.'

'I've seen no evidence yet of your so-called respectability. Anyway, let's hope the remaining Tyler brothers are respectable enough to be sitting round a table eating their tea when we get there. Especially Marcus Tyler – there's still no trace of him. We've checked out all the addresses Dean Tyler gave us, and we're left with brother Josh, dead, pegged out in the

Hernmouth estuary; brother Ernie, killing himself with heroin in a bedsit, and brother Marcus, vanished God only knows where. That leaves us with Dean, sitting on his tod, all warm and snug in a house which he claims to own.'

'Seems like he's doing all right for himself.'

'Aye, you could say that. He's sitting there like a bloody great spider in a web. I don't need to tell you who the flies are.'

'Does Dean work?'

'Aye, so he says. Off and on. And when it's off there's always the poor bloody tax-payer to fall back on.'

'And when it's on?'

'The mind boggles. Selling drugs, I expect.'

'Any evidence, sir?'

'Don't be ridiculous, man,' said Douglas indignantly. 'Of course there's no evidence! Is there ever, with men like Dean Tyler? They aren't completely stupid. That's why this whole business is so bloody frustrating – everyone clams up. People come, people go, get murdered, staked-out in the mud, chucked off yachts, and no one sees anything! Or hears anything. They're all wise monkeys round here. I feel like a blind man sometimes, trying to grope his way home along a road full of potholes.'

'Very poetical, sir. But you mustn't let it get you down. At the end of the day, it's only a job.'

'A bloody messy sort of job! I like a straightforward homicide: trace the suspects, interview, eliminate, arrest. Not these bloody wild goose chases! Well here we are – St. Bede's Road. Let's hope Dean's a bit more communicative than he usually is. You'd think he'd want to find the bastard who killed his brother.'

'Perhaps he's got his suspicions but is frightened to talk.'

'It's more than likely. This business, Venerables, is like a house of cards – take one card away and the rest fall over.'

'Depends which one you take away,' said Venerables philosophically. 'You've got to find the right one, the king-pin. Then you stand back, and the whole lot collapses before your very eyes.'

They had arrived at the semi-detached house on a housing estate in Jarrow, where Dean and Marcus Tyler made their home. Dean opened the door; a big, bull-necked man, with a shaven head and a reddish, freckled face, he glared belligerently at Douglas.

'Any news?'

'Not yet, sir.'

'Then what the hell are you doing here? You'll not find the man who killed my brother under this roof.'

Douglas refused to be drawn. 'May we come in?'

Reluctantly, Dean led the way into the living room. A large-screen television was on in one corner with the sound turned down; there was a battered sofa, one or two broken-down chairs and empty beer-cans on a stained table. Clearly Dean wasn't house-proud.

'If you're looking for Marcus, I've already told you – I've not seen him for over a week now. I'm used to his comings and goings. He's probably gone to London, looking for work – there's nowt much round here.'

'Does he ever go to Hernmouth?'

'*Hernmouth*? What the hell would he do down there.?

'Do you know a businessman called Bruce Hamilton? Owner of a boat named *Cormorant*?

'Never heard of him. Nor his boat.'

'Does Marcus know him?'

'How should I know? Marcus leads his own life. I don't know who his friends are.'

'A pity we can't find Marcus. Still, we'll keep looking. There's several things Marcus might be able to help us with.'

'Have you tried Ernie?'

'Ernie's no use. Couldn't even remember his own name when we interviewed him. Where does he get his stuff from? More to the point, where does he get the money from to buy it? Smack doesn't come cheap these days.'

Dean shrugged dismissively. 'Users always find the money to buy stuff when they want it. How should I know who sells it to him? I don't touch it myself.'

'Very wise, sir. You'll let us know when Marcus turns up, won't you? In the meantime, we'll get on with our investigations. You've no second thoughts about who might have killed Josh.'

'I've told you all I know. But mark this – when I find out who did him in, that person'll wish he'd never been born.'

'You mustn't take the law into your own hands, sir. That way it'll be you who ends up in jail.'

'I can't rely on you lot to get us proper justice! Josh and I were mates, not just brothers. We did everything together. If I come across the bastard who got him, I'll tear him to pieces. And I mean it. Save you a job. And I don't give a shit if you send me down – it'll be worth it. At least Josh'll have been avenged.'

They drove away in gloomy silence. Another dead end.

'We'll have to keep an eye on what's left of the Tyler family, Venerables. I don't trust Dean. He knows more than he's letting on.'

'Seems to be cut up about his brother, though. Quite touching, didn't you think?'

'He's a human being, Venerables. We've all got someone we love.'

'All except me,' said Venerables dolefully. 'I'm one of life's losers where love's concerned.'

'That's because you chase after the wrong sort of lassie. First Jenny – and now I suppose Lizzie's given you the boot.'

'No boot needed, sir. She won't let me get near her.'

'Better that way. You can concentrate on the job in hand.'

'I *am* concentrating sir. But there's nothing to concentrate *on*. I wish someone would make a move! I wish Marcus Tyler would turn up, either alive or tangled up in someone's fishing nets, if he was the one Lizzie chucked off the yacht.'

'We'll have to wait. Something always turns up.'

The car phone bleeped; Douglas, one hand on the wheel, picked it up. He listened in mounting agitation and Venerables looked at him enquiringly.

'The bairn's gone!' said Douglas when the call finished. Something's turned up, all right. Christ almighty, what'll Edith Laker say when she hears about this?'

'What do you mean – gone?'

'Kidnapped, Venerables! That's what I mean. The wee bairn, Clare, didn't come home from school. Una Rose phoned the school at half past four and found that Clare had left an hour ago. Now all hell's broken loose.'

He drove at speed back along the A1, glad of his old Volvo's still-powerful engine. As he turned the car into Wynwick, he saw a crowd of people standing round the main gate of St Oswald's Hall. Light streamed from every window of the house; a distraught Una Rose was waiting for them at the front door, her face ashen.

Venerables turned to Douglas. 'The house of cards might just be on the point of tumbling down.'

'Aye, laddie, it might,' said Douglas grimly. 'But will it fall down in time to get the wee Clare back safe and sound?'

Chapter Seven

Superintendent Blackburn's car had been ahead of them as they drove up to St Oswald's Hall. Blackburn had already reached Una Rose; he nodded briefly in Douglas's direction and led the way to where a grief-stricken Sister Anna was waiting for them in the sitting room.

'I'm sorry,' she said, rushing forward, 'so sorry! I should never have let her go, but I knew Donald Stirling was going to take her home, and I recognised the car, so why should I doubt him? It was getting late, and Clare was tired and cold and impatient to get home. Dear Mother of God! Pray she's safe . . .'

'Amen to that,' said Douglas, leading her gently to one of the chairs. 'Don't blame yourself. We'll get to the bottom of this, have no fear. Now, you're sure that the car was the usual one? You'd seen it before?'

'To be sure! Delrose often used it when Mrs Laker was out driving the big one.'

'And you didn't recognise the driver?'

'Well, no, but . . . Delrose told me Donald Stirling would be picking Clare up in the BMW that evening. He often sends one of his friends as a replacement when he's driving Mrs Laker somewhere. Dear God, if anything should happen to Clare, I could never continue teaching! No one would ever entrust their child to me again. And I couldn't blame them.'

She burst into tears. Una Rose came over to her; kneeling down beside the chair, she put her arms round the nun. She too was sobbing, but she recovered sufficiently to glare at Douglas.

‘What’s the point of all these questions, Chief Inspector? Sister Anna’s suffering enough as it is, and upsetting her isn’t going to bring Clare back. Why shouldn’t Sister Anna trust this Donald Stirling? To all intents and purposes Delrose had supplied a substitute chauffeur, as he’d promised, and he was driving Delrose’s car. I would have done exactly the same as Sister Anna. So let her be.’

Douglas, somewhat abashed by this feminine onslaught, found himself, for once, lost for words. But before he could vindicate his line of enquiry, a policeman came into the room and went up to Blackburn.

‘Car’s been found, sir. Abandoned in a lay-by outside Hernmouth. No signs of any struggle. Wiped clean; there are some fingerprints on the tool box in the boot, and we’re checking them, but steering wheel, doors, etc, are all clean.’

‘You’re sure it’s the right car?’

‘Yes. Black BMW, registered in the name of Edith Laker.’

‘Where’s Stirling?’

‘We’re looking for him.’

He turned to Una Rose. ‘No messages? No phone calls?’

‘There might be a message on the answerphone – I haven’t checked. It’s in the study.’

Venerables was one step ahead of them. As they went into the study a man’s voice was speaking.

‘The child is unharmed. She’ll be returned on payment of two million US dollars. I’ll tell you where to bring it later on. Don’t try to find the child, and don’t play tricks on me – or I’ll kill her. Is that clear?’

The message ended. Venerables, white-faced, looked across at Douglas. ‘The bastard! A wee bairn . . .’

‘We must find her soon,’ said Blackburn urgently, ‘otherwise you know what happens. They take the money and run. The child remains with them – a week later they increase the demand. And the child vanishes for good. Right – this is a major alert. All police leave cancelled. We’ll need extras from Newcastle and Durham. We’ll use this place as an operations centre, if that’s all right,’ he said, turning to Una. ‘Berwick’s too far away. I’ll get the equipment sent down. Poor little Clare. Let’s hope she comes through this. She’ll need to be a tough wee thing, that’s for sure.’

At this, Sister Anna burst into loud, anguished sobs. Una put her arms round her; the two women clung together as if they were drowning.

Blackburn turned impatiently to Douglas. 'You get on the trail of Donald Stirling. And you, Constable,' he said, turning to the policeman who'd brought the news about the car, 'get these two women's stories, and find a WPO. Get a recording unit in here. And make some bloody tea! Strong and sweet. This is no time for hysterics.'

'Who's going to tell Edith Laker, sir?' Douglas asked. 'She's going to be in a right state when she finds out. She worships that child.'

'We'll get on to her straightaway. And Delrose. You'll know where he is, Mrs Rose?'

I know where he's staying – in a hotel near Heathrow. And I've got Mrs Laker's phone number in Brazil.'

'I'll talk to her now,' said Blackburn. 'And Chief Inspector . . .'

'Aye, sir?'

'Major alert, I said. That means get on to all the local TV and radio stations and ask them to broadcast a request for information on their next news bulletin. Might as well go national, in fact – in case he's taken Clare down south, though I doubt that's likely. Now let's get moving.'

Douglas and Venerables drove out of the gates of the Hall, past the crowd of reporters who had gathered like vultures round a recent kill, and turned towards the coast. Snowflakes swirled madly over the windscreen, clogging up the blades of the windscreen wipers, fogging Douglas's vision.

'This weather complicates matters,' he said. 'It slows us down, for one thing – and pray God the wee bairn's well wrapped up,'

'I expect whoever's got her would have thought of that. She's not much use to them dead.'

Douglas winced. 'I don't even want to consider the possibility of that child's death. Not at this stage. So let's forget Armageddon. Finding Stirling's our first priority.'

'Delrose could help us there, sir. I expect he'll be a might put out.'

'You don't think he put Stirling up to this?'

Venerables paused. 'I doubt it. He wouldn't be so stupid. You don't pick your friends to do your dirty work for you.'

'Do we ever really know our friends, Venerables? The Devil's no respecter of friendship.'

'The Devil, sir? I'd have thought if the Devil was involved in this one, Sister Anna would have recognised him in the driving seat of that BMW. It'd be in her job description.'

'He's clever at disguises,' said Douglas bitterly. 'He slips in wherever he can. But this time we've got the measure of him. He'll not get that child. We've beaten him before, and we'll do it again.'

'I wish he'd steer clear of Northumberland,' said Venerables. It makes me wonder what we've done to deserve all this.'

'Not going out tonight?' said Lizzie, giving the washbasin a perfunctory swipe round with the J-cloth.

'You bet! Coming? Big Jim's been asking for you.'

It was seven o'clock: the end of the longest shift of the week. Everyone else had gone home. Lizzie tidied her combs and brushes, making sure they were all present and correct for the next day. *Big Jim*? she thought. *Who the hell is Big Jim?* Then she remembered: that party – was it really only last week? She'd eaten hamburgers in the kitchen and smooched with the huge, tattooed man who'd told her about the porn videos. It seemed like ancient history.

'Not tonight, Annie,' she said. 'I need an early night. Anyway, what's on? Anything special?'

'The usual. The three Bs: boys, booze, bonking.' Annie laughed, a rich, infectious chuckle. She was a good-hearted girl, Lizzie thought; she wanted everyone around her to have fun and she required no more from life than a few drinks and casual, uncomplicated sex on a regular basis. Lizzie envied such simplicity of soul.

'Things might warm up later, though,' said Annie, sweeping the bits of hair on the floor into a dustpan. 'Big Jim says there's a new shipment coming in tonight. Ecstasy. Dennis the Menace! Reckon he can get us a free sample, know what I mean?'

'How does Jim know these things?'

Annie giggled. 'He doesn't just pack prawns, you know. He catches lobsters as well – owns a few pots, and he's got a mooring buoy down at St. Waleric's. He's on the ball, is Jim. And a bit of the old Dennis brings in more brass than slaving in a factory, that's for sure.'

'I didn't know Jim had a boat.'

'He doesn't *own* a boat. He uses a mate's. They're in it together. Anyway, he'll be well stocked tonight. There's nothing like the big E to liven up a party!'

'Just as well it's your day off tomorrow.'

'I'll say. Just think what all those perms'd look like after a night on the tiles with Dennis!'

She shrieked with laughter; Lizzie couldn't help but join in. Most of their clients were old-age pensioners and most of them liked the same hair style; a cast-iron perm, to keep their hair in place for months.

'Maybe I'll look in later. Same place?'

'Aye. Home from home!' And she laughed until the mascara streamed down her face in brown rivulets.

Lizzie picked up her leather jacket and fastened on her crash helmet. According to the weather forecast she'd heard on the salon's radio, the temperature was dropping fast.

'Watch out how you go,' Annie called out as Lizzie opened the front door. 'The roads'll be a bit tricky.'

'The bike's safe.'

'You and your bike! You only ride it because you know it turns the boys on.'

'Really? That's news. I thought it was because it's cheap to run and easy to park.'

'That's what they all say about me! Cheers!'

Lizzie left the salon and went round the back where she'd parked her motorbike. As usual, it started on the first press of the ignition button. She waited a few seconds with the engine ticking over, then drove off, not home, but down to the quay. She stopped outside the Customs and Excise Office and propped her bike against the sea wall. A few partygoers would be disappointed tonight, she thought. Big Jim ought to stick to prawns – you knew where you were with them.

For a long time, Clare lay curled up on the bed, too frightened to call out, too shocked to move. Someone had untied her and taken the sticky tape off her mouth. Someone had wrapped her up warmly in a couple of blankets. She remembered that the girl, Sammy, had given her some orange juice – but she hadn't drunk it because it was too sour. She thought of Una and hot chocolate; of Aunt Edith, wanting a hug. She thought of Teddy, his warm, cuddly body and sympathetic face, and she started to cry.

She went on crying for a long time until her head hurt and she couldn't breathe properly. She looked across at Sammy. She didn't like Sammy. She was young and could have been pretty, but she was too thin and her face was white and pinched. Her hair, which was long and dark, might have been nice if she'd washed it. She couldn't have a Una to brush it smooth for her, tuck it back behind her ears. Sammy was wearing grubby jeans, which were torn at the knees, trainers – one without a lace – and a long-sleeved T-shirt. She was asleep now, her head down on the table.

Most of the time she'd sat at the table. She'd fiddled with a piece of silver foil and some powder which she'd tipped out of a little plastic bag. Then she'd heated the underneath of the silver paper over the candle and when the powder started to smoke she'd breathed in the fumes. Clare seemed to remember her mother doing the same thing, a long time ago. Clare had watched Sammy change after she'd breathed in that smoke. She'd seemed at peace. After she'd had a long rest, she'd opened a tin of soup and heated it up in a saucepan on top of the heater. She'd made a sandwich and brought it over to Clare, who'd thrown it on the floor; she was angry and didn't feel in the least bit hungry. Then Sammy had smacked her hard across the face, and Clare had started to cry again. Sammy hadn't eaten the soup. Instead she'd sat staring at the wall, until finally she'd put her head down on the table and gone to sleep.

Clare realised that she wanted to go to the lavatory. Would she get into trouble, she wondered, if she got up? She could see a bucket over by the stove – she could use that. Cautiously, she stretched out one leg and wriggled her toes. They still seemed to work. She put one foot on the floor and pushed aside the blanket. She stood up; Sammy didn't move.

Then she had another thought; what would happen if she went up the stairs? Was there a door at the top of them? If so, she might be able to push it open and just walk out, shutting it behind her. She pulled the blanket tightly around her shoulders – it was so long that the end trailed behind her like a train – and made for the stairs. She started to climb: the first stair, then the next; and the next. It seemed to get colder as she climbed higher, and she pulled the blanket round her more tightly. One of the stairs was higher than the previous one, and she stumbled and banged her knee. It hurt, but she tried not to mind.

Suddenly she heard a noise from below. Sammy had woken up! Sammy was there behind her, dragging her back down the stairs, pushing and pulling her until she was back in the dark room again. And Sammy was really angry. So angry that Clare felt warm liquid trickle down her legs. She'd wet herself: something she'd not done for a long time. The pain of Sammy's boney fingers and the shame of her wet knickers made her very angry.

'You're wicked! A wicked girl. Why are you doing this to me?'

'Shut up,' said Sammy fiercely, picking up the long, shiny object which Donald had given her. Clare could see now it was a chain. She wound it round Clare's waist, pulling it really tight, and dragged her across to the wall.

'See that ring? That's where they used to chain prisoners in the olden days, when they were naughty and tried to run away. Now it's your turn.'

Clare looked with horror at the ring. Terrified, she began to scream. Sammy took no notice. She flung the blanket on the floor, forced Clare to lie down, then she pulled the chain tight and fastened both ends to the wall with the padlock.

'If you're good I'll move the bed over, and you can lie on it. But if you don't stop screaming, I'll have to tape up your mouth again,' she said. 'In a minute, I'll make you another sandwich. And you've got to eat it this time, or I'll force it down you.'

Clare curled up on the blanket, the chain painfully clasping her body. She tried not to think of her wet knickers, of how cold she was, how hungry. Instead she tried to imagine what

Aunt Edith would do to Sammy and Donald. She couldn't think of a punishment bad enough. Quietly, she began to cry. She wondered what time it was, whether it was dark outside, whether it was tomorrow yet. She watched Sammy put some more powder on the piece of silver paper, and make more smoke. She sank into a twilight state, halfway between sleeping and waking.

Chapter Eight

Lizzie pulled on warm leggings and rummaged in her wardrobe for a suitable shirt. She wanted to look her best for her lunch with John Chance. She'd really enjoyed the last occasion on which they'd met, in the pub; she'd felt herself beginning to respond to his shy but obvious admiration. It was purely a chemical reaction, she told herself, as she extracted a silk shirt which didn't seem to need ironing: just hormones talking to hormones. What else could it be? He was in his thirties, devoted to his boat, had never married; had never, apparently, had a long-term relationship. Not ideal love-affair material. Yet it was good to feel desired, she thought, as she gave the shirt a shake. It was worth going to the trouble of taking care over make-up, digging out her best underwear.

She was feeling particularly pleased with herself that morning. Fred Waring had phoned early to congratulate her on busting the delivery of drugs in St Waleric's Haven. The police had retrieved several kilos of Ecstasy – better still, they'd caught the two men who'd come to empty the lobster pots. They'd both denied any knowledge of why one of the pots should contain not a lobster but a stash of Ecstasy tablets, but they were being questioned now in Berwick, and, with sufficient persuasion, might come clean. Annie's friends would have been disappointed, but no doubt they had made up for the loss with extra booze and more bonking.

Now she was going to go off and enjoy herself, and forget the feeling of unease which she always experienced when she had to betray her friends. Drugs were murder weapons, in her eyes, and Mike's death six years ago had persuaded her that sometimes the end really did justify the means. *What a good little moral crusader you are*, she said wryly, as she studied her reflection in the mirror. However, even crusaders were allowed to have a day off sometimes, and this day was going to be special. John would cook a delicious lunch in his tiny kitchen; they'd eat it with soft music playing in the background. Then they'd sit and talk, discover common interests, and as the afternoon wore on he'd pile more logs onto the fire and slide close to her on the sofa. And this time, she decided, she wasn't going to move away.

Satisfied at last with her appearance, she put on her heavy biker's gear. It had stopped snowing; there was a faint hint of spring in the cold, pale sunlight. The roads would be treacherous, she thought, as she drew on her thick gauntlet gloves – but she'd go carefully, and John's place was only three miles outside Hernmouth. She went out of the cottage to where her motorbike gleamed enticingly in the sunshine. Sleek, powerful, sexy – its name, 'Virago', painted boldly on the side – she was proud of it, and proud of herself for learning how to control it. She'd chosen it for its power, its effortless acceleration, and its low, comfortable seat which seemed to have been designed with women in mind.

She pressed the ignition and drove carefully out of Hernmouth and along the coastal road towards Cresswell. There wasn't much traffic about, although it was Saturday lunchtime. Presumably the weather was keeping everyone indoors. She registered the presence of a red Bedford van on her tail, but took no particular notice; her machine could leave most vehicles behind.

However, the van didn't drop back and the gap between them, already small, was narrowing. Surely, she thought, it wasn't going to overtake, not on that narrow, icy road, not with those bends ahead. She accelerated, and the powerful engine responded. She glanced in her wing mirror; the van was close behind her now and she glimpsed the driver in his dark sunglasses, a woollen hat pulled well down over his forehead. The collar of his jacket was pulled up around the lower part of his face, but she could see the determined set of his mouth, and she began to feel uneasy. This was not the way Bedford vans usually behaved.

Then he began to pull out, and she sensed the driver's intentions. *Dear God*, she prayed, *Don't let him cut in*! Now he was alongside her, pressing her into the narrow verge. Beyond the verge was the cliff-top and the drop down to the sandy sweep of Druridge Bay. The van swerved in front of her; she braked sharply, using the handbrakes; more than sufficient to handle any emergency. But there was no response. The brakes felt as if they were made of cotton wool; she realised, suddenly panic-stricken, that they must have been tampered with. There was no brake fluid. Someone must have loosened the nut on the handbrake hose.

Instinctively she twisted the handlebars towards the verge and the bike went into a sickening skid. As it went out of control, she remembered the half-joking words of her instructor, at the end of her final lesson: '*At the last moment, jump clear. Never let the machine fall on top of you.*'

And Lizzie jumped, clear of the bike, clear of the verge, and straight down a slope covered in coarse grass towards the sea glittering below her. She came to a halt, crashing against a boulder with such force that she heard the bone crack in her arm, felt a jarring pain in her shoulder. Looking up, she saw the gleam of yellow metal. It was her motorbike, coming to rest upside down in a thorn bush.

She waited. Nothing happened. Above her a gull screeched derisively. She tried to move, but the pain in her left arm was excruciating. But she could still move her right arm. She pulled the gauntlet off, using her teeth, and slid her hand down into the pocket of her thick, waterproof trousers. Her mobile was still there, intact: a miracle. She drew it out and, propping herself up on her right side, dialled John's number.

'John? I won't be able to make lunch, I'm afraid. I'm on the side of a cliff, wedged up against a boulder, and I can't move my left arm. Could you be very kind and call me an ambulance?'

She didn't hear his reply. The sunlight faded, and she passed out.

The moment which Douglas had been dreading had come. Edith Laker stood in front of him. She was almost unrecognisable; deep lines were etched under her eyes and round her mouth and her eyes were glittering with a fierce anger. She reminded him of a lioness who'd lost her cub: a lioness out for revenge. Blackburn, standing beside her, was trying to be conciliatory.

'Best to wait, ma'am – it really is. It's only a matter of time before we find the child.'

'Time, Superintendent, is the one thing we haven't got! Clare is only six. God knows where they're hiding her, what hole she's been stuffed into. She could die of hypothermia, dehydration, suffocate . . . Children of that age haven't our strength and resilience. We must pay up, Superintendent! You heard what that monster said; he wants us to meet him in the car park outside St Walerick's. No police presence, just one person carrying a holdall. Then he'll hand Clare over. What's two million dollars to me? It's *nothing*, compared to the life of that child.'

Douglas intervened. 'It's best we don't give into him, ma'am. There's no guarantee that, even if you hand over the money, you'll get Clare back. Try to keep calm. We all sympathise with your distress, but we must remember what sort of person we're dealing with. We usually get there in the end. House-to-house searches are taking place, people are being interviewed – everything is being done that can be done. To give in to the kidnapper at this stage would be fatal.'

'And leaving Clare in his unspeakable clutches wouldn't be fatal? Listen, Superintendent – and you, McBride. I want Clare back, whatever the cost. She's all that matters to me, all I've got. Understand? Now, do as that man says. Tuesday, he said – that gives me a day to get the money.'

'I really don't advise . . .'

'To hell with you and your pussy-footing! If you don't take me down to that car park, I'll go on my own. It's time someone took some action round here.'

'It'll not work,' said Douglas helplessly, 'people will only end up getting hurt. Believe me, we've had experience of these situations.'

'No doubt you have some bureaucratic procedure you'd like me to follow. But this is *my child* we're talking about! I take full responsibility for Tuesday. No strong-arm tactics, no guns – just me with a holdall.'

'You're not thinking of being there? said Blackburn, aghast.

'Of course. Who else? He said he doesn't want the police anywhere near.'

'I really can't allow that, ma'am. It's far too dangerous. We'll get one of our female plain-clothes officers to make the handover. We do know what we're doing. It's not the first time we've dealt with this sort of event.'

'It's the first time for Clare, though, isn't it? And it's going to be the last. I shall be there, Superintendent. You can't stop me – I'll sue you if you do. This is my business. I am responsible for that child – I want to deal with this in the way I think best.'

Blackburn paused and stared at Edith's set face. He turned to Douglas and Venerables. 'Very well. Do as the lady says. Remember – no guns, no intervention unless it's absolutely necessary.'

'Presumably we know where the calls came from,' said Douglas, on his way to the door.

'Both from Berwick. Phone boxes. It means nothing. Bastard could be anywhere.'

Douglas and Venerables walked slowly out to where Douglas's car was parked.

'The woman's gone stark, staring mad,' said Venerables. 'It's no way to get the bairn back. He'll not play ball – its happened before. She'll hand over the money and get nothing in return.'

'Well, we'll have to go along with her. Up to a point. I'm sure we can reach some sort of a compromise. She means what she says, all right. And Blackburn can't upset her – she's much too important round here. A very generous lady, too; she never forgets the Police Benevolent Fund. Blackburn won't want to tread on her toes. So what did Delrose have to say about all this, Venerables?'

'Swears blind that he knew nothing about any plan to kidnap Clare. He confirms that Donald Stirling is a friend of his. Says he originally met him in a pub in Newcastle – apparently Delrose goes into the City quite regularly on Edith's charity business. According to him, Stirling travels round the ports, getting crewing work wherever he can. That's why he doesn't have a fixed address, or a phone number – he's never in one place for very long, and he's usually at sea. Stirling occasionally gives Delrose a ring when he's in the North East and they meet up for a drink. A couple of days before Clare was kidnapped Delrose met Stirling in The Boomers and mentioned that he was off down to Heathrow soon and needed to sort out a substitute chauffeur for Clare while he was away. Apparently the friend he usually relies on was visiting relatives in Wales – we've confirmed that part of his story. Stirling offered his assistance – said he'd always dreamed of driving a BMW. Delrose was a bit dubious at first, but couldn't think of a good reason to refuse. After all, he has no reason not to trust Stirling. He says he's always found him very reliable and honest – "straight as a die", is how he describes him. Of course, Delrose is really cut up now. Blames himself. I think he was worried that Edith Laker would sack him – but she could see how upset he was and she gave him the benefit of the doubt.

'Anyway, Stirling picked the BMW up from the Hall just after Delrose arrived back from delivering Clare to school in the morning. Delrose handed the car keys over, gave Stirling very specific instructions about what time to pick up Clare and so on. Then Delrose drove Mrs Laker down to London in the Mercedes. He told Stirling to ring him at the hotel in Heathrow if there was a problem, but he never got a call. He reckons that after Stirling collected Clare from school – Delrose thinks that the man driving the BMW probably was Stirling, from Sister Anna's description – the car was somehow forced to stop. It wouldn't be difficult to do in this weather – cars have been skidding all over the shop and if you were driving along and found one of those narrow country roads was blocked by a car slewed across it, you wouldn't necessarily be suspicious. And if Stirling is the helpful, friendly soul that Delrose says he is, he might just have made it all that much easier for the kidnapper.'

'So Delrose is adamant that Stirling isn't behind the kidnapping?'

'He's sure of it. I played him the answerphone message and he says he doesn't recognise the voice. He pointed out that plenty of people know Edith Laker isn't short of a bob or two – and know that he and Mrs Laker make regular trips to

London. It wouldn't be that difficult to find out the details. They never kept it secret – they had no reason to.'

'So it looks like Stirling's been taken along with Clare. Either that, or . . .'

'More likely that they've got rid of him and hidden the body where we won't find it. They wouldn't want to drag an adult hostage along, especially a young, fit male who might spring a few surprises on them. And Stirling isn't a rich man. He wouldn't be worth anything to them.'

'I'm very much afraid that you may be right, laddie. Poor old Stirling! He couldn't have been in a worse place at a worse time. So what time's the handover?'

'Seven o'clock, Tuesday morning. So do you think Edith Laker can lay her hands on that amount of money at short notice? Two million dollars is a hell of a lot – and I thought most of her cash was tied up in De Profundis.'

'Seems as if she's got a bit more stashed away somewhere for a rainy day. Where are you off to?' he said, as Venerables began to set off down the drive.

'To my own car. I want to go to Ashington.'

'Ashington?'

'To see Lizzie.'

'Oh, no, you don't! You stay right here with me. We've got a handover to organise for the day after tomorrow, and you're not seeing anyone except who I tell you to. There's a child's life at stake here. Lizzie's not going to die. I'm sorry for the lass, but a dislocated shoulder and a broken arm never killed anyone. She got off lightly.'

'What about the shock?'

'The sight of you will only add to it. The hospital'll let her go soon – then you can see her.'

'She'll be needing visitors.'

'John Chance'll see to that, never fear.'

'She'll think I don't care.'

'Well, send her some flowers! Not now – later, from Berwick.'

'It's not the same, sir.'

'In your case,' said Douglas, looking thoughtfully at Venerables, 'it's better.'

Chapter Nine

After her father and mother left, Lizzie sank into a deep, healing sleep. She woke up late on Sunday afternoon to see John Chance standing awkwardly by the side of her bed, clutching a bunch of flowers.

'Roses,' he said unnecessarily, looking round for somewhere to deposit them.

'Wonderful! Here, dump them on the bed. I'll get the nurse to bring a vase later.'

Gratefully, he laid the bunch down between the small humps made by Lizzie's legs.

'I think this proves that mobiles can be useful after all,' he said, grinning.

'I was amazed it still worked! Better to break an arm than one's mobile – at least when one hits a rock. I'll never let it out of my sight in future.'

'You'll have to get rid of that motorbike now. I told you it was a recipe for disaster.'

'It wasn't the bike's fault! Someone had tampered with the brakes.'

'Aye, I know. There was no brake fluid left at all.'

'You've found the person responsible?'

'Not yet. You know how long these things take. We've found the van – stolen, as you'd expect. No sign of the driver. We'll want a full description now that you're back in the land of the living.'

'That'll be difficult. His face was mostly hidden.'

'Any detail helps. But don't think too hard just yet. You look a bit rough.'

'I'm sorry. I'm not at my best right now.'

'No offence. How are you feeling?'

'Much better for seeing you. It just happens that I can't move my left arm, and my head hurts like hell.'

Lizzie gingerly waved her plastered arm in John's direction, and immediately regretted it; a stabbing pain made her gasp. 'Ouch. That hurt,' she said.

'Take it easy, now,' said John, clearly concerned. 'Try to keep still.'

'I've got to move soon. They're sending me home tomorrow.'

'*Tomorrow*? You're not fit. Where are you supposed to go?'

'Home, I suppose. Mum and Dad want me back in Seaton, but I'm not going. I want to be around when you find that bastard who pushed me off the road.'

'You can stay with me. I'll look after you.'

'Thanks, but Douglas wouldn't wear that. He says I'm still a target.'

'Has he been to see you?'

'No. Too het up over that child. She's taken priority, and rightly so. Kidnapping children is a different kettle of fish from picking up a couple of kilos of Ecstasy in a lobster pot. If you'll excuse the metaphor. Anyway, Douglas phoned – that was nice of him. Says I'm to join Holmes in the police house in Hernmouth when they let me out of here. I can help out in the Incident Room for the time being and when they've cleaned up this gang, I can go home again. Suits me. I can answer the telephone and no doubt make umpteen cups of coffee, but at least that's better than sitting around watching TV all day.'

'You can't stay in the police house!' said John vehemently. 'Venerables lives there.'

'So? He won't bite! Think how nice and cosy we'll be.'

'He fancies you, Lizzie. You must see that.'

'He must be kinky to fancy me like this,' and she waved her arm again, wincing with the pain.

'It'll only take six weeks to mend and then you'll be fit again. A lot can happen in six weeks. He'll have all that time to butter you up.'

Lizzie shut her eyes. *Men*, she thought. *Always the same. Always eyeing each other like rutting stags.*

A nurse came into the cubicle. 'You've got another visitor,

Lizzie. More flowers! I'll be back in a moment to put them all in water.'

Lizzie tried to sit up, but metal hammers began to pound vigorously in her head. As she collapsed back onto her pillow, Sergeant Venerables came in. He had gone to trouble over his appearance, she noticed; his neat, grey overcoat looked newly cleaned and he was wearing a blue silk tie spattered with white polka dots. He was carrying a huge bunch of yellow chrysanthemums.

'Why, aye, hinny,' he said. Lizzie winced; she didn't like being "hinnied". But she knew he was only trying to be friendly.

'How're you feeling?' he went on. 'My, but they've done a good job on you! You'll not be riding motorbikes for some time. We told you they were trouble. Where can I put these flowers, now?'

'Next to mine,' said John sharply. 'You've gone a bit over the top,' he said, glaring at the dozen large yellow heads wrapped in transparent paper and tied with a giant satin bow. 'You're turning the place into a bloody morgue.'

'It's lucky the lassie's not *in* a morgue! But here you are, alive and kicking, Lizzie, my love. Only the best for the best of girls.' And he dumped the flowers next to John's modest bunch of roses.

Uninvited, Venerables drew up a chair and sat down. Lizzie closed her eyes again. She realised that she'd been lucky to have a room to herself; but it did mean there was no escape from visitors. At that moment, she could have done without John and Venerables locking horns and stamping their hooves at each other.

'When are they letting you out?' said Venerables companionably.

'Soon. I'm coming to live with you, Frank, have they told you?'

'Why, that's good news,' said Venerables, beaming. '*Great* news. Did you fix that?'

'It's not up to Lizzie to decide where she goes,' said John irritably. 'They'll not let her loose until they've banged up the men who sabotaged her bike. They think she'll be safe enough with you.'

Venerables ignored the irony. 'Of course she'll be safe with me! Let's just hope we take a long time to catch the bastards. I can bring you breakfast in bed every day, love.'

'You'll not have time for that,' said John, sitting down on the edge of Lizzie's bed in a proprietorial manner. Really, she thought, if they staked their claims any more obviously they'd be sitting on top of her. 'I'm surprised Douglas let you come here today. Have they all dozed off in Berwick?'

'He'll not miss me for half an hour. They're all running round in circles trying to find the child.'

'What's happening on that score, Frank?' said Lizzie, opening her eyes again. 'Douglas sounded as if the end of the world had come when he told me what had happened.'

'He's certainly taken it hard. I've never seen him like this before. The handover's on Tuesday. I'll not say more – only that Billy Ransome's on his way from New Zealand.'

'Ransome?'

'Aye. The child's father. A New Zealander, husband of Bridie Ransome of this parish, now deceased. He's as gung-ho as they come, wants to join in the hunt. Better if he keeps out of the way, I say, but we can't stop him from coming over.'

'You can't blame him,' said Lizzie, praying that the two men would leave her in peace. 'After all, she is his daughter.'

'Edith Laker won't like him interfering,' said John. 'She'll want to run the show.'

'She'll have to put up with him,' said Venerables. 'Now who's this? More visitors? It's too bad of people to come uninvited when you could do with a bit of rest and relaxation, lass. Why, it's Clinker,' he said, 'with Lady Nevill. Must be party-time.'

Clinker and Hilda came into Lizzie's room just as the tea trolley arrived. Lizzie began to feel desperate. This was just what she needed: visits from aristocratic ladies doing charitable works. Her head was throbbing badly, and she needed a painkiller.

But Hilda was understanding, and quickly saw what the situation demanded.

'I thought you might like some snowdrops – I picked them this morning,' she said, filling a small vase which she'd brought with her, with water from the bedside jug. 'The first sign of spring. They were under a holly bush where the frost couldn't get at them.'

'They're really beautiful,' said Lizzie gratefully. 'It's very kind of you to come and see me in this weather.'

'Clinker wanted to come and I agreed to bring him. I've always wanted to meet you,' said Hilda cheerfully. She put the snowdrops down on top of the locker, where Lizzie could see them, and went over to help the lady with the tea. 'He was very concerned when he heard what had happened. You seem to have a lot of admirers.' She brought a cup of tea over to Lizzie. 'Do tell us when we're no longer welcome, won't you? Visitors can be exhausting when you're not feeling one hundred per cent.'

Clinker was rummaging in his pocket. Shyly, he came over to Lizzie. 'Here, I bought these for you,' he said, extracting a long, thin packet of after-dinner mints. 'I reckoned you'd have enough flowers.'

'Thanks, Clinker! Let's eat them now. It's well after lunch, at any rate. Open them, John. I don't think I can, with only one hand.'

John, resenting his loss of an opportunity to have an intimate hour alone with Lizzie, sulkily obliged.

'You'll not be allowed home on your own, surely?' asked Clinker. 'That shoulder's not going to heal in a day.'

'She's coming to stay with me,' said Venerables smugly.

'That doesn't sound ideal,' said Hilda firmly. 'My dear – I'd be delighted if you'd stay with me. For as long as you like. I've got plenty of room in my flat and I'd enjoy the company. You can sit and look out at the estuary, watch the birds setting about their spring activities. All very restful.'

'Do you know,' said Lizzie, wearily, 'I might just do that, if they'll let me.'

'Of course they'll let you!' said Hilda, collecting up the tea cups. 'We'll have to have a police protection but I'm sure that can be arranged. Then there'll be more room in the police house for someone who really needs it. I'll have a word with the Chief Inspector.'

John brightened up visibly: better to have Lizzie looked after by motherly Hilda than chatted up by lecherous Venerables.

'Sounds good to me. Nice of you to offer, Hilda.'

'Only too pleased to help. Now, what news of that poor child. Sergeant? Edith Laker must be beside herself.'

'Aye that's for sure,' said Venerables, grumpily. 'But we're doing our best. Investigations take time.'

'You still have no clue as to who's behind it?' Hilda wanted to know.

'We've not made as much progress as we would have liked. It looks like Delrose is in the clear, at any rate. But there's still the chance that it could be an inside job. An insider would be best placed to know exactly how much money Edith Laker's got immediate access to.'

'That's what I thought, when I heard the news,' said Hilda quietly. 'And that reminds me – I must go to Durham tomorrow, if the snow keeps off. I've got to investigate something.'

'You doing a bit of amateur sleuthing, Hilda?' said John amiably.

'I'm just being nosey, that's all. Keeps me occupied whilst Frank gets on with the refurbishment of *Sirius*.'

We rely on people like you,' said Venerables more warmly; he knew Lady Nevill hadn't meant to queer his pitch. 'At the moment we're drawing too many blanks. However, Drugs Squad have got one result: two drug smugglers have been brought in to Berwick for questioning, thanks to Lizzie here. They still say they were only going after lobsters, but we won't give up.'

'I don't envy you lot one little bit,' said Clinker, reaching for a second mint. 'Unless you catch the devils red-handed, you can't prove a thing. I'll keep an eye on things down in the harbour and let you know if I see anything that seems out of the ordinary. You'll get there in the end, John – I'm sure of that.'

'Thanks for the vote of confidence, Clinker. Any news of *Cormorant*?

'Still moored, but no sign of life. Hamilton's not taking any risks.'

'Bruce Hamilton?' said Hilda in surprise. 'I know him! He's one of Edith Laker's friends. And I've seen him out and about with Delrose. Surely he's not involved in smuggling?'

'We can't rule anyone out, Hilda,' said John. 'It's a matter of keeping track of everybody and being there when the action starts, so we can see for ourselves who the real villains are.'

Lizzie was dozing off. The nurse came in and took her temperature.

'It's time for you all to go,' she said briskly. 'The poor girl's exhausted. She had a nasty bang on the head, remember, as well as broken bones. She'll not get better if you wear her out with your chatter.'

Hilda got ready to go. 'Come on, Frank,' she said, turning to Clinker, 'let's be away. As I said,' she went on, 'I'm willing to look after Lizzie for a few days when she comes out of hospital. I'll leave that to you to arrange, John.'

They left the room. Quietly, Lizzie began to snore. Venerables looked at John Chance.

'You can go, John. I'll keep watch here.'

'No – she's my responsibility. After all, it was me she was coming to meet when the bike went out of control. I'm staying.'

'Why do you always have to butt in?'

'You think she fancies you? Since when? How come she didn't want to stay with you then?'

The nurse looked irate.

'Out with you both! This is no place for a quarrel and I've got things to do. Come back tomorrow, when she'll be feeling a bit brighter. The poor lassie can't be expected to cope with the likes of you today.'

John looked stoically at Venerables, whose face had turned quite red with emotion.

'Come along, Sergeant. We're in the way. Besides, Douglas will be missing you. Mustn't keep the Chief Inspector waiting.'

As they drove into the car park, the cold, white light of dawn melted before the radiance of the sun as it appeared over the horizon. Douglas, more nervous than he had ever been in his life, prayed that nothing would go wrong; still he feared the worst. They had tried to persuade Edith Laker that it really wasn't in Clare's best interest for the money to be handed over, but she had refused to change her mind. A policeman, rather than herself, would carry the holdall: that had been the only compromise she had been prepared to make. Both Douglas and Blackburn had begged her to take their advice and stay away from St Waleric's that morning; yet despite their pleas, she had turned up with Delrose, and he had had to deploy two of his constables to keep her from any precipitous action. Minimum police presence had been the order. There were two members of the firearms squad hiding behind the hedge of the conifers which bordered the left-hand side of the car park. If they were spotted by the kidnapper, in all likelihood a shoot-out would develop. And it could be the child who got hurt.

He glanced anxiously around the small square of tarmac which constituted St Waleric's Haven's only car park. There was no sign of life from behind the conifers. On the right hand side was a path where the kidnapper would have to halt before handing over the child; at the far end was the sea wall. On the other side of the wall a path ran along the edge of the estuary. Today, however, this presented no means of escape; it was high tide, a particularly high tide as it happened – he could see spray from the more energetic waves breaking over the top of the wall. It all looked safe enough. On the main road, opposite the wall, were two cars: one containing himself and Venerables, the other, Edith's Mercedes, parked a few yards away, with Delrose in the driver's seat and Edith Laker in the back, guarded by a policewoman.

He looked at his watch; almost seven. The sun had cleared the horizon now and was rising in an aura of golden haze. Despite the freezing cold, it was going to be a glorious late winter's day. More glorious still if they succeeded in getting the child back in one piece.

Suddenly a car – a nondescript black Renault coming from the direction of the A1 – came into view. It slowed down and parked in the side road. A man was in the driver's seat, a small child by his side. Douglas felt every muscle in his body stiffen with tension as Venerables spoke quietly into the radio. No one moved.

Douglas got out of his car. To steady his nerves, he took in great lungfuls of the wintry air, which crackled with frost and seemed to turn his lungs to ice. He opened the boot and pulled out the holdall containing the money. Quietly, feeling like a traveller who had been dropped onto an alien planet and was being watched by hundreds of inquisitive eyes, he walked to the middle of the car park. He put down the holdall, and waited. There was no sound. Just the muffled booming of the waves dashing against the sea wall, and the derisive screech of two black-backed gulls hovering in hopeful expectation of sharing the breakfast of a few hardy tourists.

As instructed, Douglas returned to his car. The man in the black Renault got out. Of medium height, he was dressed in waterproofs, boots, and a terrorist-style balaclava helmet, which covered his face, leaving only a slit for his mouth and two slits for his eyes. He walked round to the front passenger seat and hauled out a small child dressed in the grey uniform raincoat of St Hilda's Convent, with a royal blue scarf wound round her throat and covering the lower part of her face, and a blue uniform beret pulled down over her hair. Douglas held his breath as the man drew out a gun and pointed it at the child's head. Then the child, her arms tied behind her back, was pushed forward towards the holdall.

She seemed stiff and unresponsive, moving like a sleepwalker. Douglas could do nothing but watch the gun. He knew that Edith would be frantic with worry; he prayed that the policewoman had a firm hold on her. One false step, and the man would shoot without hesitation.

Suddenly the man pushed the child forward; she stumbled and fell over. He seized the holdall and dashed to the sea wall, flung the bag over and jumped after it. The noise of a powerful marine diesel engine shattered the silence. The police marksmen ran out from behind the conifers and leapt up onto the wall, their semi-automatics crashing out.

Then Edith Laker broke free from her guardian, forced the car door open, and rushed over to where the child lay crying on the tarmac. Douglas went after her. She picked up the shivering child and went to hug her – but something was wrong. Instead of a loving reunion, Douglas was confronted with a wild Edith who turned on him, her face contorted with rage.

'You fool! You stupid, incompetent fool! Why couldn't you have done it my way? This is not Clare!'

Douglas couldn't believe it. After all the care they'd taken . . . 'What's your name, pet?' he asked as gently as he could.

'Miney,' said the child. She sounded terrified.

'Good God, it's Hermione Pringle,' said Venerables who'd

run over to join them. 'From Morpeth. She was reported missing twenty-four hours ago. Her parents will be over the moon to get her back.'

'What about my Clare?' said Edith, turning on him. 'Where is she? Why didn't you ascertain that this girl wasn't Clare?'

'We couldn't risk her life,' said Venerables quietly. 'Remember, the man had a gun – he would've shot the child if we'd hesitated. You wouldn't want a child killed, surely? Even if she isn't your Clare?'

Douglas had knelt in front of the child. 'Come here, lassie,' he said, filled with pity for the little girl who was crying and shaking with fear. 'You're safe now.'

Then the child came into Douglas's arms, and he knew for the first time in his life what it might have meant to him if he'd had children of his own. WPO Polly Staples had to prise the child away from him.

Douglas glared angrily at Edith.

'You might call me an incompetent fool, ma'am,' he said, 'but I hold you responsible for this. Didn't we tell you it wouldn't work? Didn't we tell you to hold your horses? All you've done is lose a mint of money, and the bairn's still missing. That bastard knew he could get even more out of you if you agreed to go along with him, and that's why he snatched Hermione Pringle. He intended this to happen all along. Now there'll be another ransom demand – and who knows whether it'll stop there? We can't allow him to set the agenda. Mark my words, we'll find Clare – but only if we play it our way.'

'*Your* way? And wait till Clare's dead? I thought I could trust you, Chief Inspector! And as for you,' she snarled, turning on the police marksmen who, having failed to stop the motor boat, had come over to join them, 'call yourself crack shots? You couldn't hit a rabbit at close range!'

The leader of the firearms contingent glared at her stonily. 'Aiming at a boat which is zig-zagging over a rough sea isn't easy,' he said reproachfully. 'We did our best, ma'am.' He turned to Douglas. 'There's a fog out to sea, sir. Coastguards'll not find him.'

'Then *we* will, laddie,' said Douglas. 'We won't rest until we do. Come on, Sergeant – let's get Miss Pringle home to her parents. At least some good's come out of this.'

Chapter Ten

Douglas had been at his desk for nine hours. Endless phone calls; endless questions to be answered. He vaguely remembered someone coming in and putting a sandwich and a cup of coffee down on the desk beside him, but he hadn't touched either. It had been a long time since he'd got as emotionally involved in his work. It was something he generally avoided, something he advised against most strongly in his lectures to recruits. But he couldn't dispel the memory of that small child in his arms. It was easy to be dispassionate about people like Josh Tyler; that was the risk people took when they embarked upon a life of crime, and as far as Douglas could see they weren't much loss to humanity. But he had cared about Bridie, whose poor, abused body he'd seen in the Auckland morgue; and he cared very much about Bridie's daughter.

For all their efforts, the police had not yet come up with anything useful. No sign of Stirling, alive or dead; no suggestion that anyone might have seen him on the day of Clare's disappearance. Someone remembered seeing the BMW parked in the lay-by outside Hernmouth; that was all. They hadn't seen who dumped it there. The weather wasn't helping; not many people ventured outside for long in these freezing temperatures. It was too early for serious bird-watchers – usually an invaluable source of information – to be out in force; in a couple of weeks they would be swarming all over the estuary, but now their hides were well and truly empty. John Chance and the Drugs Squad were naturally keeping an eye on McLoughlin and Dean Tyler, but there was no evidence to connect them to Clare's kidnapping. It was felt that neither

McLoughlin nor Dean Tyler had the brains to organise such an ambitious enterprise in any case. There were easier ways of making money, and neither of them would have had access to Edith Laker's financial affairs. But they both knew Delrose. Everyone knew Delrose. As the driver of Edith Laker's white Mercedes, he was hardly inconspicuous. Yes, thought Douglas, as he looked up from the computer monitor, the finger of suspicion could be made to point in the direction of Edith Laker's chauffeur. The fact that he happened to have been at Heathrow airport on the day Clare disappeared was irrelevant; he'd given himself the perfect alibi. And there was no real proof that Stirling was the innocent victim Delrose had made him out to be.

And yet Edith seemed to trust Delrose. And she was no slouch where judgement of character was concerned. He had a doting wife, a more than comfortable berth in St Oswald's Hall – was he really prepared to risk all that? *People will do anything for money*, Douglas reminded himself gloomily. And two million dollars would provide Delrose and Una with a luxurious retirement.

Too many what-if's and maybe's, he chided himself, as the phone rang yet again. All the same, he ought to get down to St Oswald's Hall and have another chat with Delrose . . . He picked up the phone: Superintendent Blackburn. Billy Ransome had turned up, demanding to see Douglas. With resignation, Douglas turned off the computer. In the last week, he thought, he'd witnessed enough emotional outbursts to last him a lifetime. He hoped to God that Ransome wasn't going to involve him in another one.

Blackburn came in, followed by a young man with a tanned face and dark good looks. Douglas remembered him well: he was distinctive, with the blue tribal tattoo on his left cheek and his long, curly hair tied back tidily. Ransome dumped his back-pack down on the floor; Douglas rang for coffee, and pulled up two chairs.

Billy was dressed for cold weather. His brown, Polynesian eyes were full of sadness and anger. 'So you haven't found her yet,' he said bleakly.

'Not yet. Take a seat, man,' Douglas said, as Billy hovered awkwardly in front of him.

'What are you doing about it?'

'Everything we can,' said Douglas wearily, conscious suddenly of his lack of sleep. 'The county's swarming with police. House-to-house enquiries going on at this moment. We're interviewing everyone in sight.'

'And how long is all that going to take?'

Why, Douglas thought, suppressing his irritation, was everyone assuming that the police were deliberately dragging their feet?

'We'll get there in the end.'

'The end might be too late for Clare. Have you talked to that bitch Edith Laker yet?'

Douglas looked up, surprised; the word sounded harsh, incongruous. 'Of course! But we're ready to see her again. Here's coffee. Take your time now – and try to calm down.'

'Look, mate, this is my daughter's life we're talking about! And you tell me to keep calm?'

'Pity you didn't think of her before you disappeared to New Zealand, sir. A child in those circumstances must have needed her father.'

'You think I left of my own accord? It was Edith Laker who drove me away . . . I didn't fit in with her plans. But let's get down to the Hall and hear her side of the story.'

'I'll set up an interview right away,' said Blackburn, standing up and making for the door with obvious relief, glad to dodge such a fraught encounter.

'Get Venerables down to the Incident Room in the Hall, sir. I want to have another talk to Delrose, and it might be a good idea if we tape the interview – with his permission, of course.'

'Anything you say, Chief Inspector. I'll get things going.'

He left the room, and Douglas was left with the young man. Now he'd dropped his confrontational stance he looked hopelessly lost, out of his depth. It was natural that he should be angry, Douglas thought; the difficulty was going to lie in stopping him from upsetting the apple cart. The last thing they wanted at this stage was to have an amateur detective with a personal axe to grind blundering around the countryside, sending every crook in the vicinity rushing headlong for cover.

'I'm truly sorry about your daughter,' Douglas said. 'But we'll do our very best to find her. Try and have faith in us.'

Blackburn returned at that moment and announced that Edith Laker was ready to see them whenever they wanted.

'Like hell she is!' said Billy furiously, picking up his backpack. 'She'll never be ready to hear what I've got to tell her.'

Una Rose opened the front door of St Oswald's Hall and ushered them into the sitting room. She seemed strained, nervous even, but she recognised Billy. He barely acknowledged her.

Edith was standing in front of the fire, which crackled and spat sparks onto the hearth and up the chimney. She was, as usual, elegant, but this time her stylishness seemed oddly superficial; her face, though perfectly made up, looked gaunt, and her hair, although immaculate, was dull and rigid with lacquer, as if she hadn't bothered to wash it for several days. There were deep shadows under her eyes.

Billy ignored her outstretched hand. 'I've come to find my daughter,' he said. 'Any idea who's got her?'

'If I knew that, Billy, there'd be no point in the police coming here.'

'To hell with the police! We'll only get Clare back if you and I work together. You've got your suspicions, I'd stake my life on it. What's going on? Bridie had something important to tell me, but the bloody Hohepa clan got to her before I did. So are you going to enlighten me?'

'My, you are an angry young man,' said Edith. 'You're a fine one to throw stones at people! Who abandoned Clare? Who left his wife when she needed him most? Call yourself a father and a husband? You're no damned good! And you have no right to come back here, criticising me. I gave Bridie my best shot.'

Douglas made no attempt to intervene. This was grist to the mill. Let them tear each other to pieces; it was all evidence.

'Call yourself a mother and a grandmother? I might have left Bridie, but I was more than prepared to stick around and support her and Clare if she agreed to go for treatment, and you know it. But you did not want me around, did you? I might have put a spanner in your works. You swore to me that if I went back to New Zealand, you'd make Bridie enter a clinic – a pack of lies that turned out to be! You just wanted me out of the way so you could get your claws into my daughter. And Bridie was just an obstacle and an embarrassment, wasn't she? When I wasn't there to keep an eye on you, you could help Bridie to hit rock bottom all the faster. I shouldn't be surprised if you sold her the stuff yourself. You'd washed your hands of your own daughter, so you decided to go after mine!'

Edith had lost her composure. She sank down into the armchair by the side of the fire and stared at Billy, her face white.

'You knew all along?'

'Bridie told me. She wrote to me, after I'd left. Poor cow, she actually believed you were trying to help her – but I put two and two together. She even asked me not to tell anyone else in case it upset you! Christ, it wouldn't do for the lady of the manor to have a junkie for her only daughter, would it?'

'If you were so concerned, why didn't you come back?'

'I thought I'd only make matters worse for Bridie. And I knew she was back on the smack in a big way – I couldn't stand to see her like that. I knew Clare'd be all right. Oh, yes, whatever happened, you'd always look after Clare.'

'There's hope for Clare. There was no hope for Bridie.'

'But she was your daughter, for God's sake! Didn't you have any feeling for her?'

'My feeling for her died the day she first used heroin. For a year I watched her slowly destroy herself. I didn't throw her out, you know. I would have continued to offer her a home. She made her own decision to leave, to go to New Zealand.'

'My only regret is that I didn't meet up with her in time. The Maoris saw to that. Oh yes, I know . . .' he said, as Douglas started to remonstrate, 'you all think she topped herself. Maybe she did, but Jimmy Hohepa and his friends helped her along the road. They didn't want her either. God, what a bloody mess! Why did I ever get mixed up with the Laker family? What did you *do* to her?' he said passionately. 'Have you ever thought why she became an addict in the first place? What was she looking for? She needed love. And not the sort of love I could give her. What sort of mother are you? You gave her nothing!'

'I tried to persuade her to go to a clinic – but she refused.

She was an adult and it wasn't my place to interfere. She was beyond my help.'

'That's maternal instinct for you,' said Billy grimly. 'She had nowhere else to turn, so she came to me – the father of her child. It must have been something mighty important to bring Bridie, in the state she was in, to the other side of the world. Something she couldn't even tell me on the phone . . .'

'And you, Billy?' said Edith furiously. 'What did you give her? You dare to speak about love? I gave her more love than you ever did.'

'I gave her Clare. Clare was the best thing that ever happened to her. To either of us. So why didn't you look after her properly? Why didn't you collect her from school yourself, if you're such a dutiful grandmother?'

'I was in South America. Delrose drove me to Heathrow, as he always did, and stayed there overnight. When that happens, one of his friends always picks Clare up – that's the arrangement. I couldn't possibly have known.'

'Aye, that's right,' said Douglas, flabbergasted by the revelations, but feeling that the time had come to put an end to recrimination. 'No one could have foreseen that the child would be kidnapped.'

'The whole thing stinks. Someone's got to know something! Have you spoken to Delrose yet?'

'Of course we've questioned him,' said Douglas tetchily. 'But I do want to have another talk to him. Is it all right if I have a word with him now, ma'am?'

'Of course. I'll get Una to fetch him. By the way, do you know Sergeant Venerables is waiting for you in the study?'

'Yes, I asked for him to join us. We'll not be needing you for the time being,' he said to Billy. 'Can you occupy yourself?'

'I'll not hang around here for long. I'll wait until you've finished and then maybe you can drive me to some bed and breakfast place. In the meantime, I'd like to see Clare's room.'

'Very well, said Edith, gradually regaining her composure. 'You know where it is.'

Billy, looking as if he'd kill Edith later given half a chance, left the room, made his way upstairs and Douglas went into the study, which had been furnished with police equipment.

Venerables raised his eyes inquisitively as Douglas came in.

'A right kettle of fish we've got here, laddie,' said Douglas. 'Edith Laker's little Clare's grandmother! Wouldn't acknowledge her own daughter: worried about what the neighbours would say. And it sounds like Bridie's death couldn't come too soon for Edith. Ransome's going to need watching. Bit of a loose cannon, I suspect. Now for Delrose.'

'Time the pot was given a stir, sir.'

'Let's just hope it doesn't boil over.'

Douglas decided on a gentle approach. If he set alarm bells ringing, Delrose might slip away between his fingers.

'Take a seat, sir. You don't mind if Sergeant Venerables tapes our conversation? Just for the record. Saves time later. I never have been able to read my sergeant's handwriting – and I'm not sure he can either!'

'I don't mind in the least.' His voice was soft, placatory.

'We appreciate your cooperation, sir.'

Douglas despised himself for his false heartiness, but he had to put Delrose at his ease, or the man would smell a rat. 'We're having to reinterview everyone who had a connection with Clare,' he went on. 'Someone might have remembered something – noticed something – even subconsciously.'

'You've heard my story. Do I have to go through it all again?'

'If you don't mind, sir.'

'I was at Heathrow – and just as well that I was. I could get Edith off her flight and drive her back here as quickly as possible.

'So the kidnapping came as a total surprise to you?'

'I loved that child!' said Delrose indignantly. 'We were her constant companions, me and Una. And she's everything to Edith. How could I possibly want to harm her? And don't forget, Stirling was my friend. There's a good chance that he's dead.'

Douglas decided to change tack. 'I know you're devoted to Edith Laker.'

'*Devoted*? That's putting it a little strongly. I'm grateful, certainly. She's given me a job for life and more than enough for Una and I to live on.'

'You're most fortunate, sir. Fallen onto green pastures. How did you come to meet Mrs Laker, if you don't mind me asking?'

'It was a long time ago. When her husband was alive.'

'Remember the year, sir?'

'That's a tall order!'

'Take your time.'

Delrose looked thoughtfully at the ceiling. 'It was in the mid-seventies, when they were living on the Hamble. 1976, I think. They wanted help with the house and advertised for a handyman. When George died, Edith went travelling in the South of France, and I went with her – as a sort of manservant.'

'A manservant. Not her lover?'

Douglas knew he was being provocative, but he wanted to shatter Delrose's composure. And he certainly succeeded.

'God God, man, are you mad? Mc, Edith's lover? She'd have me for breakfast and still be hungry. I was never in the running.'

'She had other lovers then?'

'Maybe. She certainly always had an eye for a good-looking young man. She was quite a looker herself, when she was younger. She never played around when George was alive, but she might have had one or two male friends later on. I wouldn't have blamed her. She'd gone through a lot, looking after George.'

'Did you get on with George?'

'He was one of the best.'

'And the girl? Bridie? What happened to her after George died? Don't worry, sir – we've heard the truth about Bridie.'

'No one was supposed to know. Edith was ashamed of her.'

'So we gather. Didn't you realise that sooner or later someone would spill the beans?'

Delrose shrugged his shoulders dismissively. 'Seems only natural to me that a parent of Mrs Laker's background wouldn't want to acknowledge a junkie daughter. After all Edith did for her! And she just threw it back in her mother's face. If you ask me, Bridie didn't deserve to be acknowledged.'

'What did Edith do for her, exactly?'

'When she went to the South of France, she left Bridie with friends. Made sure she was well looked after. Sent her to an expensive boarding school. What did Bridie do? Kept running away! Finally disappeared altogether and we didn't see her again until she turned up here with Clare and that layabout New Zealander. Edith gave her a job, took her in. But it was hopeless. She was already hooked on drugs and she wasn't capable of kicking the habit. All the money Edith gave her was spent on heroin. The more money she got, the more she took. Ransome didn't stick around for long. In the end, all Edith was interested in was saving Bridie's daughter.'

Douglas frowned. 'It isn't that clear-cut, though, is it, sir? Think about it. A teenage girl, fatherless, needing her mother like she's never needed her before. And what does Edith Laker do? Abandons her and goes off to make a new life for herself in France. Oh, I'm sure she had good reasons for going, and I expect she thought she was doing her best for Bridie, but you have to see it from the girl's point of view. She'll have felt unloved, unwanted. A classic reason for turning to drugs.'

Delrose sighed. 'With respect, that's sentimental twaddle, Chief Inspector. The girl was well provided for and she chose to kick over the traces. When she came back here it was for money – that's all. Edith didn't want any trouble.'

'So she paid her daughter hush money. Not nice, is it, sir?'

'As I've said, I've no time for sentiment. I'm just stating the facts. Edith knows what she wants and she knows how best to achieve it.'

'So it appears. And you, sir – what do you want?'

'To live in peace. And get the child back to Edith.'

'Very commendable. No ambitions to become lord of the manor one day?'

'Me? Don't be bloody daft! The Hall will go to Clare.'

'Suppose we don't find her? Or we do find her and she's dead – who'll get the Hall then?'

'I don't know. I've never seen Edith's will. It's none of my business.'

'I thought you were her business manager?'

'For the charity – not for her personal concerns.'

'Who looks after those?'

'Her solicitor. I don't know his name, but I think he's based in London.'

'Let's return to George Laker. He left Edith a lot of money?'

'I don't know the details. I suppose he must have done. Enough for her to tour France, and come back and buy this place. And set up De Profundis.'

'And to keep a yacht down in Falmouth. And a crew on permanent stand-by.'

'Look here, Chief Inspector,' said Delrose, jumping up angrily, 'I am not her confidential adviser. I know nothing about her affairs, and never have done.'

'Of course not, sir.' Douglas was unctuous. Thank you, sir, for your help – you've been invaluable. There's no need to go back through your previous statement. Still no news of Stirling, I'm afraid. Incidentally, exactly how long have you known Stirling? A good while, I suppose as you were happy to entrust Clare to him. I don't think you mentioned it in your original statement.'

'I've known him for years. Almost as long as I've been living here. He's one of the best. I hope to God he doesn't turn up in the morgue. I hope you get the bastards responsible.'

'Oh, we will, sir. I'm quite sure of that. One last question: do you happen to know Bruce Hamilton?'

Delrose looked startled. 'Hamilton? Yes, of course. He's a frequent visitor here.'

'Anything special about him?'

'How do you mean? He owns *Cormorant*, likes sailing and shooting. He's always up with the Border gentry at their house parties.'

'Do you do any work for him?'

'Good God, no! We're on polite social terms – that's all.'

'Been out in *Cormorant*?'

'Never! The sea doesn't suit me. I'd be as sick as a dog.'

'Been out in Edith's yacht?'

'No. For the same reason.'

'Must take a lot of money to run a big ketch like *Cormorant*. Where does Hamilton get his money from?'

'He plays the stock market, I believe. Like Mr Laker did.'

'Lucky for them. And Edith inherited the lot?'

'I imagine so. As I said, I only manage the charity. She gets nothing out of that, I know. All the money she raises is ploughed straight into De Profundis.'

'A worthy cause.'

'Edith is an admirable and generous lady.'

'A pity none of that charity ever came near her daughter, if you don't mind my saying so.'

'Bridie didn't deserve charity! She was her own worst enemy.'

'She needed help. Love. Isn't that another word for charity? What is it, Mrs Rose? Douglas said, as Una came into the room, looking like a frightened rabbit.

'Excuse me interrupting, but Madam's ready to go out,' she said to Delrose. 'Will you be long?'

'We're almost finished,' said Douglas briskly. 'Now, sir, I'd be most grateful if you'd not stray far from home. We'll probably want to see you again very soon. You've been most helpful today. Do let us know if you think of anything else.'

'I've told you all I know.' He sounded defensive.

'It's enough to be getting on with. Oh, just one other thing: have you ever heard of Hermione Pringle?'

'No. Sounds like a film star!' Delrose gave a little laugh.

'Never mind. Just a thought. Come along, Sergeant, we'll be off. Ransome still here?'

'He's waiting for you, sir,' said Una, looking timidly at Douglas.

'Then we'll make a move.'

Ransome was in the entrance hall, back-pack in position. Douglas nodded to Edith Laker and promised to be in touch soon, hopefully with good news. The three men walked towards Douglas's car.

'The Boomers will put you up,' Douglas said to Billy.

'The Boomers?'

'A pub down at Hernmouth Quay. Named after a gang of eighteenth-century smugglers. We've had our fair share of trouble around here in the past and unfortunately it looks like nothing's changed. But it's not rum and baccy they're delivering today. You'll have to get a permit if you're planning to stay here long.'

'As soon as we find Clare I'm off home, taking her with me.'

'Mrs Laker'll not like that.'

'To hell with Mrs Laker!

Chapter Eleven

After they dropped Billy Ransome off at The Boomers, Venerables turned to Douglas with concern. 'You look all in, sir. Anything wrong? Anything in particular, I mean?'

'Everything's wrong, Frank.'

Venerables was stunned; Douglas usually only addressed him by his Christian name at moments of high drama. Clearly something was very wrong.

'We're up against the forces of evil here,' Douglas went on. 'Not just normal, run-of-the-mill criminality: pure, unmitigated evil. Smuggling's bad enough but it's always gone on. People will sell anything to make money. But what kind of monster in God's name, would abduct a child? Two children in this case – there's little Hermione Pringle as well as Clare, That bastard just made use of her – who knows what effect all this will have on the rest of her life? She's so terrified she won't even talk to us. An ordinary little girl, loving parents, waiting for her mother to come and pick her up from school in Morpeth. She only went a few yards . . . She shouldn't have got into that car, but the child had a trusting nature. Someone had done his research, laddie. Now look at the child – can't stop crying. She'll never trust anyone again. Who could stand by and watch an innocent child suffer fear, hunger, cold, and God knows what else? And all the time, he's one step ahead of us! I feel incompetent, useless. Old. It's time I retired, laddie. I'm past it.'

Venerables was pleased, for once, at Douglas's return to the more familiar – and patronising – epithet; all the same, he was concerned. Douglas was becoming far too emotionally involved in the case, and that wouldn't do at all. It was the road to disaster, both personal and professional.

'It's not your fault, sir. We're doing our best. Not like you to give up so soon! If you'll excuse the liberty, I think you need a stiff drink, a meal and an early bed. You've been in front of that computer too long.'

'Thanks for the sympathy, Sergeant, but the day's not over yet. Let's get back to the Hall.'

'No one'll be there. Don't you remember, Delrose was ferrying Edith Laker somewhere?'

'It's Una Rose I want. Let's go and have a wee chat with her. She's Delrose's wife, after all – a wife generally knows what goes on in her husband's head. And I thought she looked as nervous as a kitten earlier. I want to know why.'

'It's late.'

'So? You've nothing on this evening, have you?'

'I was going to see Lizzie,' Venerables admitted reluctantly.

'Still barking up that tree? She's got her protector well and truly dancing attendance. You'll not get anything from that quarter. Anyway, I need you with me. I *am* weary, I'll grant you that, and that makes it all the more imperative for me to avail myself of your sharp wits.'

Venerables felt a glow of satisfaction. He'd been feeling the lack of appreciation just recently – and he'd come to value a compliment from Douglas, who wasn't given to effusive praise, more than almost anything.

'You're sure this trip's worth the trouble?' Venerables said as they drove off towards the Hall. 'I still feel you'd be better off with that drink and a wee nap.'

'Oh stop your nannying, man! I'm not ready for the rest home just yet. To answer your question: yes, I definitely think its worth paying a little call on Una Rose. I can't get Delrose out of my mind. I can't believe this story of his friend Stirling, however plausible it might seem. Kidnappers wouldn't have held on to Stirling – he'd be nothing but a bloody nuisance. So why haven't we found him? Wouldn't they have wanted to leave his body in as public a place as possible – to show they mean business?'

'I agree with you – in principle. But would Delrose really do something that would well and truly blot his copybook with Edith Laker?'

'If he's got two million dollars waiting for him somewhere, he won't give a damn.'

'Then why didn't he take the money and scarper? He's still with us, sir. Still smiling.'

'That's because he wants to put us off the scent. And maybe bleed Edith Laker dry before he makes his exit. So let's see what his wife has to tell us.'

Una Rose peered round the door of the Hall, her eyes dark-ringed and anxious. She was clearly reluctant to let them in. Douglas tried to reassure her.

'We only want to ask a few questions, Mrs Rose. We'll not keep you for long. We'll be off and away before the nine o'clock news.'

'I've nothing clsc to say, Chicf Inspcctor.'

'Come on now, lass – let us in. It's freezing my ears off standing out here.'

'Grudgingly, she led them into the kitchen, where a gas fire hissed away and a plump armchair was placed strategically in front of the television. The table was cleared; all was neat and orderly. Douglas looked round approvingly.

'Nice and cosy, Mrs Rose.'

'I like it in here. I always stay here until Edith gets back, then me and Delrose go off to our own place. Sit down, if you're going to stay. Like a cup of tea?'

Douglas remembered his empty stomach. A sandwich wouldn't have gone amiss, but he didn't want to push his luck. 'Just the job! Mind if I take off my coat?'

'Go ahead. Make yourself comfortable.'

She filled the kettle, flicked on the switch, took mugs out of the cupboard.

'Now sir,' she said, 'what's this about?'

'It's about Clare. What else? I assume you're as concerned as we are by her abduction?'

She whirled round to confront him, her homely face red with indignation. '*Concerned*? We're devastated! Edith's nearly out of her mind. Del blames himself – he's hardly slept since Clare went. And I'm so upset I hardly know what I'm doing. We all love her, Chief Inspector. She's everything to us.'

'Did you know Edith is Clare's grandmother, Mrs Rose? That Bridie Ransome was Edith's daughter?'

Una seemed to crumple. 'Aye. We knew that. She hated Bridie for what she'd become. She was ashamed of her, thought people would think less of her if they knew about Bridie. I could never see much harm in the poor wee lass, but – but Mrs Laker loved the child. We hoped she could find some comfort in Clare.'

'How long have you known about Bridie?'

'For as long as I've known Edith.'

'Which is?'

'About ten years. The same time as Del and I have been married. When Edith bought this place, Del came with her. I was working up at the castle for the Harrisons – lovely job, but Edith offered me more money and a nice little lodge to live in. She also introduced me to Del. So that's how I came here, and happy I've been until all this happened. It all goes back to Bridie, see. She should never have brought that Billy home. He's no good. What could she have been thinking of, to marry the likes of him? She was Edith Laker's daughter; she could have inherited all this, if she'd played her cards right. And now look what's happened. Dead in a mud hut, and her daughter missing. She threw it all away.'

'How friendly are you with Edith Laker, Mrs Rose?'

'She's an employer. Not a friend. I cook, clean, do my duties. We don't – gossip.'

'And Mr Rose? Does she confide in him?'

The kettle began to scream; Una made the tea, clearly glad of the chance to consider her answer. 'Del knows her better than I do,' she said, handing them each a mug. 'What they talk about is their business. He doesn't tell me, and I don't ask. That's as it should be.'

'Do you get many visitors at the Hall?'

'Not as a rule. Edith keeps her own company. Sometimes she has people round for drinks. Like the wine and cheese party for the charity – you were here, sir, if I remember correctly.'

'Aye. A memorable occasion. But she must have friends, surely?'

'She's not got many. She's choosy about who she mixes with. Lady Nevill – now she's a nice lady. She comes sometimes.'

'Anyone else? Bruce Hamilton?'

'Bruce? Aye, he's been here. Usually with other people, like the Harrisons.'

'Does he ever drop in to see Delrose?'

'Good heavens, no! We're just ordinary people, Chief Inspector. We don't hobnob with the gentry. Del sees him occasionally in the pub, I think. He's always very friendly to us.'

'Does Delrose do any work for Hamilton?'

'Not that I know of. Mrs Laker keeps him busy.'

Douglas finished his tea, feeling deflated: no joy from this line of enquiry. And yet Una still looked uneasy. Perched on the edge of a kitchen stool, she clearly wasn't relaxed. Still, he thought gloomily, that was understandable. It didn't necessarily mean she had anything to hide. She'd no particular reason to trust them, not after they'd failed to deliver Clare that fateful Tuesday. However, he wouldn't retire from the fray just yet.

'Do you know where Edith's gone this evening?'

'To see her accountant. He lives this side of Newcastle. Paying that ransom's left her in difficulties.'

'It can't be easy to lay hands on a sum of money like that. All to no purpose – but we did warn her.

'She'd do anything for Clare. And I don't blame her. I wouldn't put it past her to sell the Hall, if it'd do any good.'

'Let's hope it doesn't come to that . . . How about you and Delrose? Got much put away for a rainy day?'

Una laughed mirthlessly. 'You do ask daft questions, Chief Inspector! Do we look like millionaires? We've got the use of the Lodge for as long as we want it, but Edith doesn't pay more than the going rate for the job. Oh, it's enough for our needs – I'm not complaining. But we've not got anything in the piggy-bank, not even for a holiday. I've always wanted to go to one of those villas in Spain, lie next to the swimming pool and sip cool drinks all day . . . I'd like that. It'd be nice to get away from these Northumbrian winters. But we haven't got that sort of money.'

Douglas rose from his armchair and put on his coat. Una too slid down off the stool, seeming relieved that the interview was over. She walked briskly over to the door.

'I'll see you out, sir. Sorry I haven't been much help.'

'Oh you've told us a great deal Mrs Rose. Don't get cold, now. We'll let ourselves out.'

Back in the car, Douglas turned on the ignition and the heater; the inside of the car was like a fridge. Venerables looked at him speculatively. 'So she told us a great deal did she?'

'It wasn't what she said – it was her face. That's what's bothering me. I'd expect to see sadness – she's obviously upset over the child; but there was more. And that's what interests me. Now, my body's telling me it needs food, and that bed you mentioned a while ago seems like a good idea. I'm going to sleep on it. Tomorrow I'll have a wee talk to a couple of bank managers I know, see if I can twist their arm a bit. They won't be able to tell me much, but they might be able to tip me the wink if Mr Rose's bank account has suddenly taken a turn for the better.'

'Surely that's a breach of client confidentiality, sir?'

'Put it this way – I happen to know a couple of people who work in a bank and I've done one or two good turns for them. And one good turn deserves another, isn't that what they say? Nothing definite – but a wink's a wink.'

'Glad to hear you sounding a bit more positive, sir.'

'There's nothing like good, honest work to get rid of a fit of the miseries! As long as we're busy, we'll keep the Devil on his toes. As soon as we sit back, he'll ride again. And he'll be our master.'

The following afternoon Lizzie decided it was time to pack her bag; not easy with only one arm in operation. But the moment was right. Hilda had gone to Durham and wouldn't be back before five – and Lizzie knew that if she didn't go now, she never would, not once Hilda came home with her offer of hot suppers and early nights.

It wasn't as if she was ungrateful, Lizzie thought – for Hilda had been all kindness. She had installed Lizzie in her best room – part bedroom, part sitting room – with a magnificent view across the river to the ancient burial mound marked by a wooden cross. That afternoon the tide was out, exposing mud flats rich in nutrients, feeding grounds for flocks of waders, probing and scratching for the minute organisms which constituted their staple diet. It was freezing outside and the sky was overcast, but there was a tinge of brightness in the light which made the seabirds restless. Lizzie too, perhaps.

Certainly she no longer felt inclined to dwell on her aches and pains. Her head still ached, but only with a gentle twinge now and again, to remind her of that ghastly moment when she had plummetted over the cliff and come to rest at last against that strategically-placed rock. Her left arm was stiff and useless, but the rest of her worked perfectly and she felt her old energy returning. It was time to offer her thanks to Hilda: time to return to the dust of the arena. She *needed* to work. The incident with the motorbike had affected Lizzie more than she realised. It was the first time she had suffered a physical attack on her person and she felt, not fear, but fierce anger. She'd see her attacker behind bars if it was the last thing she did.

She took her holdall out of the wardrobe; the effort made her wince with pain. She walked across to the window and looked down into the road; the policeman who guarded the house was talking to another man, tall, athletically built, wearing jeans and a black leather jacket. John Chance. When John rang the doorbell Lizzie felt her heart turn somersaults and she struggled to fight the emotion. She glanced at herself in the mirror, grimaced at her tired face, and pressed the entry switch to let him in. She heard his footsteps coming nearer, her heart still in turmoil.

'Hello,' he said, when she opened the door. 'On your own?'

'Yes, Hilda's out. Come in.'

He entered the room, looked round at the pile of clothes on the bed, the holdall standing open on the floor.

'You're not leaving, surely?'

She nodded. 'It's time to move on.'

'But that arm's not nearly better! And what about your head?'

'I can function perfectly well with one arm. And my head's just fine.'

'Like hell it is! You look terrible. Hilda will be furious when she gets back.'

'She'll understand.'

'Douglas'll hit the roof.'

'Douglas doesn't own me!'

'No, but he's the boss.'

'He's not *my* boss. Look, why don't you sit down? Why have you come here? Nothing else to do except nag me?'

'I came to see you, of course. I feel responsible for what happened.'

'You didn't drain my brake fluid.'

'I should have come to fetch you. The roads weren't safe – they still aren't.'

'Look, John,' said Lizzie wearily, 'will you please stop trying to nanny me? I'm a big girl now, or haven't you noticed?'

'Big enough, I'll grant you that. But let's be serious for a moment. If you are thinking of getting back into harness, then I'd better give you an update.'

'Have they found the driver of the Bedford?'

'Not yet. But they've found Marcus Tyler – or rather, what's left of him.'

'Who's Marcus Tyler?'

'Brother of Josh Tyler, deceased, and Dean Tyler, still alive and kicking. The Tyler brothers – the North East's answer to the Kray twins. You gave us a rough description of the chap you chucked overboard a week ago. You mentioned his jacket, which seemed pretty distinctive. Well, he's still wearing it. Or he was, when Dean Tyler identified him. So we're pretty sure he's your man. His body was washed up on the shore near Creswell. They want you to get down to the morgue, when you're feeling strong enough, and tell us if you think this chap Marcus Tyler could conceivably be the man you chucked into the sea.'

Lizzie looked startled. She sat down heavily on the bed. 'There can't be much left to identify, can there?'

'Enough. The sea's pretty cold at this time of the year, and the fish didn't seem to fancy him much. Can you blame them?' He looked at her and grinned. 'Still want to go back to work? Relax – it's Marcus Tyler, all right. Dean's furious! Two brothers down, and he's still pretending that the Tyler brothers were one happy family, sitting around playing Scrabble in the long winter evenings.'

'I didn't kill him, John,' she said quietly. 'I only tipped him overboard and I saw him holding on to that dinghy. I wouldn't leave a man to drown! There were others on that boat. They could easily have pulled him out.'

'Maybe they did. And maybe they threw him back in later on, when they'd realised that you might be able to identify him. I suspect they acted on the spur of the moment. If they'd stopped to think, they'd have remembered that bodies do surface after a time, and the tide's got a nasty habit of bringing them ashore.'

'Any chance Dean will shop his brother now he's dead?'

'Not a hope. Claims he has no idea what Marcus got up to, knows nothing about any hardcore porn, and has never heard of a boat called *Cormorant*. As you'd expect. But I'm worried about you, Lizzie. Someone's already tried to bump you off. If it gets round – and it will – that you intercepted Marcus Tyler, and stopped a consignment of videos from reaching their destination, the chances are that they'll take another pot-shot at you. They'll want their revenge. You're a prime target, Lizzie – and that's all the more reason why you should stay here with that nice, safe Hilda and be guarded by Pete out there.'

'Thanks for the lecture, but I'm leaving all the same. Dean might not have known what his brother was up to the night I stopped him going ashore with the videos – unless Watson and Spicer told him, and I doubt that, because I gather from Douglas that they're still in custody. Incidentally, if those two bumped Marcus Tyler off, then they'll be facing a murder charge, won't they? I suppose they'll wriggle out of it, deny that there was anyone on board when they hijacked the yacht . . . And why isn't Dean Tyler more cut up over the death of his brothers? Why isn't he acting the avenging angel over Josh's death?'

'I think he knows who killed both his brothers but is too frightened – of reprisals, of the police sticking their noses in – to accuse anyone. He's got too much at stake. But at the moment, this is pure supposition. If he *was* involved with what happened on *Cormorant*, and he was the one who tried to kill you on your motorbike, he might just think you've had a big enough scare to keep you out of action for the time being. It still doesn't alter the fact that it's dangerous for you to be seen around Hernmouth.'

'Oh, I won't go out. I propose to take up residence with Holmes and Venerables.'

'You're not back on that tack, Lizzie? What a persistent woman you are. Most people would be asking for a transfer to the Orkneys.'

'I've never fancied the Orkneys. I'm not a country girl. Besides, I've got a vested interest in all this. I want to find out who sabotaged my bike. I worshipped that machine, you know.'

'Then you're not only persistent, but unnatural. Why can't you worship a nice chap like me? Surely I've got more going for me than a motorbike? And I bet I'm cheaper to run.'

She laughed, and although the movement jarred her arm she immediately felt better. He looked so bewildered, so utterly unsure of himself that she stood up and went over to kiss him gently on the cheek.

'There – I like you too. Really. But I doubt you quite come up to my bike's standards. You can't beat that accelerator . . .'

'Don't tempt me, Lizzie. You've never put my accelerator to the test.'

'I'll take your word for it,' she said, as he came closer. 'Don't come any further,' she shouted in alarm, hugging her wounded arm protectively.

But with gentle firmness he drew her to him, keeping her wounded side away from him, and kissed her long and deeply. At first she tried to twist away but found that her shoulder protested, so she let him kiss her until her body responded and she kissed him back. Eventually they drew apart, breathless.

'For someone who's just had a brush with death, you're amazing. Just as well you're *hors de combat*, or I'd have thrown you on that bed.'

'Don't you dare! I don't want to end up in hospital with the surgeon re-setting my arm! How would I explain that one?'

Just then they heard the front door slam, and footsteps came up the stairs. A pause, and Hilda came in. She looked cold and tired, and made at once towards the fire.

'I hope I'm not interrupting anything,' she said, smiling across at John.

'Unfortunately not,' he said. 'Lizzie's a bit tied up at the moment, but she'll soon be back in action. It's nice to see you again, Lady Nevill.'

'Please call me Hilda. Everyone does. But what's all this?' she said, looking towards the bed. 'Are you thinking of leaving me, Lizzie?'

'It's not that I don't like being here, Hilda,' said Lizzie, full of contrition. 'You've been so kind – it's been marvellous staying with you. But I have to make a move. I'm feeling so much better, and I'll be quite safe in the police house in Hernmouth.'

'It's up to you. I shall certainly miss you, but I do see that you must be bored here. It suits me – I love watching the birds out there on the estuary – but it's not suitable for young people.'

She took off her coat and stooped to plug in the little kettle that stood on the table by the fire. For once, she looked like a woman well on her way to old age; on impulse, Lizzie went over to her and put her good arm round Hilda's shoulders.

'It's been *wonderful* here. See how much better I am! But I want to get back to work. So much is going on, and I'm beginning to feel left out.'

Hilda smiled and returned the hug. 'I've done all I can for you. That arm will heal itself now, if you look after it.'

The colour had come back to Hilda's cheeks. Lizzie knew that she approved of her decision to rejoin the real world; Hilda wasn't one for burying her head in the sand.

John came over and made the tea whilst Lizzie, with Hilda's assistance, bundled the pile of clothes into the holdall.

'Did you have a good day in Durham? said Lizzie, packing her hairbrush.

'It gave me a lot to think about. And plenty to do. It's so cold, and the roads are treacherous, but I must set off again tomorrow. Further south, this time – I want to see one of my husband's friends.'

John came over with the tea. 'We've a new man at The Boomers,' he said cheerfully. 'Billy Ransome, a New Zealander. Charlie was thinking of taking on extra help for the season, and Billy fits the bill – no pun intended. He's an interesting chap; half Maori. Nice bloke. Likes sailing. Charlie Wheeler felt sorry for him and found him some work. Billy's none too happy at the moment, though – he's the child's father. Poor little Clare. He wants fast action and it's going to be a job stopping him from forcing our hand. God help the kidnappers when Ransome gets his hands on them!

'Let's hope that will be soon,' said Hilda fervently.

Chapter Twelve

On Thursdays, Delrose always drove Una to the big supermarket in Morpeth to stock up for the week. Today, just over a week after the kidnapper had failed to deliver Clare to her grandmother, was no exception, even though Edith Laker was too anxious and distressed to eat much; meals had become sporadic and the amount eaten negligible. But life had to go on. There were household items to replenish and Una, conscientious over these matters, insisted that the Roses keep to their normal schedule.

The day was fine. High pressure had set in and the ground crackled with frost; breath hung suspended like smoke in the clear air. But the sun was shining, and anything was better than the black skies, icy wind, and driving rain of the past few weeks.

Una had gone into Wynwick – to buy stamps, she'd said, but Delrose knew that she'd be gone a good hour. She'd drop in to see Mrs Hawkins, ostensibly to ask if she wanted anything from the supermarket. That would mean a cup of coffee, a biscuit or two and a good old gossip. So Delrose decided to make good use of her absence and clean the car. Usually he drove the BMW to Morpeth for the shopping, but the police hadn't yet released the car, and Delrose was currently using the Mercedes for household expeditions.

Delrose loved the Mercedes with a passion he'd never felt for a woman. Never, in his wildest flights of fancy, had he seen himself owning such a car; it was enough that he was able to look after it and drive it whenever Edith needed chauffeuring. He loved its sleek, sexy lines, the contented purr of its engine. He even loved cleaning it.

Today, in the brutally pale spring light, it looked grubby. During the winter, the local roads had been heavily salted and covered with grit, and the residue now coated the lower half of the car's bodywork. Delrose shook his head disapprovingly and set about unwinding the hosepipe. He flipped open the garage door with the remote control and went to find a bucket, polish and dusters, and a chamois leather. This was going to be a proper job: not just a sloosh of water and a wipe-down. The whole household might be in chaos as a result of Clare's disappearance, but that didn't stop him from doing his duty, restoring the car to its pristine state, making it shine like a knight in armour, all ready to face the spring.

He turned on the outside tap, muttered a prayer of thanks that it hadn't frozen, and walked back to the car, carrying the dripping hose. He stooped, turned on the car radio, and settled down to work.

He started on the side of the car nearest to him. After a while he stood up to admire the result. The white paint gleamed through the grime – like a good deed in a naughty world, he thought, pleased with his turn of phrase. Then he bent down again to tackle the rear wheel. He never saw his attacker. He didn't hear the soft plop of the silenced gun, didn't feel the bullet thud into his back. He stood quite still for a second, then dropped the hosepipe and fell face-down onto the cobbled courtyard.

The voice on the 'Jimmy Young Show' droned on inexorably. What ought one to do, a listener was asking, when one's husband walked out on his family and one had to pay off the mortgage on one's own?

'He's lucky to be alive,' said Venerables.

'Aye, laddie, he is. The bullet just missed his heart. Two ribs won't take long to heal,' said Douglas, pulling out onto the A1 from the Ashington road. 'Pity he didn't catch a glimpse of his attacker.'

'No one ever sees anything around here! There are no footprints, no tyre marks. Maybe they'll find some broken twigs in the shrubbery: boy scout stuff. When are we going to get a break, sir? I'm fed up with hitting my head against brick walls.'

'That's what detective work is, laddie. We hammer away, and sooner or later someone squeals, or makes a run for it, or walks into a trap. But I agree it's frustrating. There are just too many people in this district determined to keep stumm. If we go on as we're going, we'll have Scotland Yard on our heels. But the breakthrough *will* come. And God knows what we'll find when we take the lid of this particular can of worms. At least we know now that our friend Delrose isn't all that popular round here.'

'It's like the poem, sir. 'Watch the wall, my darling, while the gentlemen go by!'

Douglas turned his eyes of the road and looked at Venerables in blank astonishment.

'Have you finally flipped, Venerables? What's poetry got to do with any of this?'

'It's Kipling, sir. My old man used to like Kipling.'

'Did he now? You surprise me.'

'There's no need to be patronising, sir. Not everyone from Tyneside has criminal intentions.'

Douglas snorted derisively. 'You could have fooled me. Bunch of ignorant pigs, if you ask me. Bellies full of brown ale and both feet in the trough.'

'If that's how you feel, Chief Inspector, I think maybe you'd be better off with someone else sitting beside you. I'll not be your whipping boy.'

Douglas, his heart pounding alarmingly, pulled off the A1 into a parking lay-by. He switched off the engine, and opened the car door. 'I'll take a wee walk, laddie. So we can both calm down.'

'You're the one who needs to calm down, sir. We'll not get anywhere by calling each other names like kids.'

Douglas got out of the car, and slammed the door shut and walked away. Venerables was right. Douglas was tired, anxious, at breaking point. And Venerables was an essential part of his team. They'd worked together for two years now, come through a lot. He'd been wrong to cast aspersions. There was nothing for it; he'd have to apologise.

Douglas went back to the car and found Venerables smoking a cigarette.

'Come off it, laddie,' said Douglas gruffly. 'You know

you've finished with that muck. Jenny persuaded you to give it up, so don't start backsliding. Besides, if you want to attract the lassies, you oughtn't to soak yourself in tobacco. Chuck it out of the window. It's a filthy habit.'

'Why should I worry? You've just said we Tynesiders are pigs wallowing in our own filth.'

'Aye, and you're a pig with a bloody great chip on your shoulder. But I can't do without you, laddie, so why don't we call it a day and get on with the job? I'll not be happy with any other sergeant.'

'You could get one from Durham.'

'Durham? They're a sad lot over there! No, there's nothing for it – we'll live and die together. Come on, out with that fag.'

Venerables threw the cigarette out of the window. He said nothing, and Douglas too retreated into his inner thoughts.

'Who'd want to kill Delrose, sir' said Venerables after a long pause.

'I can think of several people who might want to shut him up. If he'd double-crossed any one, or fouled things up in some way. You see, I think Delrose, McLoughlin, the Tyler brothers, Hamilton and those two who stole *Cormorant* – Spicer and Watson – are mixed up in this together. *Have* to be. It's just too much of a coincidence otherwise, in an area this size. We've got a lot of dubious characters in a few square miles. I'd say we've got one, maybe two, gangs. That's one of the problems. Could be some of these characters are working for more than one boss and keeping quiet about it. But things aren't running that smoothly. A drug landing at St Waleric's Haven went wrong and Drugs Squad picked up the lot. A landing of porn videos was intercepted – we know what happened to Marcus Tyler. Lizzie's definitely identified him, by the way. There was just enough left of his face for her to say that she was almost one hundred per cent sure he was the man with the holdall on board *Cormorant*. And his jacket gave him away. Whoever killed him should have thought about that. Now, someone's to blame for all these slip-ups. I think they blame Delrose and want rid of him. Because why else should he be shot?'

Venerables had to admit there was a crazy logic in Douglas's theory.

'So who's lost the most? Who'd have most reason to punish him?'

'In human terms, Dean Tyler. He's lost two brothers. But funnily enough, he doesn't seem to be all that bothered.'

'Sir?'

'Look, lad, if Dean's part of this, then he'd be prepared for possible alterations in the size of his family. He'd know the risks and the rules. And if he's getting plenty out of it all, financially speaking, then he'd be happy to say nowt, wouldn't he?'

No one could be that callous. Not where a brother's concerned.

'Aye lad, they could. Money's the root of all evil, there's no doubt about that.'

They fell silent. It was freezing in the car; Douglas turned on the ignition and the heater.

'Will Dean be any better off with Delrose out of the way?' said Venerables suddenly.

'Could be. One less for the share-out. And perhaps you're right – perhaps Dean does have some brotherly feelings. If he thought that Delrose was to blame for killing either of his brothers, he might have decided to take his own, personal revenge.'

'Then we ought to get back to Dean?'

'Maybe so, laddie.'

'Do we bring him in?'

'Not yet.'

'Someone's checking his alibis?'

'Of course. We'll get back to him soon. One thing's for certain: *Cormorant* won't be going out to sea at the moment, not if the skipper's got his head screwed on right. I saw the forecast – fog's on the way. It gets bad at this time of year. So with no activity on the smuggling front, we can concentrate on Delrose.'

'We ought to report back to Mrs Rose.'

'Indeed. And watch out for Edith Laker's reaction when she hears her chauffeur will be around for a bit longer.'

'She'll be pleased, surely?'

'Unless she suspects that he might have something to do with the kidnapping of wee Clare. She's hardly going to tell

Delrose, if that's what she really thinks. And there's someone else in the family who might be keen to bump off Delrose, if he thought Delrose was involved in the kidnapping.'

'Billy Ransome?'

'That's right, laddie. He wants his daughter back more than anything. And he's her father – he'd be ready to hurt anyone he thought had harmed her.'

'That's just supposition, sir.'

'That's a big word, laddie.'

'Well, we Tynesiders do sometimes use words of more than one syllable.'

Douglas accepted the sarcastic admonition humbly. He eased the Volvo into gear. 'I reckon I owe you an apology. I stepped out of line. It's just that—'

'Think no more about it, sir. We're all under stress and, as you said, we've got to stick together. It won't help that poor wee girl if either of us deserts the sinking ship.'

'Any news, Constable? said Douglas, winding down the window of the Volvo as he eased it into a parking space in front of the Hall.

'They've found out that the attacker came up to the garage by way of the shrubbery, sir.'

Douglas nodded impatiently. 'Anything else?'

'No footmarks on the cobblestones,' Constable Wilberforce went on. 'The firearms squad say they know roughly where the attacker was standing when he fired the shot because of the angle at which the bullet went into the man's chest. But they haven't found the bullet.'

'They won't have. It's still inside Delrose. Surgeon at the hospital's going to take it out for us.' Douglas gestured towards the house. 'How are the ladies taking it?'

'A right carry-on. WPC Stride's in there with them.'

'Polly?' said Venerables, coming to life. 'She's a great girl! Me and her go back a long way—'

'Down, boy,' said Douglas affectionately. 'You've had enough excitement for one day. Stick to Lizzie. She's got one of her arms in a sling so she can't hit you too hard.'

'There's too much competition in that quarter,' said Venerables, 'and I don't like competition.'

'Aye, I can tell that. Anyway, what makes you think that Polly Stride'd look twice at you? The whole Force has been after her at one time or another and no one's had any joy. Why should she break the habit of a lifetime?'

'It must be good to be like you, sir. Never after the lassies.'

'I won't say I don't take a wee peek at them from time to time. But I know my limitations. Unlike some . . . Come on, laddie. To work.'

Una Rose opened the door. Understandably, she looked distraught, and her face was tear-streaked, but there was something else. Something which caused Douglas's heart to accelerate. Fear. Over the years, Douglas had taught himself to smell fear. It was a distinctive scent; follow it, and you'll not go wrong, was the advice he gave to police cadets. He glanced at Venerables; his sergeant had recognised it too. His face was tense, alert.

'How's my Del? said Una, as she led the way into the study.

'He'll survive. Couple of cracked ribs and they've still to dig the bullet out. He'll be home soon. But he won't be doing any chauffeuring for a wee while.'

'Oh, thank God! Thank God. Can I go and see him?'

'I should check with the hospital first. How'll you get there?'

'I'll take her,' said a voice behind him; Douglas turned and came face to face with Edith. 'We'll go as soon as the Chief Inspector and Sergeant have left. Have you any idea who attacked Delrose?' she said evenly, looking at Douglas.

'We have our suspicions. Perhaps you can help us. Did Delrose have any enemies? Anyone who didn't see him as flavour of the month?'

'A man like Delrose doesn't have enemies!' said Una passionately. 'He's the most upright man I have ever known. And he keeps himself to himself, doesn't he, ma'am?'

'I'd agree with that assessment,' said Edith.

'Does anyone come to the Lodge to see him, Mrs Rose?' said Douglas. 'Anyone you don't know?'

'What are you suggesting, Inspector? That he uses the Lodge as a meeting-place for all the lowlife in the neighbourhood?'

'I didn't say that, Mrs Rose.'

Venerables had wandered off towards the desk. Suddenly he stopped; then turned to face them.

'Did you know there's a message here on the tape?'

'Damnation! I ordered a constant watch on that machine. Get Constable Wilberforce in,' he said to the blonde policewoman who had just come into the library.

'He's been guarding the shrubbery,' said Venerables. 'He can't be everywhere at once.'

'He forgot, more likely. Like everyone else. They're all too busy looking for footprints in the shrubbery, like a bunch of bloody Sherlock Holmes's.'

'For God's sake, stop it! Both of you,' said Edith vehemently. 'Let's play the message. This is Clare's life at stake here. We don't have time for your petty squabbles.'

Venerables played the message back: a man's voice, with a slight Newcastle accent.

'It didn't work, did it? And whose fault was it? I told you – no police, just you and me. I saw you sitting in that fancy car of yours, a policewoman cosied up next to you. So let's have another go, shall we? Same place, same time, next Thursday. But one thing's changed. I'll need a further two million US dollars if you want the child back. If I see any signs at all of police presence, then you'll not get her. And don't cheat on me this time, or you'll get a little gift in a jiffy bag in Friday morning's post. And Clare won't be learning to play the piano in a hurry. Now here she is. She wants a word with you.'

Faintly at first, then louder, came the sound of a child sobbing quietly. Then the dialling tone sounded. No one moved until, with a soft moan, Edith Laker fell to the floor. 'Trace that call, Sergeant,' Douglas said. 'And Polly – look to Mrs Laker.'

'It's most likely a mobile, sir,' said Venerables, picking up the phone. 'He wouldn't want to risk a call box, not at this stage of the game.'

'Then get on to Network Security! We're running out of time.'

Chapter Thirteen

Douglas stood over Edith, watching her regain consciousness, appalled at how much she seemed to have aged during the last few minutes. Gradually, recognition and remembrance came back into those heavily-shadowed eyes.

'Chief Inspector,' she said, her voice weak and hesitant, 'tell me it isn't true. Tell me I've just had a bad dream. If I don't pay up in time, they'll cut off Clare's fingers. That is what he meant, isn't it? He wouldn't dare do it, would he? Not to a child?'

'There's a great deal of difference between a threat and an action.' Douglas tried to sound convincing. 'The child's a wee innocent. He'll respect that, unless he's a monster from hell.'

'That's what I'm afraid of!' said Edith, her voice growing stronger. He must be a monster, to have kidnapped a child in the first place! Two million dollars – well, he can have it. Money's nothing to me, not when Clare's safety is in question. I won't have a hair on her head harmed. And this time, Inspector, I shall deal with it on my own. This time there'll be no mistake.'

Douglas winced. Would she never learn? 'Ma'am, on no account take the initiative. We don't want a second fiasco. They might kill you *and* the bairn when they've got four million dollars out of you. They might decide it's safer to get rid of the pair of you. The dead can't give evidence. Don't do anything rash, ma'am, I beg of you. We know what we're doing.'

'If you think I'm going to wait around for you and that incompetent sergeant of yours to get off your fat backsides, then you're making a big mistake. This is my business,

Inspector, and I'll handle it as I see fit. One of us will get Clare back – and I know who that will be.'

'You can't dismiss years of police experience of—'

'*Police experience?* What do I care about police experience!' shouted Edith, jumping to her feet, contempt flashing from her eyes like the beam from a lighthouse. He recoiled, thinking for a moment she was going to attack him physically. Instead she spat at him, like a wild cat cornered by her adversaries. The gesture – so unexpected, so uncharacteristic – took Douglas completely by surprise. Instinctively he wanted to back away, to leave the wild cat to shout her defiance at the world. Instead he took his handkerchief out of his pocket and wiped the spittle off his tie.

'Shout and curse, ma'am, if it makes you feel better. I do sympathise. I know how you must feel, though I've no bairns of my own. If I had, I expect I'd be spitting as well. But it's not the way to do things. We've got to work out a rational plan of action, and we've got a week to do it in. First, we have to trace that message. I never thought I'd be thanking God for living in an electronic age.'

Edith, white-faced, was as tense as a tightly coiled spring. Douglas had never seen her like this. He knew she cared for the child, but never had he reckoned on such savage devotion. Never for one minute had he thought that civilised, elegant Edith Laker could lose all control.

'Chief Inspector McBride,' she said, enunciating every syllable, 'my grandchild is everything to me. *Everything*. One day, when I'm gone, she'll be rich, successful and independent. That's what I want for her. Her mother was a dreadful disappointment to me. Never will Clare go along that road. I'll see to it that she doesn't.'

'Ma'am—'

'I understand these people,' she said, breathing rapidly. 'They want money. Well, they can have it next Thursday. All they ask for. And I give you my word that this time, I won't interfere with your arrangements. You go your way, and I'll go mine. Now, if you'll please excuse me, I have some phone calls to make.'

She pushed past him and left the room, followed by Una and WPC Stride.

Douglas stood silent, lost in thought. What was Edith planning to do? She seemed capable of anything, where Clare was concerned. And Venerables rushed in, his face flushed with excitement.

'Sir!'

'What is it, man? You look like you've just won the lottery.'

'Feels like it! Network Security have traced the phone message. Bloody fast going, eh? It *is* a mobile – and it was sold to someone local. And you'll never guess who.'

'I don't want to play guessing games with you, man! Out with it.'

'Bruce Hamilton! Bought the phone last January.'

'The devil he did! Come on, laddie. He only lives down the road at St Waleric's. And this time there'll be no excuses.'

Clare didn't know which Sammy she hated most; the sleepy Sammy who sat and gazed into the distance after she'd breathed in the special smoke, or the bad-tempered Sammy who sat moping by the table, shivering and sniffing, waiting for Donald to come.

After a while, Sammy had taken the chains off and allowed her to lie on her bed with her feet tied together with a rope. But she'd tied the rope tightly; Clare could feel it biting into her ankles like a swarm of angry bees. She'd tried to loosen the knots by wriggling her feet, but it hadn't helped. There was nothing to do but to lie down and pretend that she wasn't in this cold cellar with its stone floor, and Sammy looking paler and grimmer each day.

Clare knew how to tell the time; Edith had taught her. Her watch, a present from Edith on her sixth birthday, was still on her wrist, so she always knew when Donald was due. It was always two o'clock in the afternoon when he clumped in with his heavy oilskins and big boots. He never stayed long: just threw a little plastic bag at Sammy, emptied the bucket which they used as a lavatory, and brought them more water in a second bucket. A couple of times he brought a carrier bag with bread in it, and a packet of butter, and a jar of jam. Another time he came with a box of tinned food: Clare saw baked beans and spaghetti hoops.

But Sammy didn't always bother with the food. At first she'd made tea in a little metal teapot, but soon even this seemed to be too much trouble. Clare couldn't understand why Sammy never felt hungry, or thirsty. She remembered with regret the sandwiches which Sammy had made for her when she first arrived – which Clare had rejected – and the mugs of lukewarm tea which she'd left untouched, telling Sammy that she wasn't allowed to drink tea or coffee, she wasn't old enough. How she longed for them now.

One day, Donald was late, and Sammy got very cross. When she heard his steps coming down the stairs she stormed across to confront him. Clare, very cold and sleepy, couldn't find the energy to sit up, but she listened.

'You're late!' Sammy shouted. 'It's nearly four!'

'Shut your mouth,' said Donald. 'What's in an hour or two?'

'A lot's in it!'

'You're a right little junkie, aren't you? Here, take it. I'm told it's good stuff – thought I'd bring you a treat.'

He threw the bag down on the table. Sammy ran over to seize it, like a dog chasing a lump of meat.

'And make it last. I won't be over tomorrow, it's getting too dangerous. The Bill's out in force and I don't want to attract attention to this place. Soon the wardens will be arriving, and then we'll have to move. Keep a low profile for a few days. And watch the child.'

'When's the handover?'

'We're still talking.'

'So there's no money yet?'

'Relax – you'll get your share. Then you won't have to rely on me for your stuff.'

He came across to where Clare was lying on her bed. Sammy, ignoring them, began to fiddle with her silver paper. Clare shut her eyes.

'The child doesn't look too good,' Donald said. Are you feeding her?'

Sammy nodded vaguely, intent on what she was doing. Donald went over and looked in the carrier bags.

'You've hardly touched these! Christ almighty, Sammy, you've got to feed her. That was part of the deal.'

'She don't want much. Not much of an appetite. I can't force-feed her.'

'For God's sake, make her some toast or something and tea, I don't want her dying on us.'

Sammy shrugged her shoulders indifferently. She was already heating the foil, settling down to take her first hit.

Donald looked at her, grunted, and went up the stairs. There seemed to be a lot of stairs; Clare listened to his footsteps fading away into the void above her. From a great height, she heard the trap-door to the cellar close, and she was alone again with Sammy.

She couldn't help it; she couldn't be brave any more. Tears trickled down her face and onto her school coat. She wanted her Teddy – and Una, with her cups of hot chocolate – and Aunt Edith.

Next day, Donald didn't come. Nor the day after.

Chapter Fourteen

'We're getting there, Venerables. We're tightening the net. Any minute now we'll be able to haul in our catch.'

Venerables stared out of the window into the darkness, where patches of fog swirled across the windscreen like inquisitive wraiths. The fog was going to get thicker, he'd heard on the local radio. Tomorrow it was going to be really bad . . .

'Well, Venerables?' said Douglas. 'Aren't you pleased with this new development?'

Venerables jumped. 'Sorry, sir. I was thinking.'

'Aye, so I noticed. You were in what my mother used to call a brown study. What's troubling you, man? Not lassies again?'

'No sir,' he said, equably. 'I do sometimes think of other things than lassies. To be honest, I don't know what's niggling me.'

'Then try a bit harder, laddie. Might be important. When something niggles a policeman, it pays to give it a bit of attention.'

'I *know* it's important. That's the reason for my brown study – I'm trawling my brain for ideas . . . It'll come to me. God, what a night! Freezing cold and foggy.'

'Don't complain, laddie. In this weather people have a habit of staying put in their warm houses and with this shoal of fish we've got on our hands, I'd rather have it that way. No wriggling free.'

'Hamilton's going to wriggle right enough.'

'I expect he will. But we've got him! And here we are. Mighty fine house. Opposite the golf course, very convenient. Pity we've got to interrupt his evening meal.'

Sure enough, Bruce Hamilton was about to have his supper. A decanter of whisky stood on the small table in front of the open fire in his living room; the glass next to it was half full. Or half empty, for Bruce's face was flushed, but he looked calm enough.

'Drink, Chief Inspector? You, Sergeant?' asked Hamilton, very much the bluff and genial host. He looked surprised when Douglas shook his head.

'You're not on duty, surely? Not at this time of night?'

'I'm afraid this is not a social visit, sir . . . We need information on your whereabouts today. All day, in fact.'

Hamilton picked up his drink and swallowed a sizeable mouthful. 'What's all this about, Chief Inspector? Don't tell me you're "making routine enquiries" . . . Well, I shall do my best to be of assistance. I've been in and out most of the day, though I haven't left St Waleric's. I've been up to the Golf Club – the AGM's next week, and they want me to stand as Chairman. I had lunch there – you can easily check that out. We were quite a crowd.'

'What time did you leave the club, sir?'

'About four, I suppose. There was nothing to come home for, so I stayed on and had a few drams after lunch. There was a lot of – gossip. Conjecture. Poor old Delrose came a cropper, didn't he? I was going to see him this evening, but I was told there's no point because the surgeons want to open him up.'

'To extract the bullet. That's right. So everyone knows about the incident?'

'Of course, man! You don't expect something like that to be kept secret. Is there any news of Delrose?'

'He'll live. A few broken ribs, but the bullet missed his heart. And his attacker's still waiting to be caught. Any idea who that might be?'

'Good God, I hardly know the man! We have a drink together occasionally, but he doesn't mix in my circle. I haven't the faintest idea who would want to take a pot-shot at him.'

Douglas, glancing at the mobile phone resting on the table next to the decanter, decided to change tack. 'Have you used your mobile today?'

'Why on earth do you want to know that? As it happens, I have. I'm supposed to have retired from my financial consultancy, but I'm still handling a few shares for friends. Peter Whittaker in Durham, amongst others. I rang him from the club to advise him that the time was right to sell one of his holdings.'

'Mr. Whittaker won't mind if I check on that?'

'Why should he?'

'And it was this particular phone that you used?'

Hamilton put down his glass abruptly. 'What exactly are you getting at, Chief Inspector? What the hell does it matter what phone I used? Yes, I did speak to Whittaker on this phone. Normally I would have called him from the house, as I don't like to mix business with pleasure, but it slipped my mind and I didn't remember until I was in the middle of lunch. Now, if you don't mind, it's getting late, and I want my supper.' He glanced meaningfully at the whisky decanter.

'Just a few more questions, and then we're through,' said Douglas doggedly. 'At about three thirty this afternoon, a message was left on Edith Laker's answerphone. From the kidnappers. I regret to tell you that the call's been traced to your mobile.'

Hamilton's face flushed angrily. He strode over to Douglas, and pushed his face, its bearded chin jutting aggressively, close to Douglas's.

'Look here, Chief Inspector, I might be semi-retired, but I'm not senile! I make a point of never letting my mobile out of my sight. I don't want any Tom, Dick or Harry running up huge phone bills on my behalf.'

Douglas refused to be deterred. 'That phone call, the one on Edith Laker's answerphone, was about the wee Clare. A new ransom demand.'

Douglas felt a tap on his shoulder. 'Sir, one minute . . . I've just remembered.'

'For God's sake, Sergeant, can't it wait?'

'No sir. It can't.'

But Douglas scented victory and pressed on. 'Bruce Hamilton, unless you can give me a good explanation of why that call should have been traced to your mobile phone, I shall have to take you down to the police station and charge you with the kidnapping of Clare Ransome.'

'Then you're a blethering idiot who should have stayed

north of the Border! You should have done your homework, Inspector. So you traced that call to my mobile, right?'

'Network Security checked it out.'

'Did they now? Did they also mention that my house was burgled back in February? That all my equipment was stolen: television, video recorder, microwave oven? Including my mobile phone? Which I subsequently replaced. Now get out of here, and do something useful! If you'd caught the burglar at the time, you wouldn't be in this mess now.'

He turned away, and sat down heavily on a chair in front of the fire. Venerables could contain himself no longer.

'I remembered the robbery, sir. It's what I wanted to tell you.'

Douglas whirled round on him. 'Then why didn't you, Sergeant?'

Venerables' agitation turned to instant indignation. 'I tried to, sir! But you'd have none of it.'

Hamilton looked up. 'If you two are going to start a punch-up, could you do it outside in the street, and not in my house? Get out and leave me in peace.'

Outside, Douglas got into the car and, unusually, opened the passenger door for Venerables. 'Damnation,' he said. 'I was so sure he was the one responsible! It all made sense – he's a clever man, he knows about money, he'd know how to launder four million dollars. And he had to be mixed up in that business over *Cormorant*.'

'That may be, sir. Meanwhile, we're left with egg all over our faces. And a bugger of a journey ahead of us. Look at the fog!'

A great, white bank of cloud was drifting in from the sea, settling down over the golf course, hiding the houses, obscuring the road ahead.

'We'd better get on, sir. Back to Hernmouth. There's an extra bed in my room in the police station, if you'd care to make use of it. You'll not reach Berwick tonight.'

'Fair enough, laddie. If you don't mind sharing with a blethering idiot who should have stayed north of the Border.'

Such self-abnegation was unlike Douglas, and Venerables looked at him with concern. The Inspector's face was drawn;

he looked old, defeated. Venerables felt an unexpected pang of affection.

'Chin Up, sir! This is just a temporary setback. I don't think Hamilton's as squeaky-clean as he'd like us to think. He might be a big fish – but even big fish get caught.'

But Venerables was as disappointed as Douglas by the failure of their mission. He'd hoped for a big breakthrough – God knew they needed it – and yet again it had eluded them. Now it was back to square one.

From two miles out to sea, the Nautophone on St Hilda's Island gave out a mournful wail. Venerables knew how it felt.

Chapter Fifteen

By midday on the following day, Friday, the fog had clamped down in earnest. Billy Ransome, part-time barman at The Boomers, polished glasses and tried to be patient.

He disliked playing the waiting game, but he knew it was the only game he *could* play. This was not the time to waste energy dashing round the countryside making accusations; yet his time would come. The place was swarming with police, poking their noses into people's affairs – that was their job. He was to watch and wait; and strike.

He was becoming familiar with the social scene in Hernmouth, St Waleric's and Wynwick. The usual Pommy set-up, he thought sardonically, as he finished with the glasses and turned his attention to the optics: the so-called gentry at the top of the pile, living the life of Riley. Then there were the professionals: the police, the coastguards, the fishermen. Not many of the latter around these days – his heart went out to them. Theirs was an ancient trade, diminished now to too few fish chased by too many people.

The factory just south of the town employed the sort of person Billy felt most at home with: ex-fishermen, coming onto dry land to pack prawns and lobsters which were sent all over the world. They were hard-working men and equally hard drinkers. Big Jim Tate, who liked his booze almost as much as he liked the girls, was the most regular visitor to the pub. Sometimes, when the factory was particularly busy, extras were brought in from Newcastle by coach. Dean Tyler was one of these. No doubt he'd be in later, with Big Jim. Billy had seen their doubles in New Zealand: big, tough men, dangerous only when the drink got into them. Tyler was morose; but who wouldn't be, with two brothers dead, one chucked overboard into the North Sea and the other pegged out on the estuary at low tide in what was known as a smuggler's hanging.

Then there were the eccentrics: folk like Clinker, fitting out his boat for the time when he and Lady Hilda Nevill, a weird old bird if ever there was one, set off to sail round Britain. It was Clinker's job to keep her happy; she saw to it that he was paid well for his trouble.

And all these people, with the possible exceptions of Clinker and Hilda, seeing nothing, caring even less! None of them bothering to look more than a step in front of them, everyone born with two proverbial blind eyes.

And that left himself. A bloody misfit, he thought savagely; but a misfit with a mission. And that was to get Clare back safe and sound. Clare, the light of his life. Why had he abandoned her to his feckless wife and her bitch of a mother? He'd never forgive himself. And somewhere out there, in the freezing fog, the person who kidnapped her was at large. But he wouldn't be at large for long. Billy couldn't join the police in their investigations, but he had ears and a good brain, and he knew that someone, sometime, would let slip the one vital piece of information that would lead him to his daughter. And when that time came, he was ready.

He replaced the optics, and went over to stoke the fire, piling on more coal. As he stood up he caught a glimpse of his face in the battered mirror hanging over the fire-place, between the mock-antique advertisements for Guinness and Veno's Cough Syrup. The glass was dirty and speckled with age, the fake-baroque gilt frame tawdry, like the dress of a tired whore. Nonetheless, Billy saw strength and endurance in his gaunt face; saw, too, a terrible resolution in those Polynesian eyes.

'You'll get there, boy,' he said. 'Just hang in there. You'll get the bastard.'

The door opened and Clinker scuttled in. He made straight for the fire and stretched out his hands to the cheerful blaze.

'By God, it's a foul day out there,' he said to Billy, who nodded and went back behind the bar. Billy liked Clinker: a down-to-earth sort of a bloke.

'The usual?'

'Make it Guinness. It'll keep out the fog.'

'What's the forecast?'

'Better tomorrow. The wind's shifting, and by tomorrow it'll be in the west. That'll mean warmer, wetter air – thank the Lord. Anyway, here's to you, Billy. Cheers.'

'How's her ladyship?'

'Funny you should ask. She's been down south to see one of her husband's pals – I got a phone call this morning. She wants to go out in *Sirius* tomorrow. Can you believe it? Apparently she's heard the forecast too. I said, no way, but she's adamant. Says I ought to test the new mainsail. I hope the engine's up to it. I was wondering, Billy – are you a sailing man? I'm going to need another pair of hands tomorrow if we go out. Hilda's got plenty of determination, but isn't too much use if I have to get sails in quickly.'

'I know how to pull on a few ropes. Before I took up sheep-shearing, I used to take tourists out along the east coast of South Island to watch the whales and the dolphins.'

'I thought a Kiwi would be used to the sea! So are you on? Early start. As soon as the visibility improves – I'll not go out in fog. It'll take your mind off things, and *Sirius* is on her pontoon now, so you've only got to skip down to the harbour. Only a short run, mind you; I'm not risking that boat in a swell.'

'When are you off on your round-Britain trip?'

Clinker raised his eyebrows and took a long swig of Guinness. 'When I say so, and not before. Hilda will have to bide her time.'

Billy's sombre face creased into a grin. 'Want a bet?'

The bar was filling up now. The group from the police house were drifting in; quite a party going on there, Billy'd heard. What with the girl Lizzie with the broken arm in one room, and the old fool of a Chief Inspector shacked up all cosy with his Sergeant in another, there wasn't much room for Sergeant Holmes, whose house it was meant to be. Now John Chance from Durham CID was muscling in; and that meant trouble. John fancied Lizzie, like everyone else, and Venerables's nose was being put decidedly out of joint. *Silly bugger*, he thought, watching Venerables sidle up to Lizzie on the oak settle. *He obviously knows nothing about women. All that brawn and boasting is useless if you haven't got what it takes.*

Not that *he* was one to talk, Billy thought, as he rapidly filled glasses and took orders. Look at the mess he'd made of his marriage: one disaster after another. Just his luck to fall in love with a junkie! All the same, Bridie had trusted him to help her. She'd left Clare to the tender mercies of Edith Laker in order to go out to New Zealand and find him. . .

Again he felt that uneasy nudging at his conscience. He should have *listened* to her when she made that phone call! But they'd got on to the subject of drugs straight away, and that had been the end of Bridie as far as he was concerned. He remembered his feeling of revulsion when she'd told him she was desperate for another fix, that her money had gone. He'd put the phone down, hadn't waited to hear what she really wanted to say. She'd found out something, by watching and listening, and that was what he was going to do now. But time was running out. Less than a week now . . . He thought of Clare, of her vulnerable body, her frail childishness. The thought was unbearable, and he turned sharply away from the bar. Where the hell was Charlie Wheeler? he thought irritably. He desperately needed another pair of hands. There were too many people calling for drinks – the lunch-time rush was on. He poked his head into the small room at the back of the pub where Charlie lived, and saw that he was on the telephone. He hesitated, not wanting to interrupt. Billy was grateful to Charlie for giving him this part-time job. Not many people walked into jobs like that, not in the North East at any rate.

When Charlie caught sight of Billy, he put the receiver down hastily.

'What is it?'

'Bar's filling up. Four cheese and ham toasties required – and pie and chips for the Chief Inspector and his Sergeant.'

'I'm coming. Get back to the bar. Just give me a shout next time you need me – you shouldn't leave the bar unattended.'

'OK. Sorry.'

Now, what are you hiding? thought Billy, as he went back to his place behind the bar. *I'll need to keep tabs on you. What didn't you want me to hear?*

*

There was no sunset that day. The fog that had cocooned the coast of Northumbria blanketed out the sun along with everything else. It muffled sounds too; the silence was eerie, accentuated rather than broken by the wail of the Nautophone on St Hilda's Island, sounding for three seconds at thirty-second intervals. Down in the galley of the thirty-six foot auxiliary sloop, *Flying Dutchman*, the clock showed that it was five o'clock. It might just as well have been midnight.

Not that anyone on board the yacht, just returned from the Netherlands, minded the fog. Back from picking up a ton of skunk, with a street value of over a million pounds sterling, they welcomed it, as smugglers have always done. It provided an efficient cloak for their activities. In the past, fog had been both a godsend and a hazard; today it was rendered comparatively harmless with the help of the Global Positioning System, available to navigators for the price of a few hundred pounds: a small price to pay, in view of the prize on offer.

It was time to leave the comfort of the saloon. The two men pulled on their warm waterproof jackets and climbed down the stern ladder into the sturdy wooden tender which they'd trailed behind them for the rendezvous with the bigger yacht, out in the North Sea. No one said anything; they'd been through the procedure so many times it was now routine, mundane. The bales were lowered, followed by the folding trolleys. The tender sank to its waterline. There was an outboard, but they would not use it; oars would propel them silently towards St Hilda's Island. The fog signal would guide them until they came in sight of the beam from the lighthouse, not yet visible through the impenetrable bank of fog.

The men settled down to their rowing. Both of them stared intently at the GPS secured to the forward thwart, as if they were worshipping a precious icon. Without it, the warning sounds and the faint beam of light, when it came, would all be useless, and they would be drifting around in the sea one and a half miles off the coast of Northumbria like blind men deprived of their guide dogs.

It was heart-stopping out there, the boat lifting to the swell of the short, choppy waves. Both men, experienced sailors as they were, had a superstitious dread of fog. It could disrupt navigation, distort reality. They could see nothing; no one could see them.

Suddenly the front man in the boat stopped rowing, and listened. This was what he'd been waiting for. It terrified him, as it had terrified other smugglers in times past, but it meant that the tiny navigational instrument was spot-on. It was the sound of waves breaking on a rocky shore: the sound of waves dragging back into the sea millions of small stones from a shingle beach.

They shipped oars and allowed the swell to bring them up on the beach. The front man jumped out when the keel touched bottom and held onto the bow. Then the second man disembarked, and together they dragged the boat higher up onto the beach. They began to unload the shrink-wrapped bales, dragging them up above the high waterline. They stacked the first of the bales onto the trolleys and made their way up to the pele tower at the far end of the ruined monastery, which would house the skunk as it had housed the brandy and tobacco of the old-time smugglers. They knew the timing was right, The RSPB Warden hadn't yet arrived. Kevin McDonald, the former lighthouse keeper now required only to ensure the smooth running of new technology, would already have made his afternoon visit to the island to check, on behalf of the Hernmouth coastguards, that all was well. They could take their time, knowing that the fog was on their side.

The trolleys were awkward on the sand; they paused to rearrange the bales. But the fog, once their salvation, proved their undoing. They didn't see the two men running down the sand dunes towards them. Too late they turned and took the knife thrusts full on the chest, and in the throat. They fell on the sand, knocking over the trolley. No one noticed that one of the bales broke lose, rolling over the top of the sand dune and coming to a halt in a clump of marram grass. Their attackers waited just long enough to check that both men were dead before they began to reload the bales and carry them off on the trolley.

There was nothing new in the scene. A customs officer in the eighteenth century would have found it all too familiar: two smugglers hoisted with their own petards, outwitted by a rival gang who had prior knowledge of their coming. He would have sighed with nothing more than resignation as he came upon the body of Kevin McDonald, stabbed to death as he arrived on the island to check on the Nautophone gantry.

'Enough's enough,' said John Chance, switching off his computer monitor. 'Come on, Lizzie. It's five o'clock and the fog will keep everyone in tonight. Let's get back to my place.'

Venerables looked up. 'She's not allowed out,' he said primly. 'She's what's called a hot property.'

'Oh give over, laddie,' said Douglas wearily. Trying to work in a room with a *ménage à trois* was getting him down. And he was feeling badly in need of a good night's sleep. His own bed in his solid house in Berwick was beginning to seem more and more appealing, despite its distance from Hernmouth and the atrocious driving conditions. 'Stop fussing ovcr the lass! She's got John to look after her – though I sometimes doubt whether Durham CID could look after a pet hamster.'

Lizzie too switched off her computer. She also was finding the constant sniping between John and Venerables distinctly irritating; why didn't they just call it a day? It was bad enough having to work in an overcrowded room and live in a poky police house, without having to cope with the attentions of a pair of competitive males. It was, she supposed grudgingly, good for her morale; clearly they still found her desirable, even if one side of her body was immobilised in a plaster cast and a sling. But she could have done without the compliment.

'Ta, John, for the invite – but I think I'll stay here. Holmes has got food in, and there's always the television.'

'You could have a hot bath at my place. Pine-scented bath oil. You could wash your hair, relax in front of my log fire. I've got a pretty eclectic assortment of CDs. What more can a girl want?'

Lizzie weakened. It sounded perfect on a cold, foggy night; she could relax, knowing that nothing important was likely to happen, at least on the drug-smuggling front.

'I don't think I like the sound of this,' said Venerables petulantly. 'She can take a bath here! Holmes has got a bathroom.'

'Have you seen it lately? It's freezing – condensation on the walls, bare lino to stand on,' said John incredulously.

'Seems all right to me. I suppose you want to be drying our Lizzie off in front of that log fire of yours?'

'I would if she'd let me.'

Lizzie stood up. She'd had all she could take. 'No one's going to dry me off anywhere,' she said. 'Just take a look at this, Frank. She waved her sling in Venerables's direction. 'And this.' She pulled down the neck of her pullover to reveal the strip of surgical plaster across her shoulder. 'John might have a powerful imagination, but he's got no common sense. There's not much of me that can get wet at the moment. But I will take you up on the offer of supper, John. There's something I want to talk to you about. Something I doubt you'll approve of – but sometimes you have to stick your neck out, if you want to get problems solved. Don't worry, Frank,' she said pityingly, as she saw the look of disappointment on Venerables's face, 'I'll come to no harm. This sling's as good as a chastity belt.'

'She's got a point there, laddie,' said Douglas wryly. 'Now, let the lass be. We'll be off to the pub later – I don't fancy Holmes's cooking.'

Venerables, faced with another evening of Douglas's company, and a second night of sharing a bedroom with his boss, lapsed into gloomy silence. Typical. Another man walked off with the lassie, right in front of his nose.

Later, in John's cottage – a modernised fisherman's two-up two-down affair on the outskirts of Hernmouth – Lizzie unwound over an Indian take-away and several glasses of red wine. Despite her best intentions, there'd been no talk of work. Instead, they listened to Schubert as John periodically stoked the fire. She felt pampered, safe from the dangers of the outside world. There was, she thought, a lot to be said for domesticity.

The Schubert quintet finished. John looked up. 'Ready for that bath, Lizzie? The heater's been on for hours.'

'I'm filthy. I've not been near a bath since the accident.'

'All the more reason why you should take advantage of my offer. Look, I'm a thoroughly trustworthy chap. You go up and get undressed while I run you a bath, then you can wrap a towel round yourself and I'll help you into the bath. I promise

I won't peep. I'll be a perfect gentleman. I'll just help you into the tub and leave you to it. When you're ready to get out, just shout, and I'll be up to help you out. More nifty manoeuvring with the towel – same as when you got in. Then downstairs you come, to a lovely roaring fire.'

'It does sound tempting . . . Promise you won't look?'

'Would I do such a thing? Remember, I'm used to helping people *in extremis*.'

He was as good as his word. The bathroom was warm and relatively luxurious; the water was soft, scented and just the right depth. John had switched off the electric light and brought up a candle; as she watched the shadows dancing on the ceiling she thought that it wasn't so bad after all to be a wounded policewoman. She felt cherished. John had been so gentle when he helped her into the bath; and he hadn't looked at her once, not even when the towel slipped. She rested her head back on the curved end of the bath and thought of the fog outside, the freezing, icy roads. Yes, she was definitely in the best place.

The water soon cooled down and the taps were a long way away. She tried to haul herself up with her good hand, but couldn't manage. *I'm like a beached whale*, she thought ruefully. As instructed, she shouted for assistance, and John came in wearing a blue towelling dressing gown.

'Can I be of service, madam?'

'I *could* do with a bit of help . . . Eyes closed!'

He bent down and carefully pulled her up out of the bath, wrapping her in a big yellow towel. Then he carried her downstairs and laid her on the sofa in front of the fire, where the logs hissed and spat out sparks.

'Now – let me dry you. I insist.'

Slowly, starting with her feet, he began to rub her caressingly with the towel. She gave herself up to it, relishing every moment of the contact. Instinctively, she reached out a hand and touched him on his thick, brown hair. He looked up and grinned.

'You like that, don't you?'

'Umm. Don't stop.'

And he didn't And somehow the sling and the plaster didn't seem to matter as her body responded to John's careful massage. And when he took his dressing gown off and lay down beside her on the sofa, she didn't push him away.

That night it seemed the most natural thing in the world to sleep with John in his big, white bed which almost filled the small front bedroom. Just before she went to sleep she heard the fog signal coming from St Hilda's Island. Thank God for fog, she thought contentedly. There'd be no need to rush in the morning.

Chapter Sixteen

For once the weather forecast was right. By Saturday morning, the fog had lifted and a brisk south-westerly wind had brought in milder, damper air. The sun, lurking behind dark clouds at the start of the day, become bolder as the day wore on.

Hilda drove down to the Marina at Hernmouth, and parked her car alongside the harbour wall. She was eager to go out to sea again; she'd found the confinements of winter trying and had been living in expectation of spring ever since New Year's Day. Now the signs were all around her. She could look down from her balcony window onto a carpet of snowdrops; out on the estuary the waders were well advanced in their courtship rituals. It would do Clinker good, too, she decided as she walked down to where *Sirius* was moored on the pontoon. It was time it was brought to his attention that a boat, however venerable, was for *using*. A new sail was not meant to be folded away in a sail locker like a wedding trousseau in a bottom drawer. It had a job to do: to work with the wind, like a living thing.

She climbed aboard the little wooden ketch. Clinker was tinkering with the engine, and Billy Ransome, whom she'd seen in The Boomers, was studying the coastal charts at the navigation table down in the main cabin. He glanced up as she climbed down the companion-way, took in the heavy-duty oil-skins and stout sea boots, and decided she'd do.

'Have you come to give us a hand?' she asked Billy.

'Seems like it. It's a bit brisk out there.'

'We're not going far – only to the island. We ought to start getting the feel of her.' She took in Billy's melancholy face; she felt desperately sorry for him.

'This must be terrible for you, Billy. Being here, but unable to *do* anything.'

'Thanks for the sympathy. Yes, I'm not the most cheerful of men right now. But don't worry about me – I'll get the bastard who's got Clare. Just you wait and see.'

'Any news yet? The police . . .'

'Are a lot of bumbling fools! I don't expect them to be much use. But I hear a few things in the course of my job at the pub, and I'm biding my time.'

He turned back to the charts; Hilda felt her compassion turn to disquiet.

'Don't do anything impetuous, Billy. I know the police are slow, but they usually get there in the end. It's only too easy to make a drastic mistake, once you take the law into your own hands.'

'Don't worry. I won't make a mistake. Now, where the hell's Clinker? We ought to be off if we want to make use of the tide.'

As if on cue, the engine coughed into life, and Clinker's head appeared, framed in the hatchway.

'Ready, you two? Let's get going.'

Sirius chugged stoutly out of the harbour and set course for the island with the wind on the beam. It was good to be out in the fresh air again, Hilda thought, as she tugged on ropes to get the sails up. As the sails filled with the westerly wind, and the seagulls circled hopefully overhead, she felt exhilarated. Alive. Winter never lasted for ever, did it? Despite the fact that she was an old-age pensioner, at that moment she could take on the whole world and win.

She was brought down to earth by the appearance of Clinker next to her at the mast.

'You take the helm, Hilda. You're making a right pig's ear of that sail.'

She turned to glare at him reproachfully, then noticed the considerable gap between the top of the sail and the top of the mast. Realising her limitations, she relinquished the halliard and made her way cautiously to the stern of the boat.

They were off. Even Billy began to look brighter as *Sirius* hurled herself across the North Sea towards St Hilda's Island. Clinker went below to make coffee, and Hilda, bracing her body to maintain the course, thought with pleasure of the long voyage she was soon to make. She was relieved that she'd taken that navigation course last year; Clinker, although expert with sails and engines, was not so confident when he left familiar waters. She'd never dare say so to his face, of course.

It didn't take them long to reach the island. Between them, they managed to manoeuvre *Sirius* into the tiny harbour, a mere gap in the rocks which surrounded the island. Swiftly they dropped the sails and motored up as far as they could go in the shallowing water. Then they dropped anchor, and Hilda lowered herself into the sea and waded ashore. Clinker and Billy followed. They stood together on the beach, stamping their feet and blowing on their hands, happy in the shared pleasure of the sail, and the knowledge that *Sirius* had proved herself to be a sea-worthy vessel with not a drop of water in her bilges.

Hilda suggested they take a look at the ruined monastery. In the mood for exercise, they set off towards the line of sand dunes above the beach. It was Hilda who saw them first. Two men, laid out side by side, covered with a thin blanket of sand, lying in a fold of the dunes like two people sunbathing. She stopped, horrified.

Billy dashed forward, while Clinker restrained Hilda. 'Don't look, Hilda! What is it, Billy?' he called out.

'This one's had his throat cut – the other's been stabbed. In the chest. God almighty, I know this one! It's Angus, Angus McLoughlin. You know him – sometimes he crews for Hamilton. No more sailing for him. I don't know the other man.'

'What the hell were they *doing* here?' said Clinker, going forward, Hilda refusing to be restrained any longer. 'McLoughlin wasn't out on *Cormorant*, that's for sure. *Cormorant* never left harbour yesterday, nor the day before. A bad business, Billy. Best get the police over. We can call them from *Sirius*.'

'Just one minute . . . We mustn't touch anything, of course,' said Hilda, staring down at the bodies,. but just take a look at these marks here, on the sand. Someone dragged these men to this spot. Let's just take a quick look at the beach, before we call the police, see what we can find. I wouldn't want the birds, or the sea, to remove any evidence before the police get here.'

She walked off purposefully, gazing intently at the ground in front of her. Clinker looked at her in admiration. She was a magnificent old bird, all right. Not frightened of corpses – not frightened of anything, he reckoned.

He walked quickly after her to the shore while Billy strode off towards the dunes. A few yards out to sea, *Sirius* turned her bow towards the incoming tide, bobbing up and down on the choppy waves. Hilda soon found what she was looking for.

'Here! That's where they came ashore. And look, they must have landed cargo. You can see the marks of a cart. Or a trolley. Two wheel marks, quite close together. And that's where they were attacked. There are more footmarks, all in a confusion.' Sure enough, the marks on the sand told the whole story.

'And I've found what they were landing,' said Billy quietly, coming up behind them. 'Come and see.'

He led them over to the top of the dune; they looked down at the shrink-wrapped bale which no one had noticed in the dark. 'Drug runners. And someone was tipped off and intercepted them. A rival gang? Now, where were they going to hide the stuff? Up there, in that tower? Let's take a quick look.'

They walked up to the tower, the only part of the monastery that was still intact. The reddish, sandstone walls were blackened by the pollution in the atmosphere: the great, nail-studded door firmly locked.

'We'll have to get the key,' said Clinker. 'But where the hell's Kevin McDonald? He couldn't have come over here to check the lighthouse and not seen anything.'

They looked at each other appalled, all thinking the same thing. They ran towards the lighthouse. If Kevin McDonald had seen nothing, then there must have been a good reason why. And the reason was right in front of them on the ground, in front of the Nautophone gantry.

No one spoke. 'Why aren't the coastguards here?' said Hilda suddenly.

'Why should they be here?' said Clinker. 'Fog's cleared and the light's still on.'

'But Kevin McDonald should have made an early morning call. The coastguard officer told me: the lighthouse keeper comes over by boat twice a day, in the morning and the afternoon. If he hadn't coastguards would have been here by now.'

'Then someone must have made that call. Someone must have know the form.'

'That means a local man . . . This is dreadful, Clinker. It's such a peaceful spot, where nothing ever goes on but bird-watching and rambling – and what do we find? Murder. Evil of every kind.'

'There's money involved, Hilda. Big money.'

'We must radio to the coastguard, from *Sirius*. And the police. Douglas must come and take a look at this. I don't know – sometimes I think the world's gone stark, staring mad.'

'And somewhere in all this,' said Billy quietly, 'is my daughter. That's all she means to that bastard who kidnapped her: Two million dollars, to be produced by next Thursday, on top of the two million they've already had. Let's make that call. But they'll not find anything in the tower.'

'What makes you so sure, Billy?' said Hilda.

'Because those people who killed McDonald and the other two will have cleared the lot up and taken it with them. They're professionals. And they're always one step ahead of the law.'

'A thieves' kitchen. That's what we've got round here. And the devils are brewing up a fine concoction. And *you*, McBride,' said Superintendent Blackburn, scowling belligerently, 'are sitting back and letting it happen! This coast needs a thorough purge. Three killed out on St Hilda's Island last night. Drug smugglers, ambushed by a rival gang, under our very noses. Two Tyler brothers murdered – Derek Rose in hospital. And, to top it all, one of our own Drugs Squad lassies run off the road. What next, McBride? There have been too many mistakes. Now the press are hounding me – they've caught on to the fact that this stretch of the coast is where the action is. And Scotland Yard's having a nag. They want to send reinforcements – they think we're incompetent. I'm beginning to think they're right. And they don't know the half of it yet.'

'You've forgotten the girl, sir. Clare Ransome. Kidnapped. The deadline is Thursday and today's Saturday.'

'A deadline? Who says?'

'The kidnapper says. Let me remind you: Edith Laker has got to find another two million dollars by Thursday, seven o'clock in the morning. If no money's forthcoming, they've threatened to cut off Clare's fingers. And that's just for starters. Callous bastards! The woman's frantic with worry.'

'And you do nothing, McBride! You and that useless sergeant of yours. For God's sake, man, if the press get wind of this . . .'

'They may not have to wait long, sir. Edith Laker's prepared to tell the world. She doesn't care about following the rules – she just wants her granddaughter back.'

'And what are you doing to find her?'

'We've traced the mobile phone the call came from. Used to belong to Bruce Hamilton – but that particular phone was stolen, along with other items, when he was burgled in February.'

Blackburn looked aghast. 'We're heading for real trouble, McBride! Edith Laker's a magistrate, and Hamilton's a leading light round here. Golf club, Conservative Party – you name it. For God's sake, don't go upsetting all the big noises in the area without consulting me first. Any evidence you rake up will have to be water-tight. You realise don't you, that if anything should happen to the child, you're off the case?'

'That's hardly fair, sir.'

'Fair? *Fair?* You listen to me. We've got to produce results soon, and that might mean a fresh approach. A fresh mind – a younger man, maybe. None of your dithering and shilly-shallying. That child's got to be found.'

'I agree with that whole-heartedly. I'd be getting on with my work now, if you hadn't called me up here. I'm well aware of the seriousness of this particular crime, and I'm well aware of the significance of all the other things going on along this coast. I know, too, that people in high places have had their noses put out of joint. That can't be helped. But we can't make a wrongful arrest, sir. We've got to be quite sure before we bring anyone in or we'll be the laughing stock of the whole force.'

'We're that already, McBride. So when does Derek Rose come out of hospital?'

'Rose leaves hospital tomorrow. The wound wasn't serious. And as to who shot him – before you ask, we're still working on it.'

'And who tried to kill Lizzie Teal?'

'We're working on that, too, sir.'

'And the Tyler brothers? And McLoughlin, and the other man on the island? Kevin McDonald? By God, McBride,' Blackburn stood up, his face flushing angrily, 'you've got to get a move on! Have you the remotest idea what you're doing? Have you got a plan, a proper strategy?'

The more Blackburn ranted and raged, the more phlegmatic Douglas became. *Damn the stupid bugger*, he thought; *he'd better calm down, otherwise he'll be having a coronary.*

'Of course we've got a plan. One familiar to you. One policemen learn at their mother's knee. Identify suspects; interview; eliminate; or, hopefully arrest. I agree it's slow, but it's thorough and it's effective. At the moment, the big fish are doing what big fish always do. Saving their own skins. The tiddlers are sent out to kill each other, and eventually they'll be the ones who'll lead us to the big fish.

'Now, if you'll let me get on, I have to see Edith Laker again. She's hell-bent on handing over the money herself next Thursday, and, as I'm sure you'll appreciate that isn't a good idea,'

It's a thoroughly bad idea. Especially after the disaster we had last time. And where's she going to get an extra two million dollars from? She might be rich; but not that rich, surely.'

'My own thoughts entirely, sir. And I'm just about to find out, if you'll excuse me.'

'You concentrate on the child. Leave Drugs Squad to clean up the rest of the mess. You've got no evidence that the two cases are connected. And remember – you've only got four days. Four days in which to get that child back in one piece. And tell Drugs Squad to concentrate on Dean Tyler. It seems to me he has a finger in most pies around here.'

'I've already had a go at him once – in connection with the Rose shooting. Unfortunately for us, he's got a sound alibi. He was working at the prawn factory in Hernmouth at the time Delrose was attacked.'

'Who says so?'

'It's in the factory's clocking-in book. And a colleague confirms he was working at the same bench with Tyler all day.'

'Sounds like they're in cahoots. Have another stab at him. I still think he's at the bottom of all this.;

'Not enough brain, sir. He's not one of the big fish.'

'True, but as you so perceptively remarked, he could lead you in the right direction.'

'I'll tell Drugs Squad.'

'Now go and be polite to Edith Laker. We can't have her lodging complaints. Four days, McBride – and then you're out, if there's no progress. I don't know why you should be bothered in any event. After all, you're coming up to retirement.'

Douglas stiffened with resentment. 'Nice to go out with a bang, sir, rather than a whimper.'

'Oh, get away with you, man! We've been together too long to fall out. But I'm not a happy man. I don't like this area getting a reputation. It'll drive folk like Edith Laker away, and we need people like her, people prepared to spend their money, put something into the community. Otherwise we'll just be a collection of out-of-work fishermen.'

'Aye. And pretty much all of them up to no good.'

Douglas didn't relish seeing Edith Laker again. He dreaded more emotional displays, anguished recriminations. Bruised from his meeting with Blackburn, the last thing he felt like was taking a pounding from Mrs Laker. But he had to face the music.

She was on her own when he arrived at St Oswald's Hall. Una, she informed him, had gone to see Delrose in hospital. Edith went into the sitting room and took up her usual position in front of the fire; once again she reminded Douglas of a tigress at bay. He was shocked by her appearance. She'd lost a lot of weight and her clothes hung loosely on her angular frame. Beneath the gash of lipstick and heavy eye make-up her face was ashen; the lines of tension around her mouth and across her forehead could not be concealed by the mask of face powder. She had aged at least ten years since Clare disappeared; Douglas, despite his dislike for her arrogance, felt a great surge of pity.

'Any news?' she asked eagerly.

'Nothing definite, ma'am. You've seen the BBC and ITN bulletins, I take it?'

'And a lot of good they'll do! Except to provide titillation for the masses. Do you honestly think that the animal who's got Clare will be moved by your appeals? There's only one way to get Clare back. So here it is: he's asked to see me next Thursday – same time, same place. So I'm going, and I will take the money with me. I want *no police presence*. Do you hear? No police presence. I'll see that Blackburn obeys me, if you won't. Keep out of this, Chief Inspector. I'm on my own now. I'll bring the money, make sure the child is Clare, then hand the money over. It's money he wants and money he can have. I know his type and I know how to keep him happy. I'll gladly end my days in a council flat if Clare can be saved.'

'It's not the right way to go about things, ma'am. Kidnappers always want more. As soon as they know that you're able to lay your hands on that sort of money, they'll not stop until they've bled you dry.'

'He'll never lay his hands on Clare again. And nor will anyone else. I'll make sure she's kept safe.'

'Nowhere's safe, not in this day and age. Now there's a lot of things going on around here at the moment, and it's my opinion that there'll be more. I think Clare's kidnapping may be part and parcel of this activity. This is a small community – it stands to reason the same people who've got your granddaughter are in all likelihood the same as those who bring in porn videos, smuggle in drugs. Satan's work, ma'am, carried out by Satan's emissaries. It's our job to expose these devils and rid the coast of them. It's not right to give in to them. That means they've won the battle. And one more thing, ma'am: I believe your daughter knew something about what was going on. That was why she went to New Zealand, to ask her husband for help. She felt there was no one here who would believe her, no one whom she could trust. She may even have felt she was in danger. Now that's a sad thing. You were her mother, but she couldn't confide in you.'

'She was ashamed. She knew I hated her drug habit and what it reduced her to.'

'And yet she probably bought her drugs round here.'

'Does it really matter where she got them? A determined junkie will winkle out drugs wherever he or she happens to be.

And Bridie is not the issue here. It's Clare I want to talk about.'

Douglas stared at her in amazement. He'd know that Edith Laker was a formidable woman; but he'd never believed that any mother could dismiss their own, dead child quite so easily.

'I'm well aware of that, ma'am. I just thought what I have to say might put a fresh perspective on the way we deal with the situation. What if the same person who's got little Clare is also responsible for poisoning our children with drugs, corrupting us with their foul kiddie pornography and God knows what else? Would you really want someone like that to walk away scot-free, with four million dollars in his pocket?'

His words struck home. She turned to look at him, her face distorted with fear and rage, like an animal fighting its way out of a trap.

'Don't say that, McBride. If I find out that bastard's involved Clare in drugs, pornography or anything like that, I'll kill him myself. After you've found him and arrested him. Because it's your job to do that. My only responsibility is to Clare.'

'That's right, ma'am,' said Douglas firmly. 'And that's what we have to remember: what's best and safest for Clare. Now, you listen to me. We're carrying out a full-scale investigation and the little fish are eating each other – as little fish always do. Now we've got our eyes on the big fish – one false move, and we'll pounce. But we have to do it our own way.'

'Big fish, little fish – if you ask me, you'd have been better off as a fisherman, not a policeman. Why are you here anyway, expounding your ridiculous theories, when you could be out there finding my granddaughter? If anyone hurts Clare, then I shall blame you. I shall see to it personally that your days in the police force are over for good. And my curses will go with you to the grave.'

Her voice was filled with such venom that Douglas shivered. If he had not thought it superstitious, he would have crossed himself.

'A lot can happen in four days, ma'am. Just let us get on with the job. Justice will be done, believe me.'

'Damn you and your sanctimonious stubbornness! Your caution will be the end of you. You'll never get to be Superintendent, McBride.'

Douglas refused to rise to the bait, though her jibes hit home. Let her abuse him if it made her feel better. He'd just have to bear it. 'If you'll excuse me, I've an investigation to lead. Goodnight to you, ma'am.'

Depressed and infuriated, he left her and drove off back to Hernmouth. Tomorrow was Sunday, and he'd have to go to Newcastle. People would think he was running away; let them think that. He was trying to find Clare in the best way he knew. The *only* way. There was no room for too much emotion in police work – he knew that from bitter experience. One thing Venerables had taught him, and that was to search for hard evidence. Only then could justice take its course.

Chapter Seventeen

On Sunday, Hilda woke early. She collected her thoughts, swung her legs out of bed, and reached for her dressing gown. Her legs and arms, she realised with irritation, ached: the result, she thought ruefully, of her exertions yesterday. Perhaps, after all, she was being stupid to contemplate sailing round the British Isles with Clinker. Maybe she should give in to the limitations of old age. Her spirit was willing, but the flesh, oh, the flesh . . .

She drew back the curtains and looked out across the estuary, towards the sea. In the distance, the lighthouse on St Hilda's Island flashed its warning message through the dawn. Usually the view filled her with joy, but today it was different. She looked at the island now with fresh eyes. It was no longer a peaceful place, the home of seabirds; she'd come face to face with death there yesterday. Three men killed over a battle for evil substances which could destroy body and mind. It was strange, she thought, how smugglers in the past had acquired a romantic image. Quite undeserved. There was nothing romantic about smugglers; they had always been a violent bunch. Perhaps smugglers of yesterday were glamorised because brandy and tobacco appeared less harmful than the substances modern smugglers brought in to the country. Drugs were universally destructive; in the past, brandy and tobacco had only been enjoyed by the privileged. No, Hilda repeated, there was nothing romantic about smugglers. She'd seen what they were capable of, out there yesterday, on the beach.

She padded into the kitchen, made tea, put bread in the toaster. She missed Lizzie. She'd liked her company; and, she had to admit, she'd enjoyed looking after her. For a second she thought of the loneliness ahead of her and her heart began to reproach Charles for deserting her. But she wasn't given to self-pity. She forced herself to concentrate on the day ahead and how she could make the most of it.

She added vitamin pills to her breakfast tray and carried it back to her bedroom. Then she poured the first cup of tea of the day – the first of many – and tried to enjoy the sight of waders out in the estuary. A good night's sleep had distanced her to some extent from the horrors she had seen; in any case, she had no illusions about human nature and the depravity of which it was capable. But to be confronted with evil in all its hideousness had nonetheless been upsetting. Once again, it seemed that the Devil walked out in her beloved Northumbria.

Although her body was recovering from yesterday's ordeal, her mind remained unsettled, agitated. She recognised the gnawing, nagging feeling of her subconscious trying to tell her something; and she knew she'd get no peace until she'd discovered what it was. As she drank her second cup of tea, she remembered. The visit to Charles's friend, James Turnbull – had it really only been last Wednesday that she'd driven down to Durham to see him? – had been both delightful and disturbing. She knew now that she had to see Edith Laker again. But how to set about it? She needed to catch Edith unawares, when her defences were down. Then, suddenly, the answer came to her. The sun was shining; there was a bit of mist out to sea, but nothing more threatening. A day for walking – perhaps Edith would like the exercise. It was excellent for relieving stress. She would persuade Edith to accompany her to Dunstanburgh Castle.

Edith, as it turned out, needed little persuading. By ten past nine, Hilda was dressed in walking clothes and driving to Wynwick in her little car. As she reached the village the bells in the Norman church – more like a fortress than a place of worship – were ringing for the nine-thirty service. For a moment, Hilda regretted her decision. She would have liked to take Communion on that particular morning, to reinforce her belief that good would triumph in the end, but the niggling restlessness was still there, and she knew she had to respect it.

Don't stop now, her inner voice was saying. *Go on*, So she ignored the bells.

Edith, dressed in warm tweed trousers and anorak, was at the gates of St Oswald's Hall, waiting for her. She wore thick walking boots; a yellow scarf, tucked into the neck of her jacket, added a touch of colour to her drawn and haggard face.

As Edith got into the car, Hilda thought how much she'd aged since she'd last seen her. She looked awkward in the passenger seat, hampered by her long legs. Hilda told her to push the seat back, but the catch was stiff, so Hilda stopped near the church and got out to wrestle with Edith's seat. As she shut the door, having made Edith more comfortable, she caught a glimpse of a black car parked in the lay-by opposite. *Someone won't be missing Communion*, she thought, as she got back into the driver's seat and set off along the coastal road towards Craster.

But the black car followed them all the way to Howick, then turned off into a side road. Now they had the road to themselves. Hilda needed her wits about her on the dangerous bends; she tried not to look at the sheer drop down to the sea on her left. Leaving Howick behind, she pulled over, and they both got out to marvel at the breathtaking sight of Cullernose Point, alive with kittiwakes beginning their annual battle over nesting sites.

'I'm grateful to you, Hilda, for bringing me here today,' said Edith, staring bleakly at the Point. 'It was an inspired idea. A break like this helps to ease the anguish of waiting.'

'Waiting's always thc worst part,' said Hilda compassionately. Edith had always seemed so confident, so triumphant; it was painful to see her frail and vulnerable. 'I know the police are doing their best,' she went on, fumbling over the platitudes, finding it difficult to find the right words. 'You must have faith in Douglas McBride. He's slow, but he does get results.'

'*Too* slow, Hilda. My little Clare's suffering out there, while he's doing his PC Plod act.'

Edith was clearly determined not to be convinced about the successful outcome of Douglas's methods. Hilda decided to change the subject. 'I must tell you about a visit I made the other day to one of Charles's friends, James Turnbull. You must know him! James was Ambassador in Rio, during the time when you said you were there. Doubtless you met him. He was interested to hear about your charity – of course, he knows all about the plight of the street children. He's got a place near Durham now. He said he'd love to see you, when you're – less preoccupied.'

Edith didn't react. Of course she wouldn't be interested in seeing old friends at such a time! Hilda felt churlish for mentioning it. There she went again: meaning well, but making matters worse. Gung-ho to the last.

'Come – let's get on to Craster. We can leave the car there and walk to the castle.'

Now there was a reaction. Edith jerked herself out of her dark reverie and raised anxious eyes.

'I mustn't be away too long,' she said. 'I've got to be back. Just in case there's another call. I've got to be there.'

'I understand,' said Hilda sympathetically, and they got back into the car.

The car park in the tiny fishing port of Craster was full of bird-watchers unloading their paraphernalia, so Hilda didn't see the black car drive in and park opposite them. Impatient to get ahead of the bird-watchers, she had already set off along the path which led to the magnificent, fourteenth-century Lancastrian stronghold of Dunstanburgh Castle.

The path was soft and springy underfoot and made for pleasant walking. It hugged the coast for the first part of the way, then climbed up towards the castle. Below them, the sea crashed and thundered against the ancient rocks. Ahead, the castle rose out of the haze like an enchanter's palace.

Soon they had left the bird-watchers behind. Edith, with her long legs, strode on ahead; Hilda had to run to keep up. It didn't take them long to reach the gate house. The ruined towers on either side, with their narrow windows and thick walls, reminded them that this was not a pleasure palace but a fortress, strategically built to keep out the invading Scots and the army of a furious king.

They wandered round the Inner Ward. A melancholy had settled on them as if they were under a spell, and after a while they separated, to be alone with their thoughts. Hilda made her way to the south walls, constructed to protect the most vulnerable side of the castle, whilst Edith walked across the Outer Ward towards the northern side of the castle where there was no wall, merely the natural barrier of a precipitous cliff-face. Meanwhile the bird-watchers had arrived; after a perfunctory tour, they made their way to the postern gate which provided access to the foreshore on the south side.

One of the bird-watchers, Hilda noticed, didn't keep with the herd. Tall and thick-set, he was protected from the cold in a green Barbour jacket with the hood pulled up, and was wearing heavy walking shoes. From time to time he stopped and, raising his binoculars, stared out to sea. He didn't follow the rest of the group down to the shore; instead he sauntered along the South Curtain wall towards the cliffs where Edith was standing.

Hilda didn't take much notice. There was always someone in every group with a mind of his own. She was preoccupied; she must see James Turnbull again. James knew everyone. James had a yacht which he kept down on the Hamble, so that he could sail across to the continent when the mood took him . . .

Suddenly, she realised that Edith was no longer where she'd last seen her, and the solitary bird-watcher was walking swiftly back towards the gate house. For one moment Hilda thought Edith was with him, but he was still very much alone. Hilda's heart lurched unsteadily. *Dear God*, she thought, *don't let Edith have done anything stupid. She must know it's dangerous to try to climb down to the beach that way.*

As Hilda dashed over the Outer Ward to the cliff edge, she heard Edith shouting. Back through the postern gate streamed the bird-watchers, alerted by her cries. When Hilda got near the edge, she flattened herself on the turf and eased herself towards the brink. Then she looked down. Edith hung suspended halfway down the cliff, like a spider on a wall. Below her, the sea crashed on jagged rocks. A ledge in the sandstone cliff had stopped Edith's fall, and she had managed to grasp hold of a shrub which had fallen down the cliff and taken root during one of the frequent landslides. To Hilda, the shrub looked horribly frail.

Then Hilda felt someone grab her feet and drag her back from the edge: one of the bird-watchers. The leader of the group produced a rope and threw it down to Edith, shouting to her to tie it round her waist, but she seemed paralysed by terror. Someone went to get help from the porter at the gate house, who returned with more ropes and other equipment kept handy for just such an emergency. Then two of the bird-watchers abseiled down the cliff, and Edith, shocked but otherwise unhurt, was brought up to the top. Someone produced a flask of coffee – the bird-watchers seemed prepared for every eventuality – and Edith gratefully accepted a drink. After she'd recovered a little, the leader of the group knelt down and looked at her severely.

'You must *never* go near the edge of the cliff, madam' he said. 'It's very dangerous! Didn't you see that notice over there, warning you? The cliff's made of sandstone; it erodes if you so much as breathe on it. Always stick to the path. If you want to go down to the shore, then that's the way – over there, through the postern gate. You're lucky to be alive, madam. Thank your lucky stars that bush had taken root where it did! This is a hazardous area; it's very easy to slip.'

Edith took a deep, gasping breath. 'I didn't slip,' she said indignantly. 'I was *pushed*.'

There were no more sandwiches now, and no more tea. Donald didn't come and see them any more. So no one emptied the now smelly bucket, or brought them food, or brought Sammy her little bags of powder. Clare, huddled on the bed, still wearing the raincoat she was wearing when she'd been abducted, had gone beyond crying. She lay there, motionless, staring across at Sammy, wondering what Sammy would do next.

After Donald came that last time, Sammy had forgotten Clare entirely. She'd only been interested in breathing in her special smoke. After she'd done it once, Clare had asked her for a drink of water. Sammy had come over and hit her – really hard – on the face. She'd hit her again when Clare rolled off the bed and pulled herself across off the floor, to get away from her. Then she'd gone back to the table, and made some more smoke. But it hadn't had the same effect as before. Sammy had started shaking and coughing, then she'd been very sick – that was even smellier than the bucket. The she seemed to have fallen asleep. And she'd been asleep for a long time.

Then the paraffin heater had gone out, and there was no more paraffin to light it again. It grew very cold – so cold that Clare started shivering and couldn't stop. Sammy had left a candle burning, but there wasn't much of it left. Soon it would be completely dark. And Clare was frightened of the dark. She hadn't used to be, but she was now – ever since Donald had brought her to this place.

Clare was almost sure now that Sammy wasn't going to wake up and hit her again. She looked across the room to the bucket of water and the carrier bags, and knew that, in future, if she wanted any food she would have to get it herself.

She waited a little bit longer, then slid off her bed and across the floor to the water bucket. She drank gratefully, although the water was warm and tasted dusty. There was some stale bread in one of the carrier bags, but not very much. Clare tried to get the lid off the jar of jam, but it was so stiff, and her hands were so cold, that she couldn't manage. She thought she might be able to open one of the tins in the cardboard box – she'd seen Una do it – but she couldn't find a tin opener. It was very dark, even with the flickering candle, and there were lots of shadows. Sammy didn't move. Clare prayed for someone, even Donald, to come and help Sammy, make her wake up. But no one came.

Chapter Eighteen

The hospital phoned at midday on Sunday; Una Rose took the call. Delrose was being brought home at six that afternoon. As Una couldn't drive, the hospital had managed to find him a placc on a day-care ambulance.

She heard the news with mixed feelings. She'd actually enjoyed the last few days without Delrose. It had been a bit of a holiday for her; Edith, frantic with worry over Clare, hadn't bothered about whether the house was clean, or what time food appeared on the table. Una had enjoyed making her simple meals; putting up her feet in the afternoons to watch old films on television; going to bed early to read light romantic novels: all things she wasn't able to do when Delrose was around.

Life with Delrose, she thought as she replaced the telephone receiver, had never been a bed of roses. He was a stern taskmaster. He frequently made her feel like a stupid child being scolded by a particularly strict teacher.

She knew that Delrose thought she *was* stupid. In fact, she'd never really understood why Delrose – then in his early forties and set in his ways – had chosen to marry her. It had all been Edith's doing; she realised that now. Edith had wanted both a housekeeper and a handyman, and the accommodation she could offer was most suitable for a married couple. Delrose had been an attentive suitor up to the point when they'd tied the knot – and then, perhaps predictably, things had changed. Very soon they'd settled down into the sort of routine which she supposed most middle-aged married people endured: a polite arrangement for convenient living. Delrose had made it plainly obvious from the start that what he called 'the physical thing' didn't interest him as far as Una was concerned, so Una had retreated to her own room and, given the opportunity, sought a satisfying substitute in her collection of romantic novels, borrowed from Wynwick's mobile public library.

And now Delrose was coming home. He would be in pain, exhausted, even more demanding and critical. As always when she felt anxious, she got out the Hoover and embarked on the housework. The Lodge wasn't that large, but it was difficult to clean, with lots of small, angular staircases leading to numerous tiny rooms which, in the past, must have been occupied by servants. Appropriately, Una had chosen one of them as her own bedroom.

She made the living room look as tidy as possible. She moved out into the hall, and then over to the kitchen, where washing-up was piled in the sink. Tidying the kitchen took longer than she'd bargained for, and it was four o'clock when she next looked at the clock. Panic set in. Delrose's bed needed making, and the bathroom was in a dreadful mess. With one eye on the clock, she bustled round: not for love of Delrose, nor any desire to please him, but for fear of his withering scorn when he laid eyes on her sloppy housekeeping.

She didn't bother to clean her own room; Delrose never went in there. But she did stop to look at herself in the narrow mirror on the inside of the wardrobe door. No wonder he wasn't interested in her, she thought, as she looked at the plain face, the frizzy hair fading to an unattractive orange, the hefty body. Perhaps she should buy herself a new pair of glasses. Nothing too glamorous, though; Delrose wouldn't want that.

She changed into a pleated skirt; that meant tights, of course. Slippers, not shoes, until Delrose came back, then she'd have to change them – he couldn't abide slippers. Why, oh why, had he married her? she asked herself for the umpteenth time.

There still remained the three rooms at the top of the house. They were never used, but last night she'd thought she'd heard scratching noises, the scampering of tiny feet. She knew that birds and mice had a habit of coming inside in the cold weather; knew also that Delrose would go spare if he lost sleep as a result of them.

She went quickly up the uncarpeted stairs to the attic rooms and opened the door on the right. It was icy cold in there, and she shut the door quickly, but not before she'd caught sight of droppings on the floor boards, caught a whiff of an unpleasant musty smell. *Damn*, she thought; *that means a call to the Pest Control people tomorrow. And Delrose won't like them poking around.*

But in the room on the left-hand side of the landing, there were no droppings on the floor. Inexplicably, it looked as if it had been recently cleaned. There was also a chest of drawers tucked away under the eaves; she couldn't remember seeing that before. *It must be one of Delrose's purchases*, she thought. He had a weakness for buying items at auctions. She went over to inspect it. Even more puzzling: usually, Delrose bought cheap antiques, living in hope that one of the items he purchased for a song would turn out to be an eighteenth-century gem. This certainly wasn't. It was a plain, serviceable, nineteen-fifties chest of drawers in light oak.

She pulled open the top drawer: jam-packed with blank video cassettes, none of them labelled. She pulled out the top one and made a rough calculation that there must be about twenty in that drawer alone. Strange, she thought; perhaps Delrose had bought a job lot. The second and third drawers contained more of the same. Maybe he was going to sell them at a car boot sale; he'd often said there was money to be made that way. Then why hadn't he told her? He generally couldn't wait to boast of his latest money-making scheme.

She stooped down and pulled open the bottom drawer. It was heavy, and the contents were jammed against the bottom of the drawer above. She heaved and tugged, until the drawer flew open, and she fell backwards onto her heels. The drawer was stuffed full of magazines. Unfamiliar magazines, some in plain covers. She tugged some out. The pictures on the covers made her heart miss a beat. Naked boys; little girls with grown men. One cover-girl in a thin, cotton nightie that didn't even cover her bottom, couldn't have been more than seven or eight. Her plaintive face, with its huge, pathetic eyes, made Una want to cry.

She pulled out more magazines: more pictures. But these children weren't skipping along a beach, or going to school, or enjoying a birthday party. These children pouted provocatively at the camera, revealing their pre-pubescent private parts. She flipped over the pages. More children, mostly with adults. Adults doing disgusting things, exposing their own dirty bodies . . .

Una felt her stomach lurch. She rushed to the bathroom, where she was immediately, violently, sick. Afterwards she sat on the floor next to the lavatory, too weak to move, shaking uncontrollably. Her mind was racing. There must be some mistake . . . Perhaps Delrose had found the magazines somewhere on the estate, had meant to take them to the police, had only been prevented from doing so because he was shot. Perhaps the real owner of the magazines knew Delrose had got them, had shot him to ensure his silence! Una knew she was clutching at straws, but nonetheless hope surged through her. She might not love Delrose, but she couldn't bear to think that she had married someone who . . . Again a wave of nausea rushed over her. And suddenly she remembered the videos.

Fighting sickness every step of the way, she stumbled back upstairs and took out one of the cassettes. Then she went down to the sitting room, slotted it into the video recorder, turned on the television and pressed 'play'. She knew by now what she would see, but it was still a shock. Never in her worst nightmares had she imagined such things. Children, none of them more than ten years old, used by adults in a parody of sexual gratification – it was vile, unspeakable.

Unable to take any more, she switched the television off. So Delrose, she thought, enjoyed hurting children. Delrose, her husband, was a sexual pervert. A monster. Another thought crept into her mind, a thought so terrifying that she clutched her chest in an attempt to quieten her racing heart. *Clare*. Dear God, not Clare – not that sweet, affectionate little girl, who didn't know of what iniquities men were capable . . . Had Delrose been behind her kidnapping? Was Clare, at this moment, being forced to perform unmentionable acts for the cameras? Because one thing was certain: ordinary children featured in the magazines, in the films. No trickery was involved. And most of the children had looked scared to death.

She glanced at the clock. It was almost six; Delrose would be home soon. She still felt numb with shock; her brain wouldn't function. Of course Delrose hadn't kidnapped Clare! He'd been at Heathrow, waiting for Edith to come back from South America. But Delrose had lots of friends who seemed unsuitable companions for a man like him . . . It seemed obvious that, whatever Delrose had done, he hadn't done it alone.

God help me, she thought; *what will Delrose say when he knows what I've found? He must never know. But Edith, she should be warned.* Una knew she couldn't accuse Delrose directly – she dreaded his anger – but neither could she ignore what she'd seen. A note! That was it. She'd write an anonymous note to Edith, pointing her in the right direction.

She ran upstairs to her room where she had notepaper and an envelope. Quickly she wrote a short sentence in block capitals on a piece of paper. ASK DEL ABOUT CLARE. But what on earth was she going to do with it? It couldn't stay in the house, not with Delrose due back at any moment. She searched desperately for a solution. Then the idea came to her: outside the Lodge, attached to the gate, was the wooden letter-box for the Hall. It was Una's job to empty the box every morning and take the contents up to Edith. That's what she'd do. Tomorrow morning, she'd take the note to Edith along with all the other letters, and Edith would never know who sent it. And Delrose would never know who betrayed him.

She put the note in an envelope and sealed it. Then she went downstairs out into the drive, and dropped the letter in the box. Just in time. As soon as she got back into the house and smoothed down her hair, she heard the sound of a vehicle turning into the drive. And went to welcome Delrose home.

Back home in her flat in St Waleric's Haven, Hilda drew the curtains. Too tired to light the fire, too tired to think about supper, she poured herself a stiff whisky, added water, and collapsed onto the sofa.

She couldn't stop thinking about Edith. What a formidable woman! Having fallen down a cliff – or, as Edith maintained, having been pushed – she'd refused to go to hospital for a check-up, refused to report the incident to the police, confirming the bird-watchers' suspicion that she had imagined her attacker and had not wanted to appear stupid admitting she'd disobeyed the warning notice. But Hilda wasn't so certain. She remembered the tall man who had not been with the others, who had left the scene so swiftly. Just what, she thought, was going on?

Edith had agreed to see a doctor in Berwick, and he'd prescribed sleeping pills. In the doctor's waiting room, Edith had seemed dazed, shattered; Hilda was glad she'd accompanied her. She was glad, too, that she'd driven her back to St Oswald's Hall then stayed with Edith whilst she'd had a hot bath, made sure that Edith took a sleeping pill with her cup of tea. Edith didn't want to rest, saying she wanted to see Delrose, who'd just arrived home – but Hilda, acting on the doctor's instructions, had insisted that she go to bed. And Edith had fallen asleep as soon as her head hit the pillow.

A second whisky beckoned; Hilda decided that she'd earned it. She helped herself and felt her body relax. But the more she relaxed, the more her brain cleared, and the more she realised there was much she had to do. She would have liked to discuss her thoughts with someone . . . But who was there? Douglas would have been ideal; but he'd gone to Newcastle. Heaven only knew why. There was Venerables, but he wasn't sufficiently senior. And Douglas would never forgive her. Lizzie and John? It wasn't their investigation . . .

Then she thought of James Turnbull: quiet, charming James, who knew everyone, and if he didn't, knew how to find them. Retired James, who, like her, had time on his hands. She glanced at the clock; it wasn't too late to call. Hilda respected people's privacy and knew that the telephone could be an intolerable intrusion, and besides, James was probably about to eat. She felt quite sure that James always cooked himself a proper dinner and sat down to it at a perfectly laid table with a wine bottle at hand. But this was important, so perhaps today could be regarded as an exceptional circumstance.

Taking her whisky over to the phone, she called James, ready to apologise if the timing was inconvenient. But he too was on his second whisky, and had apparently been contemplating ringing *her*.

'James,' Hilda said, once the warm preliminaries were over, 'something's happened. I wonder if you could do something for me. Just a few enquiries—'

'I might be one step ahead of you, Hilda. I've already started on my Sherlock Holmes career.'

'What have you found out?'

'I've tracked down someone you're going to find rather intriguing.'

'Who? Don't keep me in suspense.'

'My dear, I'm afraid you'll have to control your impatience. I'll be in a better position to tell you more tomorrow.'

'But time's running out!'

'I'm aware of that, after what you told me when we met; but I don't want to raise your hopes too high. Let me phone you tomorrow, after I've spoken to this person . . . Hilda, it was good to see you the other day.'

'It took me back to times past. They were good times, weren't they, James?'

'Splendid! And no need to think they're over. Can we meet again in the near future?'

'I should like that. After all this is over.'

'I'll do what I can.'

'I'd be most grateful. I don't want to miss the boat.'

'You'll not miss the boat because of me.'

'James, you're a gem!'

'Indeed! I'll draw comfort from that fact. Actually, you're not half-bad yourself.'

Hilda smiled as she put the phone down. Suddenly, she had regained her appetite. It was good to have friends.

Chapter Nineteen

After eating a light supper and watching an hour's television, Delrose retired to bed early and Una heaved an enormous sigh of relief. Every time she'd looked at him, she could see only those photographs in the magazines, the faces on the video. She'd not been able to eat, but fortunately Delrose was too debilitated to notice the state she was in.

For a long time Una stood at the window in her bedroom, looking out onto the moonlit garden of St Oswald's Hall. Her room was at the back of the Lodge; she often gazed at the elegant gravel drive, the graceful cedar tree, the fine collection of early-flowering trees and shrubs, imagining how she would feel if she were the mistress of the house. But she wasn't ambitious. She was content to look and admire – whereas Delrose, she knew, tended to envy and covet. He thought he was as good as anyone else – she accepted her position.

Tonight, in Edith's garden, the bitterly cold night air had already covered the lawns and flower-beds with a white blanket of frost. She shivered. From the cedar tree came the eerie call of a barn owl. She waited, and there it was, staring at her with its flat white face and immense eyes. It too was watching the garden, but its motives were different; the frosted grass was a perfect back-drop for small mammals scuttling home to their nests. After giving another piercing cry, the owl flapped its powerful wings and flew off, circling the lawn, swooping low over the flower-beds, then aiming for the house, passing so close to her window that, if it had been summer and the window had been open, she could have stretched out a hand and touched it. Another cry, then it was off towards the Hall, where a dim light glowed in Edith's bedroom. So she was home, Una thought; Una knew she always slept with a light on nowadays. She said she'd adopted the habit when Clare came to live with her – sometimes the little girl would wander into Edith's room in the night, needing comfort after the trauma of a nightmare.

She turned away from the window. She wished she hadn't seen that owl. Owls were omens of evil, weren't they? Leaving the curtains open, Una got into bed. She remembered the letter; tomorrow, she'd take it down to Edith with the post. She was glad she'd written it. It meant she could sleep with an easy conscience. Emotionally drained, she slipped into a dreamless sleep.

Not for long, however, She woke up, her heart pounding, to find Delrose sitting on the edge of her bed, staring at her.

'What's wrong? Are you feeling Ill?'

'I want to talk to you, Una.'

'Why, Del? What's so urgent? Won't it keep till the morning?'

'No, my love, it won't.' She flinched at the unaccustomed endearment as if he'd hit her. 'While I was away in hospital you went nosing through my things. Didn't you?'

'I cleaned up. That's all.'

'Oh, you cleaned up, all right. Don't start denying it. You forgot to take the video out of the recorder, didn't you? While you were getting supper, I put the TV on, played about with the remote control. And guess what popped up on the screen? You shouldn't have interfered, Una. You should have minded your own business.'

Una was really frightened now. How could she have been so careless. Delrose was right – she was stupid. Stupid. His quietly menacing voice struck fear into her soul. She decided there was no point in dissembling.

'Del . . . I'm sorry. It's just that – I don't understand why you need such things. I know I've never been one for bed – but if you'd told me what you wanted, I would have tried harder.' *Take the blame*. That was what Delrose liked. Play the part of the inadequate wife, bewildered by her man's incomprehensible appetites, and he might just leave her alone.

'Tried harder? I never wanted you to try at all. Don't fool yourself that I ever felt anything for you. You were useful to Edith and me – that's all.'

'To *Edith*? But what—'

'Edith and I understand one another. We're partners, always have been. She realised that I needed a wife to give the whole thing a bit of respectability – and God knows there's no one more respectable than you.'

'*Partners*? What do you mean?'

'I mean professionally. At one time, I admit, it was more than that. Edith in her heyday was a man-eater, she just couldn't get enough of it, and I was more than happy to oblige. That fool George Laker couldn't satisfy her, that's for sure. But now she's past it, and it's strictly business.'

Una could scarcely breathe. Delrose continued to talk, but she couldn't take any of it in. Her life was collapsing all around her; now she had nothing. She had lost the battle before she had begun to fight it.

'So, Una,' he was saying, 'what are we going to do with you? Now that you've shown more ingenuity than I ever gave you credit for?'

'I'm so sorry, Delrose! I won't ever do it again.' She pleaded with him, like a naughty child dreading punishment. '*Please*! I won't say anything to anyone. Let's pretend this has never happened—'

'But it *has* happened, Una. And I don't trust you to keep your mouth shut.'

He slid along the edge of the bed until he was almost level with her head. She couldn't move; she was paralysed, like a rabbit caught in the headlights. She tried to sit up, but he forced her down. And, dimly, she realised there was no hope. She'd been so blind. So *stupid* . . .

'Del, please . . .' It was no use. His face was distorted with fury as he leant forward and put his hands round her neck. She struggled, reaching up to try and tear his hands away, but he caught hold of them. Sitting astride her chest, he pinioned her arms against her side with his legs. She tried to fight him, gasping for breath, but his hands pressed down inexorably, the full weight of his body behind them. Soon it was all over, and her body lay still.

Delrose got up and stared down at his wife. From the cedar tree came the cry, low and mournful, of the barn owl.

His wife's face stared up at Delrose, her eyes fixed in terror. He made quite sure she was dead. Then he went back to his own room and dialled a number.

'I've got a job for you. Now. It's urgent.'

The voice at the other end of the line remonstrated.

'No! Now! Otherwise we'll lose everything – you as well as me. Park in the street and come to the Lodge on foot.'

Delrose went downstairs to the kitchen and sat and waited. Not for long. After a short while he heard footsteps, and a tall man dressed in heavy boots and anorak walked in without knocking.

'What's going on, Delrose? I thought you were in hospital.'

'Well, as you can see, I'm fit enough to be at home. She's upstairs. I need your help. To get rid of her.'

'Who, for God's sake? Edith Laker?'

'Don't be a bloody fool! Why should I kill *her*? Una. She found out about the porn.'

'You're the bloody fool! You could have just warned her off, couldn't you? Did you have to kill her?'

'Of course I had to! She might've gone to the police – she's daft where kids are concerned – and then it would have been all over for us. Come on – help me. I can't lift a thing with this damn plaster across my chest. We'll have to bury her.'

'*Bury* her? The ground's as hard as concrete. It'll take us all night, or what's left of it, to dig a big enough hole. I'm not digging holes tonight, that's for sure.'

'Then what do you suggest we do with her? She can't stay where she is.'

'You should have thought of that, Delrose, before you started on her. You shouldn't expect me to come in and clean up your messes. I've done enough for you already, and you've done damn all for me. I get the child for you, see she's all right, and what do I get out of it? Just a warning to keep out of the way. Get lost. I daren't put my face outside in the day-time in case I get recognised. I'm taking a big risk coming here now.'

'Forget the sermon, Stirling. You'll get your reward. And soon. It won't be long before Edith coughs up some more money, and then we can both get the hell out of this place. Just bear with me a bit longer. Anyway, how is the girl?'

He shrugged indifferently. 'How should I know?'

'Haven't you checked on her?'

'She's being looked after. I've had more important things to do.'

'No doubt. What's Hamilton up to these days? Keeping you busy, is he?'

'Hamilton's all right, as far as I know *Cormorant*'s in harbour, and she'll stay there – the Bill's watching her day and night. She's no use to Hamilton now. It's too dangerous. The Bill are everywhere.'

'So you're doing Hamilton's dirty work for him? You always like to have it both ways.'

'Don't be daft, Delrose. You know I only work for you now.'

'Aye – and when the cat's away . . . Now listen. If anything happens to that child before Thursday, two million dollars go down the drain. And it'll be *you* I'll be burying.'

'Nothing can happen to her. She's safe enough. And Sammy's keeping an eye on her.'

'That sad little junkie? I suppose you've given her plenty of what she likes?'

'She wouldn't have agreed to help otherwise. She's hitting it in a big way. It'll kill her before long, the way she's going.'

'Well, make sure that it does just that after Thursday. Take her plenty of stuff. Finish her off, if you have to. Then, if the police find her, it'll be just another smackhead biting the dust.'

'I'll see she gets what she needs.'

'Don't forget. I don't suppose you know who took a pot-shot at me? Whoever it was couldn't aim properly, so that rules you out.'

'One of these days someone'll get you. You've got enemies, Delrose. Someone doesn't like what we did to Josh Tyler, for starters.'

'He had to go. He grassed.'

'A lot of people "have to go", according to you.'

'You don't make money – the sort of money you and I are interested in making – without a few casualties along the way.'

'True enough. But the trouble with you, Delrose, is you

don't know when to stop . . . Right, let's get on with the job. Where is it?'

'Upstairs. Follow me.'

'We haven't decided where to put her yet. Where'll be safest? I suppose there's always the well—'

'Good idea! We'll have to carry her – we don't want to leave drag marks.'

'You'll not be able to carry a child, let alone a fat old woman like Una. Leave her to me.'

They went upstairs, dragged Una from the bed, and bumped her downstairs. Stirling picked her up and threw her over his shoulder as if she were a sack of potatoes. He followed Delrose out into the moonlit garden.

They walked to the yard behind the stables, where piles of logs were heaped up and an old farm cart, covered in tangled ivy, stood in the corner. Delrose went over to the far side of the yard where there was a well with brick sides; he lifted up the wooden cover and helped Stirling heave Una over the rim of the well. Then they tipped her in and replaced the lid.

As they hurried back to the Lodge, Stirling looked back at their tracks across the frosty lawn.

'Frost'll be gone by tomorrow, hopefully, and the tracks'll disappear. But if not . . .'

'Doesn't matter if they don't,' said Delrose. 'We're not banned from going into the yard. All you have to worry about is that child, Stirling. Until Thursday, after we've collected the money.'

'If there is any money.'

'There will be. Edith'll pay anything if she thinks she can get that child back.'

Stirling walked swiftly over to where he'd parked his car and drove off into the night; Delrose, exhausted, went back to bed. There was no sound now from the cedar tree.

It was late when Douglas left Newcastle. He was tired; and he'd eaten nothing since lunchtime, when he'd had a pie and a pint with Jimmy Butler in a Tyneside pub. Not that he was hungry – he was far too preoccupied with thinking over the day's events. Both Jimmy Butler and Harry Monroe in

Durham had been exceedingly obliging, both promising to get back to him as soon as they had something definite to report.

The first thing he had to do, he thought, as he turned onto the A1 and headed north to Berwick, was to see Blackburn. If it turned out that Douglas's suspicions were correct, he'd need a special warrant. It wasn't going to be easy to get Blackburn to agree to this; his Superintendent was a cautious man and hated sticking his neck out. If Douglas had got this one wrong, then they would both be for the chop.

It seemed a long time since he'd seen Venerables; much as he hated to admit it, he actually missed him. It was at times like this when he most valued the younger man's presence: chewing over the day's events while driving through the dark, stopping at some late-night cafe to sort things out over a sandwich and coffee. But in this case he had to go it alone. Serious information, he thought, meant serious responsibility; and the price one had to pay was loneliness.

The A1 stretched ahead, straight as an arrow towards Berwick. As was his habit, he gave silent thanks to the Roman legionaries who had originally built it with scant respect for the rights of the conquered Celts. As he passed the turn-off for Hernmouth he thought of his colleagues, packed like sardines into Holmes's police house. Poor Holmes: he'd never recover from this invasion. That house was his sacred little domain. For a moment he felt a pang of nostalgia for the warmth and comradeship of an evening spent between those four walls. He craved someone to welcome him, however grudgingly – someone to pour him a drink, rustle up a makeshift meal. He was tempted to turn back and join them; but then he thought of Blackburn, of what he was going to tell him, and drove straight on to Berwick, to a cold house and a bare larder and a solitary bed. There was no alternative. Time was running out. *Dear God*, he thought fervently, *don't let anything happen to that wee child! Tell her we're coming. And, please, don't let anyone or anything foul this one up*.

Chapter Twenty

The bar at The Boomers was packed out on Monday lunch-time; Lizzie and John had difficulty in finding a table. Eventually two people who'd finished drinking obligingly got up when they saw them struggling through the crowd with their trays of sandwiches and beer.

'I've never seen the place so busy,' said John, squeezing behind the table to slide onto the bench against the wall. 'Must be the rat pack. The Case of the Kidnapped Heiress. They'll be pitching their tents here until Thursday; they'll want to be in at the kill.'

Lizzie shivered. 'Don't say that, John! And don't let Billy behind the bar hear you. It must be awful for him, listening to all these ghouls positively relishing any bit of bad news. There's a lot of police here too. Where've they all come from?'

'God knows. I've never seen most of them. They'll be falling over each other before long. Anyway, the child's not our responsibility, thank the Lord. We're Drugs Squad – and we've got more than enough on our plate.'

'Don't you think there's a connection?'

'I think so, yes. But we've no evidence. Evidence is what we're all desperately short of at the moment. Let's take a look at our side of things: we've got two gangs, as far as we know, operating along this coast. The fiasco on St Hilda's Island showed us that quite clearly. Someone knew McLoughlin and his mate from Craster, name of Cyril Kerr, were running drugs to the island. So we've got a spy somewhere, who told the other gang where and when there was to be a drop. It's even possible that he works for both gangs. He'd pick up a lot of money that way, though he'd certainly be living dangerously.

'Now, once gang number two knew about the drop, it was an easy matter to get to the island first and arrange an ambush. That sort of thing went on all the time in the eighteenth century. Usually in those days, it was gangs of locals who lured unsuspecting ships onto the rocks and murdered the crews. Things aren't much more sophisticated today.'

'How far have we got with the investigation?'

'The interviews haven't revealed a lot so far. These people are expert at covering their tracks. We've checked on all the obvious people. Dean Tyler, for instance; he's always got an alibi. Butter wouldn't melt in his mouth. It's the old story: no one witnessed anything untoward that night. Mind you, the fog was so thick you couldn't see your hand in front of your face. The coastguards were sleeping peacefully in their beds – they thought the fog would mean a night off. They were taken completely by surprise. The lighthouse keeper, poor sod, didn't live long enough to alert anybody. But it's pretty obvious what happened. We've got a bale of the goods in question. Soon, we'll get the culprits. But the only way to do it is to catch them red-handed.

'The trouble is, my informants seem to have short lives; even when they were around, they weren't much use. Take McLoughlin: not only did he take police money, he also made a tidy sum for himself working for the gang he was informing on. What we need is a proper tip-off. Like the one you had when you found those videos on *Cormorant*. It won't be long now before someone gets scared and grasses.'

'John,' said Lizzie firmly, putting down her half-eaten sandwich, 'I've *got* to get back to work. I mean my real work, not this stupid desk job. Anyone can answer telephones! It wasn't what I was trained for. Remember, I'm a mole.'

John laughed. 'A mole with a broken paw, my love.'

'I might have a broken paw, but the rest of me passes muster. You should know that.'

'If it comes to a fight, one arm isn't going to get you out of trouble. I don't want you hurt, Lizzie. I care about you.'

'It won't come to a fight. And even if it does, I'm not a novice. I'm a highly trained mole, and moles have their methods. John, I'm going back to work. Those people who tried to tip me over the cliff have got more important things on their minds now. No, listen, John! Don't look so angry. I've got a plan. I meant to tell you on Saturday night, but – well – we both got distracted.

John listened, with mounting indignation. When she'd finished, he banged down his glass and glared at her.

'Lizzie, it's not on! Not that brute. He'll *kill* you!

'No he won't. Not Big Jim. I can handle him. I'll have to see Annie – she can fix up a meeting. Big Jim's a disgusting blabber-mouth who fancies me like crazy. And he can't hold his drink; not like me. I'll come to no harm, but I shall need you around to get me away when I've finished. It's the only way! You just said that we've got to catch these people red-handed. It's no use getting there too late, like on St Hilda's.'

'Lizzie, you know as well as I do that everyone will forbid it.'

'No one will know, my darling. Only you.'

Detective Sergeant Venerables pushed aside what was left of his sausages, egg and chips, and took a gulp of his beer. Never had he felt more redundant. Lizzie and John had not once looked across to where he was sitting; when they left they had been so wrapped up in each other that they totally ignored him. The room was packed with strangers who all seemed to be having the time of their lives; but he knew no one, and no one wanted to know him. Even the barman – for barmen were usually good for a gossip – was locked in his own thoughts. Poor devil, Venerables thought. Billy Ransome must be going through hell. Charlie Wheeler, usually fairly convivial, was too rushed off his feet to spare him a moment. And Douglas: where the hell was Douglas? He'd gone shooting off to Newcastle yesterday, stopping off, *en route*, at Durham: that much he knew. And since then there'd been no sign of him. He felt a surge of resentment. They were supposed to be a team: McBride and Venerables. Everyone knew that. But Douglas wasn't playing fair. He wanted all the glory this time round – didn't want anyone muscling in on his act.

Sod the lot of them, he thought. He got up, nodded to Ransome, and left the pub. He had a job to do, even if others didn't.

Feeling more purposeful, he got into his own car and

switched on the ignition. But then what? His emotions were still in turmoil as a result of seeing John and Lizzie together; he certainly wouldn't function properly when it came to police work. *Come on, laddie*, he said to himself; *pretend old Douglas is sitting beside you. What line would* he *take? What would* he *do?*

And then it came to him: Delrose. Delrose, out of hospital by all accounts; Delrose, wanting to know who'd attacked him. Delrose, who might be keen to talk, reveal what he knew, if he thought his life was in danger. They'd interviewed him in hospital, of course; but he might have something more to say now he'd had time to recover, consider the impact of what had happened to him.

So Venerables drove off to Wynwick. He turned into the Hall, stopped at the Lodge, got out, and knocked at the front door. No one answered. Una, he supposed, was up at the Hall carrying out her housekeeping duties; Delrose could be anywhere. Presumably, if he'd been released from hospital, his injuries didn't confine him to bed. He tried the door; it was locked. He paused. Obviously no one at home: end of episode. But . . .

He knew he was taking a risk. He had no reason for wanting to go into Delrose's house. He had no search warrant, for God's sake, and no reason to ask for one. But his policeman's instincts were telling him something: the old familiar feeling that things were not quite as they should be.

He sauntered round to the back of the house, which was well protected by a bank of laurel bushes. There he found a window had been left open just a fraction. Probably the downstair's lavatory window; people often forgot to shut their bathroom and lavatory windows. An open invitation to every cat-burglar in the district, Venerables thought, as he reached up, slid his hand in, and released the catch.

Venerables wasn't a bulky man. It was not difficult for him to ease himself in through the gap. As expected, he found himself in the lavatory. He dropped down onto the floor, opened the door, walked along a passage and into the kitchen. The room was warm; the oil-fired Aga glowed cheerfully and there was a smell of recent cooking. There was no sign of Delrose; no sign of Una.

He went out into the hall and paused, feeling uneasy. He'd

broken into someone's house! What if Delrose or Una should come in and find him? But, he decided, you couldn't always follow the rules. Not if you wanted to get your man – or woman. He went into the sitting room. All was in order, but the room was cold and uninviting; clearly the kitchen – Una's domain – was the heart of the house. He went cautiously upstairs. The first bedroom he went into was Una's, he presumed – recently inhabited by a woman, anyway, as a skirt was draped over the back of a chair. The fact that Una had her own room surprised him; he had thought she and Delrose the perfect married couple. He strolled over to the window and looked out across the grounds. The forecast had been wrong, he thought; the lawn was still covered with a thick white frosting of ice. It was going to be a cold, late spring. But clumps of snowdrops were appearing underneath the cedar tree, so better times were on their way.

He turned, noticed the unmade bed. Strange, he thought: Una always seemed such a neat, tidy person. He went across to it, stared down at the rumpled sheet and the jumbled heap of the duvet. *Looks more like someone's had a fight in that bed than slept in it*, he thought absently.

He looked into the next room, which seemed to be where Delrose slept. It was tidy and the bed was made. He went on up to the top floor. There the rooms were bare of furniture, except for an old chest of drawers in one room. He noted the mouse droppings in the other. Obviously no one came up to that part of the house very often.

Feeling that he'd seen enough, he went downstairs, and levered himself out of the window, leaving it as he'd found it: slightly open at the top. He walked back to the front of the house. The gravel on the drive was hard under foot, as if the pieces of stone had been frozen together. He shivered, his instincts had been wrong. Nothing to show for his visit.

Then he noticed the footmarks. He couldn't really miss them, not on that otherwise virginal expanse of lawn. They seemed to lead up by the side of the Hall, to the garages. Two sets of footmarks, he noted. Large footmarks: almost certainly men's. Few women had feet that size. Nothing out of the ordinary – people were allowed to walk across a lawn – but he thought he ought to take a closer look.

He walked quickly up to the Hall and followed the marks round to the back of the garage area where they ended in a yard which contained nothing but a pile of logs and an old cart. Then the penny dropped. Of course! Delrose and Una had needed more logs, and Delrose had got someone to help him carry them – he'd have been in no fit state to do such physical work. He turned away and walked back to his car. No, his visit had been fruitless after all; and he'd be in serious trouble if anyone had seen him.

It wasn't much fun playing pig-in-the-middle, Charlie Wheeler thought morosely, as he finished off the bottle of Bell's he'd opened only the day before. People in his position always got kicked around. A whipping boy, that's what he'd become, he thought indignantly. But not for much longer. Worms turn, he concluded savagely as he took another gulp of whisky, not caring that he was mixing his metaphors.

It was after midnight. Tuesday morning, in fact, which made him even more morose. Time was passing and he wasn't a bit tired. Despite all the whisky he'd drunk, his brain was still seething with resentment. And he knew that until he'd solved his problem, sleep would never come.

He flung himself down on the bed in his room above the bar, not bothering to undress or remove his boots. He hadn't even been able to summon up the energy to draw the curtains and the moon streamed into his room, adding to his discomfiture; he never slept well when the moon was full. Lying there, his body bloated with too much alcohol, he abandoned himself to maudlin self-pity. How he wished that Beryl hadn't mickied off to Newcastle with Rosy! She'd been a good listener when they'd first moved in together; she'd always managed to deal with crises quickly, with the minimum of fuss. Why hadn't they managed to stay together? They could surely have reached some sort of compromise. Rosy would be seven on Thursday, and Beryl didn't like the idea of her daughter being brought up in a boozer. But really, what did it matter? It was a job, wasn't it? And if she'd hated it that much above the pub they could have lived somewhere else in Hernmouth, which wasn't a bad little place. He could have driven Rosy to St Hilda's Convent every day. Anything to make Beryl happy.

Instead, they'd had that awful row, and she'd gone back to Mother, and Rosy was now at that posh school in Jesmond.

Thoughts of Rosy made him even more disconsolate. He loved the little girl, even though she wasn't his daughter. She was plump and blonde, just like Beryl. And she loved him. She was always waiting for him eagerly when he went to see her every other weekend. Her rich friends clearly hadn't spoilt her. Thursday was her birthday; he must remember to phone her. And then the nagging misery returned; his head began to throb painfully. On Thursday that other little girl, almost the same age as Rosy, was going to be maimed – or worse, if Edith Laker didn't produce the money for her ransom. And even if she did, he thought, the chances of Clare being released were very slim. Kidnappers didn't play fair, did they?

Then there was Billy, the good-hearted New Zealander, Clare's father. He'd never set the world on fire, but he was a good worker, and customers liked him. Charlie felt nothing but pity for the poor bastard. Imagine, if someone took Rosy and. . . Charlie didn't give a damn about Edith Laker; she could look after herself. Everyone knew now how badly she'd treated that daughter of hers. If you asked Charlie, she deserved all she got. But Billy wasn't like Edith. He hadn't a shred of her ruthlessness, and he kept his worries to himself. He was becoming more and more uncommunicative, more and more withdrawn. Soon it would be the tranquillisers, then the hospital ward. And if Clare didn't make it – who knew what Billy would do? It wasn't right, thought Charlie. Why was it always the good who suffered in this life? He sat up and groped for his glass, found it empty, and went downstairs to take another bottle from the bar.

Still sleep wouldn't come. Swirling images of Rosy's face mingled with Clare's features, until the two became one. With a cry of anguish, he sprang out of bed, and went across to the window. What could he do? He knew only too well what happened to people like him who grassed to the police. If he wasn't careful he'd end up pegged out on a mud bank, like Josh Tyler. And if he did go to the police, more than likely he'd end up in custody, along with Spicer and Watson. No, he couldn't go to the police. But neither could he sit back and let a child be hurt.

It was all Delrose's fault, he thought. He'd got him involved in the first place. People never noticed a barman, never thought he had eyes and ears and a brain. It only took one phone call to Delrose to tell him that he'd got wind of a delivery, or that he'd found a potential customer, and that was it. His work was over. And as long as his involvement had been limited to drug-running, a bit of porn, he'd been happy to go along with it all. He'd thought that a bit of extra money in the bank might persuade Beryl to stay, convince her that he could give her and Rosy a decent life. Well, it hadn't done that, but Charlie had to admit the cash had come in handy – there were Rosy's school fees, for a start, and six-year-olds seemed to go through more shoes than he would have thought possible. And then there was his car. How he loved that car! A bit of real luxury, the sort of car most people only dreamed about. His Jaguar XJS. Two seater; two exhausts; soft top: a millionnaire's car. Who cared about Beryl, as long as he had that car?

He supposed he knew it was wrong – the drugs, the imported porn – but he wasn't responsible for the people who bought it. People had a right to spend their money as they wished. And if they didn't buy it from Delrose and his ilk, they'd only get it somewhere else. Supply and demand, that was what it was all about. 'We're only satisfying a need,' Delrose had said, and Charlie saw his point.

But little kids – that was different. He'd managed to turn a blind eye to the involvement of kids in the films, the magazines – Delrose had assured him they were well looked after, weren't forced to do anything against their will, that for most of them it was the only way out of poverty and deprivation. Somehow, Charlie had forced himself to believe that. But abduction, deliberate cruelty to an innocent child – he couldn't explain that one away, no matter how he tried. And another thing, he thought savagely – Delrose hadn't kept to his side of the bargain. Not one penny of the ransom money they'd received so far had come Charlie's way. He'd been used, he thought, made a fool of – and by God, he wasn't going to put up with it any more. After all he'd done for Delrose! He'd even come up with the hiding place for Clare. But now things were going to change. Delrose wasn't going to call all the shots. Clare wasn't going to suffer any longer because of Charlie's indecision. *But who to tell?*

All night he deliberated. After several more drams of whisky, the answer came with the dawn. One person would understand. One person would put the child's interests first and ask questions later. One in the eye for Delrose, all right. And as for Charlie Wheeler, his conscience would be clear, and at last he would sleep.

Chapter Twenty-One

Hilda took Charlie Wheeler's phone call at eight o'clock on Tuesday morning. She listened carefully, asked no questions. She didn't enquire who the caller was, though she had her suspicions. No police, he'd said; and she understood why. This was someone, she surmised, who had something to hide, who would retreat in panic-stricken flight if she plied him with too many questions. So she said nothing.

A tower, he'd told her, on an island. The only one that fitted, in her opinion, was the tower on St Hilda's Island. But it had been locked when they'd last been there.

Once alerted, Hilda moved quickly. First, a phone call to Clinker: she couldn't do this on her own. Then she dressed at speed, donning heavy-duty thermal underwear, thick pullover and trousers, sea boots and waterproof anorak. With a woolly hat firmly pulled down over her ears, she stomped off through the frost to drive over to Hernmouth.

Clinker was waiting for her when she got to the marina.

'Billy's on his way,' he said. He saw her quizzical glance. 'I thought we might need a bit of brute force, especially if it comes to forcing locks. And he is the girl's father. I thought you'd want him to come with us.'

'You're right, Frank. As always. He must come with us – although this could be a hoax. I just don't want him to get his hopes up.'

'I've explained the situation. And surely even false hope is better than none at all?'

'Bring the crowbar with you. Remember, we might have to break down the door.'

'Aye, I've thought of that. Police will have searched the tower, no doubt – they might have replaced the lock. I know they didn't find any drugs there. Those bales never got as far as the tower that night. But we might be lucky – the police might have left the door unfastened. No point in locking the stable door after the horse has bolted.'

The boat rocked as someone came on board: Billy, his lean face taut with anxiety.

'Who was the caller, Hilda?'

'I'm not sure. All I can tell you is that it was a man. It could be some practical joker.'

'But you've got your suspicions?'

'Naturally . . . But remember, Billy, this could be some wicked prank. Some practical joker who gets a kick out of raising people's expectations. We'll ask questions later. He'll not run away, if it is who I think it is.'

Clinker started the engine, Billy slipped the mooring lines, Hilda took the helm. They made a good team, she thought. She eased *Sirius* out into the main channel and steered towards the harbour entrance. As they left the land, they chugged out into a sea that shone and danced in the spring light. This was always, for Hilda, a moment of pure magic: a moment to pause, even at a time like this, and thank God for being alive.

They reached the island, cut the engine, and allowed the tide to bring them ashore. When the boat touched bottom, they tied her fast to a mooring buoy, and scrambled out onto the beach. Clinker swung the crowbar over his shoulder; Billy patted his pocket meaningfully.

'No guns!' said Hilda.

'We might need it. I believe in being prepared. Don't worry,' he went on, 'I didn't steal it. I borrowed it. Charlie's got several, and he'll not miss it. It's not his day for the Gun Club.'

'But you're taking a big risk with a gun. People could get hurt.'

'If its the bastard who's got Clare, I hope he does.'

'It might be Clare who gets hurt. Leave the gun behind, Billy.'

'I'll not leave it. But I promise I won't use it unless I have to. Come on, let's go.'

Disapproving, but with no time to stand and argue, she followed the two men to the tower. All around them the sea birds were squabbling over nesting places, fighting one another for the new season's mates. Usually, it was a sight which would have delighted Hilda, but that day she didn't even notice them as she fretted over the things she should have done. Why hadn't she thought to phone Douglas, to tell him where they were going? What if they'd bitten off more than they could chew?

Sure enough, the police had broken the lock on the door and hadn't bothered to replace it with a new one. Hilda felt her heart sink; there couldn't be anything inside after all, not if the police had already looked. The phone call really was a hoax. Billy wrenched open the door impatiently, and they went inside, peering round in the gloom. The room was lit by two small lancet windows which had been designed not to let in light, but to let out defenders' arrows. The room was bare except for the accumulated droppings of small animals and birds which covered the stone floor like a carpet. The acrid smell was so intense that Hilda's stomach heaved. The disappointment was overwhelming. Clearly, no one had been here for years.

On the side of the room immediately opposite the entrance, another door concealed a rough-stone newel staircase leading up to the floor above. Billy led the way, taking the stairs two at a time; Clinker followed more slowly. Hilda, her feet clumsy in their heavy sea boots made her way cautiously after them. On the first floor there was nothing to see except more droppings on the rotting floorboards. Clinker had brought a torch which he flashed around the old stone walls.

'Nothing here. Let's go up further,' he said.

It was the same on the floor above; dangerously rotted floorboards and a squeaking and squealing from colonies of hidden creatures who resented being disturbed.

'No one's been here,' said Clinker, turning round and going downstairs again. Billy looked round despairingly.

'A bloody wild goose chase, after all. Sod the lot of them!'

Hilda had to agree with him. So they had been victims of a sick practical joker. They should have known. If Clare had been here, the police would have found her when they searched the tower. How had she got it so wrong? she thought, as the men went down the stairs to the ground floor, having decided to take a quick look outside the tower. She had been so sure that the caller was genuine! If she had guessed right – and the man was whom she thought he was – then he could have been told inadvertently where Clare was hidden. Maybe the caller *was* genuine and she'd picked the wrong tower. She wasn't a native of these shores – for all she knew there could be dozens of islands nearby with towers on them. She thought of the Farnes: plenty of disused chapels on those islands. It all depended on your definition of a tower. How high did a building have to be to call itself a tower? Could a lighthouse be classified as a tower, for instance? If only she'd asked a few more questions – but she'd been afraid of scaring the caller away before he'd imparted his information. Now she had to apologise to poor, pathetic Billy for raising his hopes.

She traipsed back down to the ground floor. It was very cold inside the tower; the faint rays of the early spring sun had not penetrated the thick stone walls. Hilda began to feel the cold creeping under her anorak, sneaking down her legs to her feet, which were slowly turning into blocks of ice. She began to stamp her boots, trying to keep the circulation going. The cold always found out one's weak spots, she thought.

The floor was solid and unyielding underneath its thick carpet of guano and nesting materials. The floor was made of great slabs of stone interspersed with bricks, which in some places had sunk lower than the stones, making the floor uneven. As she stamped around, in the corner of the room furthest from the door, kicking aside the guano, she noticed that in one place the floor felt strangely uneven, somehow less substantial. She stopped, looked down, and stamped again.

'Clinker! Billy!' she called out. 'Come back here, and bring that torch!'

They rushed back inside. Together they gazed down at the floor. Clinker looked mystified; he must, thought Hilda, with a grim, inward chuckle, be thinking that the old girl has finally lost her marbles.

'Look,' said Hilda, 'take a look at these bricks. They're not like the others. Get that crowbar under one of them. I think we've got a trap-door here. There's bound to be a cellar in a place like this. A dungeon, even.'

Clinker inserted the crowbar and found that the bricks lifted easily. He put them aside, and looked down on a wooden trap-door. He stared at Hilda in disbelief.

'Go on, Clinker – see if you can lift it. But take care.'

Clinker cautiously lifted up the wooden frame. Underneath was a flight of stone stairs. Billy pushed him aside impatiently and started to go down, but Hilda stopped him.

'No Billy – not you. Let me go first. It's more likely that he'll not harm a woman. I'll need your torch, Clinker.'

'He'd kill his own mother, this bastard, if he had to,' said Billy angrily. 'Get back, Hilda. This is my scene.'

But Hilda was determined; Billy, in his present state, wasn't responsible for his actions. Clinker handed her his torch, and grasped hold of Billy. She began to feel her way down the stairs, motioning to the two men to be quiet.

Quite suddenly, she was at the bottom of the stairs. The beam of the torch flashed round the stone walls of a tiny room, then focused on the figure of a person, slumped forward over a table. In the corner of the room was a bed. On it a small body lay motionless. It was bitterly cold. The smell of vomit and urine was overwhelmingly pungent. She felt her stomach heave; with effort she restrained the rising nausea.

She went swiftly across to the small body huddled in a school raincoat on the bed. She went down on her knees and whispered urgently to the child.

'Clare! Clare . . . it's all right. You're safe. Please, please, wake up!'

There was a muffled cry of horror as Billy came to join her. He knelt down beside Hilda, stroked the child's face. Slowly, like a corpse coming to life, Clare opened her eyes.

'Clare! It's me! Daddy. It's all over. You're in good hands now. My God, you're frozen!'

'Frozen and half-starved – but alive,' said Hilda gently. 'She's a tough little thing, your daughter. Come on, pet – let's get you warm.' And Hilda wrapped her anorak tightly round the child's small body.

'This one's not made it,' said Clinker heavily, lifting Sammy's head to look at her face. 'Surely the kidnapper didn't leave this kid to guard Clare! She doesn't look capable of looking after herself. I can't believe the kidnapper just left them both here to die – wait a minute.'

He picked up a small plastic bag lying next to Sammy on the table. Crumpled tin foil, the stub of candle, the empty box of matches. He peered inside the bag and sniffed. 'Some sort of residue – drugs. And judging by the shape this girl's in, it wasn't the first time she'd used them.' He gazed with pity at Sammy's wizened face, old long before her time. 'Could have been a pretty girl, too, if she'd taken care of herself. Why do these kids do it?'

'We must get help,' said Hilda decisively. 'We must get back to *Sirius*. Come on, my love,' she said to Clare, who was whimpering now, returning to life with every kiss her father planted on her tear-streaked face, 'we'll soon have you home.'

Clare made a tiny guttural sound, trying to speak. She coughed wrenchingly, and tried again. 'Aunt Edith . . .' she said faintly.

'Yes. You'll see her soon,' said Billy soothingly.

Clare began to cry, silently, as if to sob would involve too much effort. 'But Donald . . . will he come back?'

'No one will come while we're here. No one can harm you now.'

'Will you punish him? He brought us here, then forgot about us. It was so cold, and I'm so hungry. And Sammy was sick, and then she slept and slept. Is she still asleep?'

'Yes, my love. She's still asleep,' said Hilda. 'You stay with your Daddy now, while Clinker and I fetch help.'

'No!' Making a tremendous effort, Clare wriggled and twisted, trying to escape Billy's embrace. 'Don't leave me! You're Aunt Edith's friend – no one will hurt me if you're here!'

Hilda reached out and took Clare, cradling her in her arms. The child felt as frail as a tiny bird.

'You go with Clinker, Billy. I'll stay here.' She saw the pain of rejection in Billy's face. 'Don't be alarmed,' she said quietly. 'She needs time to learn to trust men again. And now we've found her, there'll be plenty of that for the pair of you.'

She turned to Clinker. 'Tell them to alert Ashington, send over a helicopter. And tell them to be quick.'

Then, rocking Clare gently in her arms, Hilda thanked God that they'd made it in time. Looking down at Clare's tiny, delicate face, she saw that the child had gone to sleep – a deep, healing sleep. Softly, almost unconsciously, she began to sing her a lullaby.

Chief Superintendent Blackburn listened to Douglas in mounting agitation.

'If you've got it wrong, McBride, then there'll be all hell to pay. Make no mistake – I'll take considerable pleasure in watching you ride off alone into the sunset. But –' and Douglas knew that he'd won this particular battle – 'I'll go along with your wild theories, just this once. It's worth a try – but by God, if you've got it wrong . . . I'll alert Willy Graham. We'll need a JP for this, these are serious accusations you're making here. Graham's discreet, thank God. He won't rock the boat. It's not as if we're dealing with any common-or-garden criminal.'

The phone rang; Blackburn took the call.

'They've found the child! And she's alive!'

Douglas was flooded with an intense joy that took his breath away. For a moment he was unable to speak.

'So – who found her?'

'Lady Nevill. Someone tipped her off, apparently. The child's on St Hilda's Island. Right,' he said to the caller, 'we'll get a chopper over straight away. Tell Ashington what's going on. Can you give us any more information?' He listened intently to the caller, then put the phone down and frowned at Douglas.

'The child's been locked in a cellar, underneath the tower on the island. What were those Drugs Squad officers playing at? They're supposed to have carried out a thorough search of that tower – of the whole bloody island – in the last week. Anyway, lucky for you it wasn't your men who buggered this one up, otherwise I'd have your guts for garters.'

Douglas looked reproachful. 'Time for recriminations later, sir. I'm just thankful that little Clare's in one piece.'

'True enough. The woman with her wasn't so lucky. She's been dead for a couple of days – looks like a combination of hypothermia and a drugs overdose. Presumably the kidnapper left her down there to look after Clare, but clearly no one had been near the place for some days. With Drugs Squad swarming all over the island, no one'll have wanted to risk being near the tower. So poor Clare's been left for days without heat, light or food. Apparently there was a bucket of water in the cellar which she's been drinking – that must have saved her life. She keeps mentioning a man called Donald. Seems terrified of him. So is this the same Donald we've been looking for? Donald Stirling – the man who collected Clare from school? Delrose's chum, who Delrose claims was kidnapped along with Clare?'

'There could be two men called Donald, but— From this moment, secrecy's needed. Keep the media away, for God's sake – we'll release the news about Clare's discovery later, when all this is over. But now we must put a watch on the tower. Stirling'll have to go back there some time before Thursday. We'll nab him then. With any luck, he'll walk straight into our trap. I'll be off now, to the island. You'll see about the search warrant?'

'I'll get on to Graham straight away. Good luck, McBride.'

'Don't you worry. I'll make those bastards squeal.'

'Take care. We're not in the Middle Ages.'

'More's the pity, in my opinion,' said Douglas.

All day Monday, Edith had suffered one of her occasional migraines. She had tried to get out of bed, get dressed, but the effort had exhausted her, and the pain in her head hammered on relentlessly. She realised that she had overestimated her strength. The shock of her near encounter with death at Dunstanburgh Castle had finally caught up with her. All she wanted to do now was lie down in a darkened room and take the medication which the doctor had prescribed for her years ago, when the migraines had first started. She didn't want to see anyone: especially Una, with her fussy concern. Neither did she want to see Delrose. Later, when the pain subsided, she'd phone Lady Nevill. But not yet.

Fortunately, it had been an easy matter to telephone the Lodge before Una was due to arrive and tell Delrose that she wanted to be left alone, that she was happy for Una to take a day off. Delrose said he'd pass the message on. He'd told her he was going to sort out some business in Newcastle – as he couldn't drive, he was going to take a bus and train. And Edith gave herself up to the throbbing hammers in her head.

On Tuesday morning Edith, after a night's drug-induced sleep, got up early. Another day: one step nearer to the time when she would have Clare back. Because Clare was going to be released, whatever that fool Douglas said. She would have the money ready, and this time there was going to be no confusion.

Edith understood money. It was what everyone wanted. It was what she had always wanted; thank God, she thought, she now had enough for anything she needed. And she needed Clare, and would pay anything to get her back.

It was a cold day, but bright. She got up, found gratefully that the hammers in her head had subsided, and got dressed. Then she went down to the kitchen to speak to Una, ask for breakfast; having eaten nothing the previous day, she was hungry, and it wouldn't help Clare if she became malnourished. But to her surprise, Una wasn't there. She glanced at her watch: half past seven. A bit early to start creating a fuss. But she did want her post. It would have arrived, she knew; unlike most villages, Wynwick was blessed with a punctual postal service. She put on thick walking shoes and a sheepskin jacket and set off down to the gate to collect the post. There were three letters in the box, a handful of bills, and the usual pile of junk mail. She stuffed them in the pocket of her jacket. She glanced at the Lodge; the curtains were still drawn. Una wasn't officially due to start work until eight, although she usually came at least half an hour early, so there was no reason why she should disturb the Roses just yet.

She walked back to the house, where she made coffee, taking it into the sitting room. She glanced at her letters: nothing important. One mystery letter, though, hand-written in big, childish letters. She opened it. Just four words, but they punched her heart as if she'd been struck. ASK DEL ABOUT CLARE. She had to read the words over and over again before they sank in. *Delrose*. She could hardly believe it. It wasn't what she'd been expecting to hear.

Controlling her rage, she phoned Delrose and asked him to come up to the Hall. She went over to her desk, checked that her Heckler and Koch revolver was there and ready for use. Then she sat down behind the desk and waited.

Soon she heard the kitchen door open, the sound of footsteps across the hall, and Delrose came in. She saw that he looked haggard, noticed that he couldn't look her in the eyes. Edith had a good understanding of human nature; after all these years she felt she knew Delrose better than he knew himself.

'Good morning, Delrose. Where's Una? She's not usually as late as this.'

'Ah. I was meaning to tell you about that. She's had to go to see her mother. The old lady was taken ill last night.'

'Her mother? I *am* surprised. Una's never mentioned her mother. She should have told me that she couldn't come today.'

'It was an emergency. And you were poorly – so she didn't want to disturb you. One of her mother's neighbours phoned to ask for Una's help. Apparently her mother'd had a bad attack of 'flu, and it had turned nasty.'

'I see. Now, what if I were to tell you that before Una went on her errand of mercy, she wrote me a letter? A letter all about you?'

It was a bit of a long shot – but Edith was almost sure that the handwriting in the note was Una's. Una always wrote messages to Edith in block capitals – her normal handwriting was an illegible scrawl. And she was the only person Edith knew who called Delrose Del . . .

From the flash of fear in Delrose's eyes, Edith knew that the accusation in the letter was well-founded.

'What letter? What are you talking about?'

Edith handed the note to Delrose, her face set like a mask.

'But – this is rubbish! I've nothing to do with what's happened to Clare! Una's been watching too much television while I've been in hospital.'

He paused, realising that his acceptance of the letter's authorship had given him away. 'Anyway, how do you know this is from Una? Come on, Edith. You know that a man like me, doing what I do, is bound to make a few enemies along the way. This is just malicious nonsense.'

'I'm no fool, Delrose. You've known me long enough to be

aware that I'm more than capable of putting two and two together. Una goes missing – I get this letter. She's closer to you than anyone. She might be stupid, but she's not that stupid. And she's devoted to Clare. I think she found something that made her suspicious of you. For some reason, she didn't come and see me: too frightened of you, perhaps. But she could drop a letter to me in the box. I would have got it yesterday, but no one came up to the Hall. So what's been going on, Delrose?'

'Edith, you know I love Clare too. You must believe me!' He was desperate now, knowing she'd got the better of him. 'Why would I do anything to harm little Clare? I've worked with you for years! I wouldn't dream of doing the dirty on you.'

'You're like me, Delrose. It takes one to know one.' She opened the desk drawer. 'When I first met you, in the South of France, I recognised a kindred spirit. You'd do anything to make money – and so would I, back then. But then Clare came along, and I loved her from the moment I set eyes on her. More than I ever loved Bridie.' She gave a humourless laugh. 'I don't know what it was about that wretched girl – maybe it was because she reminded me too much of my useless husband. When she looked at me with those spaniel eyes, like a cringing dog, she disgusted me. Bridie was one of life's losers – and I don't like losers. But Clare's different. She's a fighter, a survivor. No one's going to exploit my Clare.'

Delrose licked his lips nervously. 'Edith, this is a misunderstanding. We're in all this together! I swear I wouldn't—'

'Come on, Delrose. Tell me what you've done with her. Or do I have to make you?'

She took the revolver out of the drawer and aimed it at Delrose's knees. With a shriek of terror, he hurled himself at her, grabbing for the barrel of the gun. Then she fired. Without making a sound, Delrose fell straight forward onto the desk in front of her. Edith had no doubt that he was dead.

She felt no remorse. Only regret that she had killed him before she had ascertained Clare's whereabouts. But now she knew who was behind the kidnapping, she knew where to ask questions. She replaced the revolver in the drawer, came out from behind the desk and heaved Delrose's body on to the floor, noting with almost scientific interest the neat round hole in the middle of his forehead. She couldn't have shot more accurately if she'd planned it that way. Delrose wasn't a hefty man, but it took all Edith's strength to haul him, inch by inch, feet first into the kitchen. From there, she tipped him down into the wine cellar. She closed the cellar door and locked it behind her.

Then the phone rang. She was proud of the fact that her voice was perfectly controlled when she answered it. It was Douglas. Unbelievably, miraculously, they'd found Clare. They were flying her to hospital in Ashington. If she got a move on, she could be there to greet Clare when she arrived.

At one o'clock on Tuesday, Donald Stirling, believing that the coast must finally be clear, came to check on Clare and Sammy. In the cellar of the pelc tower on St Hilda's Island, four armed police officers waited for him. Clare had been whisked off to hospital; Sammy had been taken to the mortuary in Berwick. Stirling went down the stairs carrying, as usual, a carrier bag full of supplies, including a morc than generous quantity of heroin for Sammy. He walked down into a battery of floodlights and police-issue revolvers. He didn't put up a fight. Soon he was off back across the water in a police launch, to Berwick police station.

All day Edith stayed by Clare's bed in Ashington Hospital. At six o'clock, Clare opened her eyes.

'Aunt Edith?'

'Yes, it's me, my darling. I've come to take you home.'

The nurse said no one was to take Clare home, not until tomorrow morning, when a doctor would confirm that she was fit enough to leave. Also, there was someone else in the waiting room who wanted to take Clare home – a long-haired young man with blue marks on his face.

'Don't let him near her!' said Edith emphatically. 'He's probably responsible for the child's present condition. He's bad – really bad. The police will want to interview him soon. Tell him to go away!'

The nurse looked alarmed and hurried off. All that night, Edith stayed by Clare whilst she slept peacefully, clutching Big

Ted, which Edith had remembered to bring with her. Looking down at the sleeping child, Edith vowed that no one would ever hurt her again.

Chapter Twenty-Two

It hadn't taken much to persuade Annie to lend Lizzie her flat: only the gift of a pullover with a plunging neckline, which Lizzie had bought on misguided impulse in a sale. Annie's services came cheaply. Annie had also been delighted to procure the doubtful company of Jim Tate for her friend. Apparently, Big Jim had not forgotten Lizzie since that evening of the party; he'd been boasting to everyone that he intended to give her one she'd not forget in a hurry.

Annie told Lizzie not to worry. Of all her friends, Big Jim was the most harmless, although he looked the most threatening. He was, she told Lizzie, all hot air and no action, but fun to play with. He wasn't Lizzie's idea of fun.

Lizzie went to Annie's flat on Tuesday evening, ready for anything. She'd bought a bottle of whisky. Then, on second thoughts, another bottle. She went over to the window and opened the curtains. John was outside, waiting in his car. The curtains were to be the signal for help if she needed it. One twitch, and John would be up.

She lit the gas fire, checked her appearance in the foggy glass over the sink in Annie's cluttered kitchen. She looked pale, she thought; the gash of scarlet lipstick across her mouth made her look like a tart. Her eyes were ringed with dark mascara, and she'd puffed out her hair to frame her face. Yes, she'd do. But she hated herself. The T-shirt was too tight and too low, but at least it wasn't buttoned down the front – she prayed Big Jim would have a job getting it off, especially with her left arm in plaster.

She heard someone push open the street door – Annie never

locked it. Then came heavy footsteps up the stairs. Lizzie opened the whisky and got out two glasses.

A knock on the door. She opened it, trying to plaster a welcoming smile on her face, and Big Jim stood there, huge in his black leather jacket, tight jeans and biker's boots. His coarse, brutal face was creased into something resembling a smile.

'Well, love, so you've changed your mind! Fancy me after all, do you?'

'I decided I wanted to see you again, yes. Come in. I thought we could have a drink or two. As you see, I'm wounded, so I'm not up to much.'

Jim scowled as he took off his leather jacket to reveal a dingy white T-shirt and two sinuous naked ladies, one tattooed on each arm. 'I'm sorry about that. Angus was a bit hasty. Anyway, he's paid for it now. That arm'll get better, won't it?'

'No problem, but I'm still a bit delicate. You must be careful with me.' Her heart gave a great leap of joy. He'd only been there a few minutes and another bit of the jigsaw had already slipped into place. Angus McLoughlin, Dean Tyler, Jim Tate; all mates and not a brain between them.

She tried not to show her excitement. 'Fancy a Scotch?'

'Aye, love – and make it a big one. I've had a couple at Annie's already, but another won't do me any harm.'

Lizzie, saying a silent prayer of thanks to Annie, poured him a drink and watched him take a big gulp. Immediately, she topped up the glass. 'So Angus was a mate of yours?'

'He was. Not any more, though!' He laughed heartily at his own joke; Lizzie, remembering the photographs she'd seen of his corpse on the beach, shuddered.

'Who got his Bedford van? The one that pushed me off the road?'

'Why me, of course. Not that I can use it round here, not yet, anyway. One of my mates took it down south to London for a respray. I'll have it back for summer. You and I can go out in it, can't we, love? To Whitley Bay, or even further south. Lots of room in the back.' And again he laughed, and stretched out his glass for a refill.

'Come on, lass – fill up the glass and let's get down to business. Forget about Angus. Put it down to experience. You're not badly hurt and you don't need two hands for what we're going to do.'

She tried to look enthusiastic, and led him over to the fire, where he slumped on Annie's worn-out sofa.

'Here lass,' he said, as he flexed his biceps, 'come and take a look at these!'

Whisky bottle in hand, she sat down next to him and peered at the tattooed ladies.

'You like them? Now watch.' And he flexed each bicep in turn, making the ladies writhe suggestively. She sniggered dutifully, and refilled his glass. He clearly hadn't noticed she wasn't drinking.

He was easy to arouse, and easy to control. The trick was to squeeze up to him on the sofa, stroke his arm, then back away and fill up his glass. The more he drank, the more talkative he became.

'God, Lizzie, you're a right tease. Who'd have thought you were a copper? Here, take that bloody top off. Let's have a look at your boobs.'

'Not yet, Jim. Don't go so fast.'

Two more refills would do it, she thought, glancing at the two-thirds empty bottle. But he'd made up his mind to kick off the action; he leant across and pawed her breasts clumsily. She fought back her rage, tried not to push his hands away. What a foul brute, she thought. Whatever did Annie see in him? Never again was she going to get herself involved in this sort of situation. She wasn't cut out to play the whore.

With difficulty, she controlled her repugnance. She didn't want him to turn nasty. *Slowly, slowly*, she thought. *Fill up his glass. Watch him fall over.*

'You're wonderful, Lizzie,' he mumbled. 'Beautiful. Just what I need.'

He grabbed her top. As she backed away, he hung on to the material and tore it off her shoulders, gazing with blurred eyes at her breasts.

'That's better. Now come over here.'

'Mind my arm!'

'To hell with your arm. I can't hurt it, anyway, it's all wrapped up. Get those bloody tights off. Your legs aren't broken. Annie doesn't keep asking questions like you do. She likes to get on with it.'

'How do you know what I like? Come on, lie down on the floor and I'll show you what I like.'

He looked at her with a dazed expression on his face, but did as he was told. Lizzie put the whisky bottle down on the floor beside him; he knocked it over, watching in disbelief as the liquid soaked into the carpet. He cursed, picked up the bottle and held it to the light.

'It's nearly gone!'

'Don't worry. There's another bottle.'

'You know how to look after a bloke, don't you? And he lifted the bottle to his mouth and drank down the dregs.

'That's a good boy,' said Lizzie soothingly, as if she were talking to an unpredictable dog. 'Lie down now.'

Muttering, he lay back on the floor. Lizzie sat on him astride. He grinned at her, his eyes watering, the whisky fumes of his breath almost making her choke.

'That's nice,' he mumbled. 'What you going to do now?'

'That's up to you.'

'Whad'ye mean?'

'Tell me something, and then I'll show you.'

His eyes glistened. 'Go on. I'm all yours.'

She pulled down the zip on his trousers, revealing black underpants. He squirmed.

'I like that,' he slurred. 'Go on, go on.'

'Tell me when you're getting another delivery. You know – Dennis thc Menace, a few rocks, maybe a bit of Charlie. Come on, Jim, you know everything. *You* should be the boss, not that fool Dean Tyler. He's a loser.'

'You must be kidding! Delrose'd do you if he heard you calling Dean the boss. Come, on girl, get me pants off, and give us another drink. It's thirsty work talking to you.'

She reached out for the second bottle and filled his glass.

'Lift your head up, Jim, and I'll feed you.'

Leaning forward, her bare breasts not far from his face, she gave him the full glass. He gulped it down as if it were Coca-Cola, and leaned back with a sigh of contentment. He mustn't pass out, she thought. Not yet, not while he could still speak.

He reached up to grab her breasts, but she pushed him back

playfully. God, how stupid he was, she thought. He had no idea what he was saying . . .

'So who took a pot-shot at Delrose? Who'd want to kill Delrose, Jim?'

Jim's eyes were shutting. Lizzie leant forward and let him fondle her breasts.

'God, you're a raver,' he said. 'Don't stop. Finish me off. I'm all yours.'

'Tell me about Dean Tyler. Why doesn't he like Delrose?'

'What do you keep on about Tyler, Lizzie? *He's* not the boss. It's Delrose! We all hate him. Dean hates him because he ordered the death of his brothers – Josh, because he grassed, and Marcus because he might be recognised. He cheats on us all the time. Doesn't pay the going rate. We don't know where we are with him. He rides two horses, see. Hunts with the hare and runs with the hounds, and doesn't tell us what's going on. Most of us work for the other lot now.'

'What other lot, Jim?'

But he couldn't answer. The whisky was doing its work. His eyes began to close.

'Another drink? she said, and then, coaxingly, 'Tell me more about Tyler. And tell me when you're bring in the stuff; I'd like some, you know. Police Officers don't always stay on the right side of the law, you know. We could have a great time together, couldn't we? I'm much better than Annie, you'll see.'

'You're the best, love. Go on, do what you like. There's some stuff coming in tomorrow, down at Craster. You'll like that, won't you?'

He grabbed hold of her violently and began to slobber all over her face. She fought down her rising nausea, tried to remain calm. She had to stay in control.

'That sounds good. You'll save me some of the old Dennis the Menace, won't you?'

'As much as you like, girl. Don't stop now.'

She raised her head and saw that his face had turned a deep red; his breathing was rapid. His chest heaved as he panted for air. He closed his eyes. Any moment now . . .

But Jim had drunk too much. With a deep groan he ceased humping his body up and down, and subsided on the floor.

When she looked up, he was asleep, a look of pure bliss on his face.

Lizzie jumped up, went into Annie's freezing bathroom and scrubbed her hands. She found a safety pin on the shelf above the wash basin, and pinned the torn bits of her T-shirt together. Then she put on her jacket and ran down to John, who came to her and took her in his arms.

'Lizzie, what happened? My God, you're shaking. Don't cry, love. What's that brute done to you?'

'Nothing. Nothing at all. He's fast asleep and won't wake up till the morning. Leave him be. Do you know, hairdressing suddenly seems a very attractive option? No more of this femme fatale stuff. It's not my cup of tea.'

'I don't like it either. Why don't you take me along in this hairdressing lark? You cut, I'll blow-dry. Seriously, Lizzie, I might be looking for another line of work soon. I've really been blown up over this business on St Hilda's Island. Clare was down in that cellar all the time, even when Drugs Squad were searching the tower. I've been over there again – to be honest, it's difficult to spot the trap-door even when you know it's there. But that's not really a good enough excuse, is it? I was in charge of that search, and I didn't spot it. And that child could have died down there. So I've got to prove myself double quick.'

Lizzie smiled. 'I might just be able to give you a hand there. Big Jim's got an interesting line in pillow talk. Tomorrow night, at Craster – a landing. Ecstasy and I don't know what else.'

'Lizzie, you're a genius! But you leave this one to me. OK?'

'Do you know, I might just do that. I think I've done my bit for Queen and Country for a while.'

Chapter Twenty-Three

James Turnbull phoned Hilda on Wednesday, around noon. It was good to hear his calm, reassuring voice; as ever since she'd come back from St Hilda's Island after they'd found Clare, her own thoughts had been in turmoil. She knew she was on the right track, but she needed help and confirmation of her suspicions, and James Turnbull could provide both.

'James, how lovely to hear from you,' she said, with genuine enthusiasm. 'What news?'

'I really wanted to know when you're coming to see me again?'

She smiled. As always, he was laid-back to the point of being prostrate. This had used to irritate her husband no end – but she'd always found it rather endearing. And at this stressful time, it was just what she needed.

'Soon, James. Let's get down to business first.'

'And you'll have dinner with me, won't you? You ought to use that smart little car more often.'

'I should love to have dinner with you. When the weather improves. But now is not the time of year for joy-rides.'

'Don't make excuses. The weather's improving all the time. Spring's on its way. Snowdrops all over the place. Birds dashing around carrying haystacks in their mouths—'

'You make it sound positively idyllic. But seriously, James, did you find that woman you mentioned last time we spoke?'

'Irene Laker? Indeed I did. I phoned a friend in South Pelham and she knew her phone number in Winchester. They'd always kept in touch, you see. Quite a coincidence, really.'

'The Foreign Office always was a good club.'

'A *network*, Hilda, please! You make us sound like the Mafia.'

'There are many similarities, James. Charles always said so. But give me your news quickly. Things are hotting up around here.'

'Really? Have they caught the evil parson?'

'What are you talking about?'

'*Jamaica Inn*. Surely you remember? The leader of the smugglers was, if I remember correctly, the local parson.'

'Nothing as simple as that, I'm afraid. But let's leave that to the police. I'm interested in this friend of mine.'

'So you are. But I shan't tell you all I know, unless you promise with your hand on your heart to come and have dinner with me.'

'I promise! Now, get on with it.'

'All right. Listen carefully . . .'

Hilda listened with increasing agitation. It was quite horrendous: far worse than she'd imagined. And the problem was, would anyone believe her? It would take far too long to get the written corroboration she really needed.

'James, you're an angel,' she said when he'd finished. 'Now, I need Irene Laker's phone number. I'll get on to her immediately.'

'She's expecting a call from you. Hilda, go gently, she's quite elderly, but she's still – what's the expression? – in full possession of her marbles. Good luck, and get back to me if you need more help. Got a pencil? Here goes . . .'

Hilda wrote down the number, rang off, then re-dialled. Irene Laker was indeed expecting her; she talked to Hilda for twenty minutes. When she'd finished, Hilda put the phone down, and put on a warm coat and boots. Then she walked round to her garage, got out the car and drove down to Hernmouth. At the moment, it seemed to be a journey she was destined to make on a regular basis.

'Come on, Charlie, you must know more. You tipped off Lady Nevill about Clare's whereabouts, didn't you? She says she's sure it was you. We want you to tell us about some of the others involved. We want names, Charlie.'

Charlie Wheeler, standing defensively in front of Douglas

and Venerables in the bar of The Boomers, looked like a rat cornered by a terrier.

'Is this a formal interview? If so, I demand a solicitor. I'm fed up to the back teeth with people asking questions! First John Chance, and now you. I've done nothing! I know nothing.'

'A right little wise monkey, aren't you Charlie? But calm down – we're not asking you to turn informant. Just a name or two. This isn't an interview – we're not going to run you in just yet. Call it a friendly chat. Mind you, once we start looking into your activities – where you found the money to buy that smart car of yours, to start with – who knows what might happen? Let's just say that if you give us a couple of names, we'll not ask any unnecessary questions. Come on, Charlie. What have you got to lose?'

Charlie had visibly flinched at the mention of the car. Of course his income from The Boomers didn't pay for it; that hardly covered the cost of its insurance. So the pack of cards was collapsing around him, he thought. The police were pulling out all the stops. Soon all the big fish would be hauled in . . . And the sergeant was right. What was the point of digging himself in even deeper? He dropped his belligerent act.

'I don't know much.'

'Anything'll be useful,' said Venerables. 'Come on, man, what's a name or two if it means we leave you in peace from now on?'

Charlie hesitated. He didn't want the wrath of the big fish descending on his head. But if it came to a straight choice between the crooks and the police, probably the latter were the best bet. At least they wouldn't peg him out in Hernmouth Harbour at low tide.

'We've got Stirling,' said Douglas, watching Charlie's face, seeing him wavering. 'He'll spill the beans sooner or later. Especially if he knows he'll get a reduced sentence if he turns Queen's Evidence. Start with the girl – Sammy, now in Berwick morgue. Do you know where Stirling found her? We haven't been able to identify her. Did she ever come in here?'

He saw Charlie swallow at the mention of Stirling's name. He was getting there.

'No big deal,' said Charlie sullenly. 'She came in here asking for a job as barmaid, before Billy turned up. She was a poor little thing. Samantha Burns, she's called. Didn't know where her parents were, lived in foster homes and children's homes all her life. Father was a bit rough when he'd hit the bottle, so the Social people took her away when she was just a kid. She got fed up with being shoved from pillar to post. I didn't want her behind the bar, but I felt sorry for her, told her that when I heard of something that might bring in a bit of money, I'd contact her. And that's it. Stirling came looking for someone. He didn't go into details – just said he needed some temporary child care, but of course I knew what he meant. I didn't ask questions; I just sent Stirling off to the address she'd given me.'

'And where was that?'

'Some dump in Newcastle. She was hitting the hard stuff before Stirling found her. Sad, really. She was a nice enough kid.'

'A classic victim. Everyone used her. I bet when she cashed her giro she handed it straight over to the likes of Stirling.'

'Have you finished with me yet?'

'This is just a wee chat, Charlie – remember? Not an interrogation.'

'What's the difference?'

'Remember the Jag, Charlie,' said Venerables quietly. Charlie flinched.

'Just one more tip and then we'll be away. There were two gangs out on that island when that delivery was intercepted. We know all about McLoughlin and Kerr, but corpses can't talk. The others got away. Any ideas, Charlie?'

Charlie said nothing. He couldn't answer this one. To do so would lead him straight to that mud bank in Hernmouth Harbour. Not even the thought of parting with his Jag would force it out of him, not while the person concerned was still alive. Douglas realised he'd come up against a brick wall.

'Chance has already asked me that one,' muttered Charlie.

'Has he now, Charlie? And you didn't tell him?'

'I've nothing to tell! How the hell would I know? I'm not Father Confessor to all the criminals in Northumbria.'

'But you do have your eyes and ears open. You pick up

things. Come on, Charlie – just one more name. Who waylaid McLoughlin and Kerr?'

But it was no use; Charlie had clammed up. The risks were too high. Douglas looked at Venerables, who shook his head.

'All right, Charlie. You stick to your story for the time being. But we'll be back. Things are moving fast now. Who knows, you might change your mind after you've had time to think about it. In the meantime, it's back to work for us, laddie.

In the Operations Room which had been set up in Hernmouth's police station, Douglas had insisted on his own desk and a set of phones for his own personal use. Messages from Jimmy Butler, the Head of the Serious Fraud Office in Newcastle, were coming in thick and fast. Soon, he'd have enough information to pounce. At any moment, the special search warrant would arrive from Berwick; Blackburn had assured him that it was on its way. *Dear God*, he prayed, *don't let me have got this wrong . . .*

Venerables, who'd been unusually silent all morning, came over to Douglas's corner, and interrupted his train of thought, a look of urgency on his face.

'Sir?'

'Not now, Venerables. There's too much going on here for me to listen to your problems. Later, laddie. I'm sorry I've been ignoring you – but this is a bit of a sticky situation.'

'I know all that, sir. But I've just remembered something, and I think you ought to know. It could be very important.'

'Well, out with it. Better now than later – there'll be plenty for us to do soon. You won't have time to draw breath. That'll stop you brooding over the Teal lassie.'

Venerables ignored the last remark; he couldn't be bothered right now to bring Douglas up to date. Later, when all the fuss was over, he'd tell him how WPC Polly Stride, whom he'd met up at the Hall the day Delrose was attacked, was now the woman of his dreams.

'You know how it is. You see something during an investigation and you don't realise what it means until later, when it comes out of the blue and hits you between the eyes.'

'It's called a detective's intuition, Sergeant. I'm glad yours is still functioning.'

'It's the Aga, sir. It was oil-fired.'

'Have you gone out of your mind? What Aga, for God's sake? We're all on coal in this place – and bloody inefficient it is, too.'

'The Aga in Delrose's kitchen. Why should he walk off across a lawn with a friend to collect logs which he doesn't need? It doesn't fit, does it?'

'I've no idea what you're on about. But do what you want to do – even if it means conducting a survey of all the oil-fired central heating systems in Northumbria. Now leave me to get on with running the investigation.'

Venerables cursed his superior silently and sloped off. Maybe he was being irrational; maybe his detective's intuition had gone haywire. He tried to get on with some routine work, but he couldn't concentrate. He glanced at Douglas, talking intently to someone on the phone. It was time, he decided, to go it alone. He wasn't needed round here, at any rate. He got up, switched off the computer, and put on his coat. He left the police house, unnoticed, and drove up to the Hall in his own car. Over the years, he'd learned to trust his instincts; it was what made him a good policeman. If Douglas wouldn't confide in him, then Douglas could go to hell. One consolation, he thought: even if his hunch proved wrong, at least Douglas needn't know anything about it.

Later on that afternoon, Hilda drove to The Boomers and was able to confirm that Charlie Wheeler had indeed made that call to her about Clare. Then she went to find Billy. She found him in his room above the pub, in a terrible state. The staff nurse from Ashington Hospital had just informed him that Edith had removed Clare to a private clinic; and the hospital had no intention of revealing its whereabouts. But when Hilda told him her news, he grew extremely excited and demanded instant action. She concurred; but first, she said, she had to see Douglas.

One look at Hilda's face and Douglas reached for his overcoat.

'It's serious, isn't it?'

'*Very*. Please listen, and don't say anything just yet.'

Douglas listened. When she'd finished, he looked round for

Venerables. *Damn the man*, he thought. *Where the hell has he mickied off to?*

'The search warrant's just come through, Lady Nevill, so I'll get started. Thanks for coming. The information which you've gleaned as a result of your enquiries, and the news which has been coming in all day to me, clinch it as far as I'm concerned. Now, please stay here. This is police work – things might get pretty hairy. Later, when the medals are handed out, we'll not forget you.'

'I've a right to be there, Douglas. And so has Billy.'

'Stay out of it, both of you. That's a police order, Lady Nevill.'

Shouting for armed police back-up from the Special Operations Unit, Douglas dashed out of the police house and drove off north towards the A1. Billy looked furious.

'They're going to botch this up, Hilda! That Douglas is a bloody fool.'

'Not a fool, Billy. Just cautious. Anyway, there's nothing to stop us from going up to the Hall.'

'There's no one there, Hilda.'

'How do you know?'

'I phoned there while you were talking to Wheeler – and again, just before we left. Remember I told you I wanted to use the lav? Well, I did, but I also used Wheeler's phone and called the Hall. No one answered. And no one answered from the Lodge, either. That's strange, isn't it? So where's she gone, Hilda? And, more to the point, where's she taken Clare? My daughter's not in a private clinic – she'd know it'd only be a matter of time before I tracked her down. I am her father, after all. No, she's gone a hell of a long way, in that Mercedes of hers, and we're going after her. In Charlie's car. I know the bitch, see, I know what she's thinking. Are you ready for a ten-hour drive? Charlie's car is made for the job.'

'He'll never lend it to you, Billy.'

'I'll not ask him. I know where he keeps the keys. Let's away, and answer questions later.'

'That's stealing.'

'To hell with your upper-class scruples, Hilda! I want my daughter back! You can stay here, if you like. Keep Charlie company.'

Hilda didn't take long to make up her mind. She wanted to be there when they made the arrest.

'I'm coming with you. You can't do this on your own.'

Douglas got to St Oswald's Hall just as Venerables was emerging from the garage area at the side of the house. Venerables broke into a run when he saw the police car, gesticulating frantically. Douglas looked at him with curiosity.

'What are you doing here, Sergeant? I needed you back there. We're supposed to be a team, remember?'

'I've not forgotten, sir. Even if it has slipped other people's memories . . . However, that's as maybe. Could you get some of your men over here quickly, sir? I think I've found something.'

'Really? What have you found? That the Lodge has log fires after all?'

'I think I've found Una Rose, sir. Someone's stuffed her down the bloody well.'

From then on, St Oswald's Hall was turned inside out and upside down. Una's body was pulled up from the well; in the cellar, they found Delrose, white and stiff. In the tower they found a ton of skunk still in its original packaging. Douglas, standing uneasily in the sitting room, still troubled by the imaginary presence of Edith Laker, received the reports with mounting agitation. Finally, he turned to Venerables.

'My apologies, Sergeant. I should have listened to you earlier.'

'Apologies accepted, sir.'

'But no time for post mortems. I see the birds have flown. Where to, laddie? *Where to?*'

'Better call up a Merc, sir. If we're going to catch up with her.'

'And the child, Venerables? My God, surely she's not taken the child with her. Yet I'd not put it past her. I know where she's gone. She'll want to get out of this country at one hell of a speed, and she's got a yacht in Falmouth. I'll get onto the Cornish police. And by God, they'd better tread carefully. That woman's dangerous.'

*

That night, John Chance and Lizzie Teal, and a contingent of Northumbrian coastguards with police back-up, watched three trawlers approach the narrow entrance of Craster Harbour on the flood tide. One of the trawlers, *Maid of Northumbria*, seemed to hold back. Just outside the harbour entrance, it changed course, and went along the coast towards Dunstanburgh.

'That's our baby! said John. 'Follow her, but keep your heads down.'

Silently the men moved off; from the direction of St Waleric's Haven another fishing vessel appeared. *Northumbrian Maid* chugged on towards Dunstanburgh. When she was a mile or so out of Craster, she came in towards the coast, then she cut her engines. Through binoculars, John watched a man appear on deck and something was lowered over the side. John spoke urgently into his radio; the fishing vessel from the south came nearer. Another bundle was lowered from the deck of the *Northumbrian Maid* into the sea, where a floating buoy marked the place of the lobster pots.

Suddenly coastguards appeared on the deck of the fishing boat from the south. There was no escape; the *Maid* had cut her engines. The fishing vessel, full of coastguards, had a powerful, well-serviced engine. And the smugglers were caught.

The line of markers just off the shore indicated, not a row of caged lobsters, but a resting place for boxes of Ecstasy tablets and a consignment of crack cocaine, picked up out in the North Sea from a Dutch vessel which had bought the drugs in Eastern Europe.

It was all over quickly. Lizzie and John watched whilst Dean Tyler, Jim Tate, and the skipper of the trawler – Bruce Hamilton – were brought ashore and arrested. Big Jim didn't spot Lizzie, but she felt her stomach churn when she saw him. John understood and put his arms round her protectively.

'He won't come near you again. They're all off for a long stretch in jail.'

'Let's hope the judge makes it a really long stay. No more Operation Delilah for me.'

Chapter Twenty-Four

When it came to the crunch, there was nothing to it. Charlie was occupied in the bar; the garage door was unlocked; Billy produced the Jag's keys.

'This is my show, Hilda,' he said as he slung a holdall into the boot and got into the driving seat. 'I'm going to beat the guts out of this car! And serves Charlie right.'

Hilda said nothing. This was going to be the ride of a lifetime. Hernmouth to Falmouth, in a Jag, driven by a madman. Compared to this, the Ride of the Valkyries was a piece of cake. But as they headed south along the A1 she wondered whether they really would make it in time. It all depended on the efficiency of the Cornish police and the state of the tide in Falmouth . . .

She glanced at Billy, who, his eyes fixed on the road ahead, his face set, his neck muscles stiff with tension, looked like one of the statues built by his Polynesian ancestors on Easter Island.

'You'll have to take a rest at some point, Billy,' she said. 'You can't drive all night.'

'I'll not be needing a rest. I'm doing this for Bridie, see. That bitch, Edith, wanted Bridie dead. How wicked can you get? They way I see it, Edith sold drugs to her own daughter. She probably gave her the money to go to New Zealand, knowing she'd spend it on drugs and would most likely never come back.

'Don't jump to conclusions, Billy. We don't know for sure Edith was involved in drugs. And Bridie was already an addict when she turned up at the Hall. Irene Laker knew Bridie when she was a child, and said she was always vulnerable. A dreamer. Not a bit like her mother. Irene wasn't a bit surprised when she heard what had happened to her.'

'You're always ready to see the best in people, Hilda. Now me, I lost my faith in human nature long ago. So tell me more about Irene Laker. We've got a long night ahead of us, and a dead straight road until we turn off onto the A69.'

'Well, Irene and George Laker were childhood sweethearts. Eventually they got married – the marriage was happy, although George was often away on business. Then Edith Murphy turned up in South Pelham – that's the village on the Hamble where the Lakers lived. Edith was much younger than Irene, and very beautiful. And she was pregnant with George's child – with Bridie.

'Apparently George had met Edith in the States during one of his business trips and he was besotted with her. As soon as Edith appeared he filed for divorce and married Edith as soon as he possibly could. And evidently he continued to worship her – and the child – until he died of a heart attack. Well, after Irene was thrown out of her own home she moved to Winchester, where she's lived ever since. She never remarried. She's an old lady now, but James Turnbull, an old friend of my husband's, was able to trace her through a friend of his who still lives in South Pelham. Irene and I have had a lovely chat – and I'm looking to having several more in the future.

'Though I reckon', Hilda went on, 'that George Laker did have reservations about Edith. Either that, or he was driven by guilt. Because he left everything he owned – his house, his yacht on the Hamble – to Irene. So Edith was left with a young daughter and not a penny to her name – though George's Will made ample provision for Bridie's upbringing and education.

'Irene, as you can imagine, has made it her life's work to keep track of Edith's whereabouts. And after George died, Edith took off for the South of France. She returned to the yachting scene, which she'd first become familiar with in the States, and left Bridie behind. Evidently she'd originally met George on a yacht, back in the Sixties. She was still a teenager then. She decided when she was very young that a life as one of nine in a Dublin slum wasn't for her and she scraped together enough money to get her to America. The Land of

Opportunity. She must have thought her dreams had come true when she met George Laker and he fell madly in love with her.'

'Did she tell you all this? Irene, I mean?'

'Most of it. It takes a first wife to know the facts about a second wife, Billy. James Turnbull also filled in a few of the gaps, via his friend in South Pelham. Edith was a sensation when she lived there – they've never forgotten her.'

'She bummed around in the south of France,' Hilda went on, 'and when she turned up again it was with Delrose. Irene called him "that man Rose"; it took me a while to work out who she meant. And there was another man hanging around Edith at that time. Irene called the three of them, "the infamous trio"'. Unfortunately, Irene couldn't remember his name, but said he definitely came from "up north". Anyway, the three of them led a high old life. Then, suddenly, no one ever saw them again. Just like that. Irene wasn't at all surprised when she heard they'd turned up here in the North East. She wasn't surprised either when she heard that Edith was wanted for questioning by the police. Incidentally, James was also deeply suspicious of Edith's charitable activities when I mentioned them to him. He says that he never heard of her charity, De Profundis, all the time he was in Rio. Well, it transpires that Edith's husband had never been in the Diplomatic Service. James checked him out in the Foreign Office bible. It was all a pack of lies, to give Edith some credibility. George Laker did travel widely, but as a businessman, not a diplomat. It seems that all her life Edith has lied and cheated and manipulated people to suit her needs.

'I wonder whose idea it was to come to this part of the world? The East Coast was ideal for their purposes. It's not quite as well-known as other parts of England, and the coast line has masses of little harbours and inlets. The old-time smugglers took full advantage of them. And it's a convenient stepping-off place for Edinburgh, Newcastle, and Glasgow. I wonder if Douglas has searched the Hall yet? If so, I'm sure he's found more than he bargained for.'

'If Turnbull's suspicions are right, then all the money that's been raised for De Profundis has gone straight into Edith's pocket,' said Billy, as he turned onto the A69 and headed off in the direction of Carlisle.

'I wonder if she had anything to do with that ambush on St Hilda's Island? I'm sure she's got a finger in every pie. Charlie'd know – he knows everything. The problem is he won't talk,' said Hilda, wincing as Billy jammed his foot down on the accelerator.

'The police'll make him.'

'How? The rack and thumb-screws?'

Billy grunted, kept his eyes on the road. They were soon clear of Newcastle and heading for the Cheviots. Hilda held on to the armrests and sent up a silent prayer that they would get to Carlisle safely. But the car slid smoothly up the steep hill, poised sickeningly on the blind summits, and plunged down the other side like a greyhound in peak condition.

'Bridie got on with Wheeler,' said Billy suddenly. 'She trusted him. I bet he was the one who told her where to get drugs. I'd not put it past him.'

'If he hadn't, someone else would have done,' said Hilda quietly.

'I suppose you're right. God, Hilda, how I wish I'd taken that last phone call seriously. I was still mad with Bridie, see. I couldn't take any more of it. I went back to my old home and my old job, and didn't for one minute think that she'd want to see me again. I can see it all now. I'm sure now she came all that way to see me because she'd sussed out Edith and wanted my help. Maybe she found out that the Brazilian charity was phoney. They could have had a confrontation. If that had happened, then Bridie knew she'd have to get the hell out of St Oswald's Hall, because Edith would have been after her.'

'She must have been really terrified, to go off and leave Clare behind.'

'She was terrified, all right. But she knew Edith would never hurt Clare.'

'Who killed Bridie, Billy?'

'Oh, it was Hohepa all right. One of his family, anyway. They're not a bad lot, Edith, you mustn't think that. But they look after one another, you see. And Bridie wasn't one of them. She poached on their patch. If she'd gone to them and asked for help, most likely they would have looked after her. Especially as they know me. She'd only got to say she was Billy Ransome's wife and they would have dropped everything. But

Bridie didn't know the rules. She'd come to sell drugs, and they'd not stand for that. One of Hohepa's family found her in that hut, and filled her up with dope. Probably when she was asleep. I don't hate the Hohepas for what they did to Bridie. I might have done the same, in their position. I just feel so guilty; I'll feel guilty all my life. But, by God, I'll get even with Edith; and see no harm ever comes to Clare. I owe that to Bridie.'

And they drove on through the night. Hilda glanced out of the window; she saw the moon rising over the Cheviots. A fine night. There was a sprinkling of snow on the high peaks, but the road ahead was quite clear.

'One good thing will come out of all this, Billy. You'll get Clare back, safe and sound.'

'At Carlisle they turned onto the M6 and headed south. Yes, they would make Falmouth, Hilda thought. Billy would see to that.

The black police Mercedes turned onto the A69 and headed towards Carlisle, Douglas at the wheel and Venerables back in his old place in the passenger seat. Behind them was the relief driver, trying not to fall asleep.

'Let's hope she's not taken off, sir.'

'No chance of that, Venerables. Cornish police will hold her there until we come.'

'Do you think she killed Delrose?'

'Looks like it. But we'll not know for sure until Forensic's had a look at him.'

'Why? Because he instigated Clare's kidnapping?'

'We'll also know that soon enough, when Stirling spills the beans – which he will, after Berwick's done a bit of horse-trading.'

'What a woman! I hope the Cornish police go careful. We don't want her alarmed, sir. She may have the child with her.'

'Don't say that, Frank. Don't even think of it. The bairn needs warmth and rest, not a mad dash across country. No, she'll not have the bairn with her. She'll be safe in that private clinic, out of harm's way. As for the local police, they'll be keeping an eye on that yacht of hers.'

'Of all the bloody cheek, sir,' said Venerables, 'she calls her yacht after that charity of hers – the charity that doesn't exist, you say?'

'No, apparently De Profundis is the name of a warehouse down on the Rio docks. The Serious Fraud Office did a great job in starting off the enquiries into Edith Laker's affairs. We've stirred up a bloody great hornet's nest! Oh, there were a couple of orphanages, but the Brazilian government closed them down. The children were being sold into the brothels of Brazil. I bet that yacht of hers has been used for everything except pleasure-cruising. What fools we've all been! She runs rings round us.'

'Couldn't be helped. Edith Laker's a clever lady. No one's to be blamed for being taken in. What put you onto her, sir?'

'Money, Venerables. Where did she get all that money to pay for the child's ransom? I contacted her Durham Bank Manager. He's a pal of mine; we shoot together. He wouldn't say much, except that her affairs are in perfect order. Not a lot in her current account – just what you'd expect from the wife of a retired diplomat on a government pension.

But look what Butler found out . . . old Butler from the Newcastle Serious Fraud Office. He's only just started his enquiries, but it looks like there's a load of money stashed away in the West Indies – on one of the Dutch Antilles – under the name of Edith Murphy – that was her maiden name. Well, she'll not get to spend any of it now. Anyway, we've got enough to go on to get her for fraud, even if we can't yet get her for Delrose's murder. And fraud can carry a heavy prison sentence these days.'

'I reckon Delrose killed his wife. But why did he have to do it?'

'She was on to something, that's the most likely explanation. Something she couldn't go along with. Probably she found out that Delrose was selling porn; wives don't like that sort of thing. Or, most likely, that Delrose was responsible for the kidnapping of the child. Wives wouldn't stand for that sort of thing either.'

'You seem to know a lot about the female psyche, sir. Can you give me a few tips?'

Before Douglas could answer, the phone rang; Venerables took the call.

'They've interrupted a drug run, sir! At Craster. They've picked up two hundred and fifty kilos of crack cocaine and a massive packet of Ecstasy. They've also picked up Dean Tyler and Jim Tate. And Bruce Hamilton! He was skippering. He owns several trawlers, it seems . . . Now I didn't know that, did you, sir?'

'I'm beginning to think nothing would surprise me any more. Anyone hurt, Venerables – anyone we like, I mean?'

'No. Lizzie was there with Chance and they're both fine. The coastguards sprung a surprise attack, tipped off by the Drugs Squad. This time, no one tipped off Hamilton and Co. Informants are in short supply round there at the moment.'

'So they've picked up Hamilton? Now we'll be getting somewhere! He's one of the big fish, all right. Now you watch. The tiddlers will start squealing.'

'Tiddlers? Rats, more likely. They always leave sinking ships.'

Douglas's spirits were lifting dramatically. 'Any more good news?'

'They've already charged Hamilton. If you ask me, they'll all shop each other. Tate's a fool, and a blabber-mouth. Tyler'd shop his own grandmother if it let him off the hook.'

As soon as Venerables put the phone down, it rang again. He picked it up and listened; a look of triumph spread over his face.

'Dean Tyler's confessed! To attempted murder of Delrose. Apparently Charlie Wheeler – he's been mighty useful to us, hasn't he? No doubt he hopes it'll look good in court – told him that Delrose ordered the execution of his brother Josh. Dean's told us this, I suppose, in the hope of getting lenient treatment later on. Good luck to him, I say. Nobody's going to miss Delrose. Dean Tyler also claimed it was McLoughlin who killed his other brother, Marcus, this time on Hamilton's orders.'

'That'll keep them all busy in Berwick, laddie. I'm glad to be out of it and heading south. There's no honour amongst thieves, is there? I wonder which one tried to push Edith Laker over the cliff at Dunstanburgh? Pity really he didn't succeed.'

'Probably one of Hamilton's hit men. Someone was going to be mighty put-out after that fiasco the other night on St

Hilda's Island. Anyone on the receiving end of that little surprise would want to punish the person responsible.'

'We'll know soon enough. Leave it to Berwick. I wouldn't like to be in Blackburn's shoes.'

At Carlisle, they turned onto the M6. Hours passed; the phone rang continuously. The pieces of the jigsaw puzzle were fitting together nicely. Donald Stirling, on being told of Delrose's death and Bruce Hamilton's arrest, was prepared to tell all; like his erstwhile colleagues, hoping for a more lenient sentence. Apparently, he'd been ordered to get rid of Edith, after Hamilton heard that his drug landing on St Hilda's had been intercepted by two of her henchmen. Stirling gave the names: Joe Bridges and Lee Worman, both Londoners and both long-term associates of Edith Laker's. So the hunt was on. The calls continued to come in. One of them confirmed that Hamilton had decided to turn Queen's Evidence; realising that Stirling had shopped him, he saw that his best course was to own up. Yes, he had used *Cormorant* for smuggling in drugs. Yes, Spicer and Watson had been in his pay. What did it matter if he shopped his friends? It was only a matter of time before those two started to squeal once they heard their boss had been arrested. Douglas took that particular call. When it was finished, he beamed at Venerables.

'Hamilton's croaked! He hated Delrose, it seems.'

'Come again?'

'Bruce Hamilton! Seems he and Delrose have known each other for years. Both knew Edith Laker – Hamilton said he and Delrose had been friends at one time. Maybe Hamilton had been Edith's lover – maybe they both were. Who knows? It doesn't matter. But Hamilton's had it in for Delrose for a long time. And then Dean Tyler comes along and does his dirty work for him. Jim Tate, by the way, confessed to providing Dean Tyler with an alibi. Signed the factory clocking-in book on his behalf.'

'What a carry-on! Berwick's got a massive mopping-up operation on its hands.'

'And that's not the end of it. They're *all* shopping one another! Stirling's confessed to working for both Delrose and Hamilton. What a double-dealing so-and-so! He kidnaps the child for Delrose, then does Hamilton's dirty work for him. If he'd succeeded in shoving Edith Laker over the cliff, he really would have landed Delrose in it.'

'Do we know for sure who killed Delrose, sir?'

'Oh yes. Edith's fingerprints all over his nice, shiny shoes. She must have dragged him into the cellar.'

Venerables whistled. 'So she must have found out he was responsible for Clare's kidnapping. It's going to take Berwick a long time to sort this one out. Edith Laker, Bruce Hamilton, Derek Rose. All pals at one time – maybe very good pals indeed. Then things go wrong, for some reason Delrose overreaches himself, Edith needs a lot of money to pay for Clare's ransom. Rakes up her pals from London to bump off Hamilton's friends, just as they're landing a nice lucrative haul of drugs. Hamilton gets shirty, rustles up Stirling – who's not above working for anyone who pays well – and sets him onto Edith. Edith survives, only to find out that Delrose has done the dirty on her and has kidnapped her beloved child. No honour amongst thieves is dead right, sir.'

They drove on. At West Bromwich, where they picked up the M5 to Exeter, they changed drivers, and Douglas and Venerables settled down companionably in the back seat.

'Like old times, sir. Working together like this.'

'Aye, I've had a lot on my mind lately. Fraud Squad wanted strict confidentiality – I had to work alone. But we're back on course now. Let's keep it this way.'

'All right by me, sir.'

At Exeter they picked up the A38 and headed west. Outside Plymouth they stopped at a garage while Venerables fetched coffee from a machine. It lasted like nectar.

'Sir?' Venerables hesitated.

'Out with it, laddie.'

'Hilda, sir – how the hell did she suss out Edith Laker? You've told me that Hilda clinched it for you. Apart from having tea-parties together, all very genteel I didn't know they knew one another all that well.'

Douglas finished his coffee and got back into the car.

'Don't underestimate ladies' tea-parties, Sergeant. Hilda's no fool. At one of those tea-parties, she was admiring Edith Laker's sugar bowl, and spotted the hallmark.'

'I don't get it.'

'Hallmark, Sergeant. In this case it was three castles in the shape of a triangle: two above one. She tested Edith, said it was Edinburgh, and Edith agreed. But Hilda knew it was really Newcastle, so she knew then Edith wasn't quite what she claimed to be. Clever old stick, is Hilda. It made her suspicious, so she went away and checked up on Edith. She's got a pal who was a friend of her husband's – James Turnbull. Now, he'd been Ambassador in Rio at the time when Edith said she'd been there, with her husband. But James Turnbull had never heard of her. Neither had he heard of her charity, De Profundis . . . It's a long story. I'll fill in the details later, when this is all over.'

Dawn was breaking as they reached Falmouth. Out to the west great storm clouds were approaching from the Atlantic. Not a night to go sailing, Douglas thought.

As Falmouth approached, Billy grew more and more restless. Except for a brief stop to fill up with petrol, he had driven without stopping. At the marina entrance a policeman blocked their route.

'No one's to go through,' he said. Billy, tense with repressed anger, snapped.

'She's here, isn't she? Has she got the child with her? Let me through, damn you!'

Quietly, Hilda took over. She was going to have to employ all her tact if they were going to get past the police cordon. Had the Berwick police arrived? she asked. The man nodded: everything was under control. No need for anyone else to go into the marina. Hilda explained that she was a friend of Edith Laker's; perhaps, she said, she could be of help. She could talk to Edith, maybe persuade her to give herself up. She begged the police to excuse Billy's impetuousness. He was the child's father, so naturally he was distressed. Finally she threw the Chief Constable of Cornwall into the conversation – he'd been a personal friend of Charles's, they'd met on a cruise . . . That clinched it. The policeman let them through, cautioning them to stay back from the pontoon where the white yacht was moored.

Once inside the marina gates, they got out, and looked towards the line of pontoons stretching out into Falmouth

Harbour. The sun was rising, bathing the marina in an ominous red light. The air was warm, moist: out to the west, storm clouds were brewing. Then her heart lurched. Down on one of the pontoons she saw Edith, standing with her back to a white yacht. Its crew had already started the engine and were about to slip the mooring lines. Clutched in front of Edith's body was a small child.

There was no sign of any Cornish police: only the solid, comforting figure of Douglas McBride, Sergeant Venerables by his side, a few yards away from Edith. They appeared to be talking to her.

Hilda walked down to the top of the pontoon. She didn't see Billy, who'd retrieved his holdall from the boot; he'd slipped away as quietly as a shadow. No one moved. Douglas turned and saw her.

'Get back, Lady Nevill!' he shouted. 'The woman's armed and she'll shoot the child.'

Hilda saw, to her horror and utter outrage, that Edith was holding a gun in one hand and Clare in the other. And the gun was pointing at the child's head. She felt the world spin round, took several deep breaths, managed to hang on. She looked steady at Edith.

'It's me. Hilda. Come on – you know it's all over. Give me the child. Don't shoot!' she said urgently, as Edith lifted the gun. 'She's your grandchild. You love her. Think what you've been through to save her. Give her to me, Edith.'

But Edith made no move in Hilda's direction. Instead, she backed towards the yacht, holding Clare in front of her.

'It's no use, Edith. You can't go anywhere. The tide's against you, there's not enough water. You can't command the elements. And look at the clouds building up – a terrific storm's approaching.'

But still Edith backed towards the yacht, its name, *De Profundis*, painted in stark black letters along the hull.

'Stop, Edith!' Hilda shouted urgently. 'We know you've killed several men – but Clare's an innocent. Don't kill Clare. Let the child live.'

Then Edith began to speak. Her voice was soft, ragged with emotion and it was difficult to hear her at first, but after a while it grew stronger.

'And what do you know about living, Hilda Nevill? You've never had to struggle the way I have. You, with your comfortable upper-class lifestyle and your superior ways – you know nothing. I had to fight may way to the top – not like you. I'm a survivor. I learnt that when I was a child, no older than Clare. My mother used to say to me: 'Don't make the same mistakes I've made. Never let anyone put you down – and make sure you've got plenty stashed away for when you need it. At the end of the day, she said, you're on your own.'

'I'm sure your mother didn't teach you to kill the thing you love most in the world.'

'She told me to let nothing stand in my way. Nothing. And nothing will. Yes, I love Clare. Perhaps too much. But she's mine, and I know what's best for her. She belongs to me. Not you. She's mine, and you can't take her from me.'

Hilda, who had been moving almost imperceptibly, had drawn level with Douglas and Venerables. Steadily, step by step, they advanced on Edith; her face distorted with hate and rage, she was almost unrecognisable. She pressed the gun into the child's head; Clare began to scream. Then Hilda knew that Edith was prepared to shoot the child. She would go to any lengths to get what she wanted. She heard herself cry out. 'No, Edith! Stop!'

But she had forgotten Billy. While all eyes were focused on the scene in front of the yacht, he'd crept off silently along the row of pontoons. Then, clutching his holdall, he'd boarded a motor-sailer, opened the bag and took out Charlie Wheeler's Remington 30-06 rifle; the one Wheeler used for culling deer. Then he climbed the mast, and took aim.

The bullet struck Edith in the head. A neat kill – a shot Charlie would have been proud of. Edith fell forward onto the pontoon. And Hilda dashed forward and took the child in her arms.

Suddenly the marina was swarming with police. A number of officers went after Billy and ordered him to come down from his perch. Quietly, he descended; he made no protest when they arrested him. As they took him away, he looked sadly at Hilda, who was trying to comfort Clare as the ambulance men advanced along the pontoon.

'You shouldn't have done that, Billy,' said Hilda.

'It was the only way. She'd have killed Clare without hesitation. She's not a woman, she's a wild beast. Selfish to the end. Bridie knew. Bridie tried to warn us. And Bridie died. Look after Clare, Hilda. I'll not be away long. There must be grounds for justifiable homicide.'

Douglas came over to Hilda, his face drawn and weary. 'So many deaths, Lady Nevill. First, this wee bairn's mother; now her grandmother. It seems a long time ago that I saw Bridie Ransome lying in that Auckland morgue.'

Hilda handed Clare over to the ambulance crew and said she'd accompany her to the hospital. She'd take care of the child until they knew what was going to happen to Billy. Then she turned to Douglas.

'As you say, Douglas; too much dying. All that remains now is to say the last words:- "*Requiem aeternam dona eis Domine*".'

Then she climbed into the ambulance with Clare.

Venerables cleared his throat. 'I don't know about you, sir, but I could do with some breakfast.'

'Aye. That'd be just what the doctor ordered. Let's away, Sergeant.'